OCEAN GRAVE

A NOVEL OF DEEP SEA HORROR

MATT SERAFINI

SEVERED PRESS
HOBART TASMANIA

OCEAN GRAVE

Copyright © 2019 Matt Serafini
Copyright © 2019 by Severed Press

WWW.SEVEREDPRESS.COM

ISBN: 978-1-925840-82-7

PROLOGUE

Carly Grayson woke and at once remembered she was on a boat in the middle of the ocean. Her heart drummed so hard the bed sheets did little jumping jacks over her chest.

She rolled onto her side with a soft groan and draped an arm over Jesh. Her hand fell instead over a mound of unoccupied blankets.

A tremor of anxiety popped her eyes wide. Her hand swept for the Xanax bottle on the nearby bed table. The boat's swells were gentle-but-constant. That should've been enough to calm her, only she didn't like being alone at night.

That was enough to bring it.

And it always started the same. An explosion beneath the ribs followed by agitation that gnawed at her brain. Once that happened, fear was the only thing she could think. And that fear spread through her body, where her hands danced jitters and her speech became sporadic stutters.

Nobody should live this way.

Carly dropped an oval pill on her tongue and knocked it back without water, then crawled to the edge of the bed and watched the private bathroom's dark interior like a curious cat, hoping to hear Jesh's familiar shuffles inside the gloom.

He was up twice a night most nights because his bladder was the size of a nickel. Tonight, though, the door was ajar and the lavatory beyond it, vacant.

Carly couldn't move off the bed. Part of her felt safe so long as she remained planted on this tiny island of Egyptian cotton pillows. Her hands pulled the silk sheets into stress balls as the Indian Ocean's constant ebbs threatened her equilibrium. Her eyes pulled shut but small trails of salt water leaked. This while her brain pleaded to be anything but stupid.

There was an explanation for Jesh's absence. They weren't alone on the yacht after all, something that had annoyed her upon leaving port. She'd known then this was going to be more than a much needed luxury vacation.

Carly stared at the floor like it was out of reach. She considered touching down, as if doing so might result in an electric shock.

Okay, she thought, reminding herself that she'd worked once for David O. Russell and could now survive anything.

Her feet warmed to the wool carpet. She took the midnight satin robe slung over the night table. The way it felt against her sun-kissed flesh offered slight relief quickly chased off by the thumping unease in her heart.

In that moment, the bedroom door appeared a serious obstacle to overcome. Carly grabbed a deep breath and stashed it in her lungs, waiting for the calm. From the rounded vanity mirror on the wall, her reflection tried slipping past unnoticed. Its sudden appearance, startling. Her ocean eyes were soaked, her blonde hair a ruffled mop.

She resented the sight. Here was a woman in no control of her emotions. In no control of anything.

Carly cursed the cliché and forced her hand around the doorknob.

It swung toward her to reveal a pitch-dark hall beyond. A check of her robe's pockets reminded her that her cell phone was just back across the room, parked beside the Xanax. Close enough, but the mere sight of her stillborn quarters filled her with dread.

Instead of backtracking, Carly pushed on—motivated to find the others. To find anyone. Certain they were one deck up. Wouldn't have been the first time they traded sleep for excesses she had no desire to indulge in.

She was through playing the Whore's Game. This wasn't Hollywood. The pay was comparable to what she got when star power could open a show, though she wasn't about to get on her knees to show gratitude. She suspected that had been Jesh's motivation for bringing others along.

The other bunks in the hall were shut, and she wasn't about to go pushing into those rooms and give anyone the wrong idea. Instead she hurried to the end of the hall, up through the compact stairwell to the next deck. The living quarters were vacant.

Carly's heart roared. A terrible moment to be passing the unmanned bar. Rows of top shelf bottlenecks returned memories of a hundred Hollywood nights. A thousand stories. A million vices. A lifetime ago. She was a mother now. But there was safety at the bottom of a glass and she needed that. More than anything, she needed that.

She reached toward the closest glass neck, pausing once she glimpsed herself in the reflection.

The mirrors aboard the *Star Time* were telling a story tonight. In this one, Carly saw the actress she used to be. The moonlight shining through the windows caught her just right. An improvement on the depressing scene below. This time, it was like she'd sauntered onto a well-lit set.

Despite the constant thrum of panic vibrating through her, Carly found a moment of solitude in her vanity. She turned her chin, admiring the contours of her face. Hard to believe she was forty-four later this year.

Carly took a second to peruse the selection, forgetting her predicament long enough to reach for the brand new bottle of Stoli. She uncapped it and reached down under the bar for a square glass. A few ice cubes remained inside a bucket of melt. It'd been years since she'd tended bar. The memory made her smile.

"Gonna stop you one way or the other," Carly whispered to her anxiety.

She slid the cabin door aside and carried the glass into the open air, sipping steadily as a lazy wind made her bed hair go dancing across her eyes.

Her stomach tightened into sailor's knots as she circled the deck and found it empty.

Her anxiety, now validated, took the opportunity to grow. It drowned out Carly's feeble chemical and alcoholic suppressants. It pained her to feel this, the panic spreading like cancer.

The glass slipped through her wobbling fingers and shattered around her bare feet. Her hands clawed at her collarbone as if a turtleneck blocked her windpipe.

Jesh had shown her once how to operate the lights. But she'd only been half paying attention, sunning herself on the bow, pretending not to notice all the other men, his "partners" leering at her.

The switches were on the helm—one level up from topside. Carly shuddered at the thought of retracing her steps through the darkened cabin interior to get there. But there was another way, a thin iron ladder bolted to the exterior of the wall.

It was easier said than done, given her panic. But she needed to get the lights back on. A trembling hand closed on one of the upper rungs, and a bare foot stepped to another. She was slow to ascend, taking her time to ensure she didn't lose her grip.

At the top, the only light aboard the ship came from inside the helm. She half expected to find Jesh there, blabbering some excuse about how the gang got blitzed and then on a drunken whim decided it just had to do some night fishing and to go back to sleep, dear. Carly would prefer that, because then this nightmare would be over.

Only the helm was as desolate as every other inch of this ship. Carly stepped through the door, pausing to get her bearings in the darkness. The door came slamming back into place, giving her butt a "get moving" smack.

Carly moved toward the control seat. The console was full of switches and knobs that surrounded the stainless steering wheel on three sides. A diagram of the ship was positioned overhead, where blinking LED lights would alert the captain to issues below. There were controls for the bow thruster, along with dual upper and lower autopilot dials. Lower helm air conditioning, as well as radar and GPS.

When Carly had been a teenager in Grand Rapids, she was placed behind the controls of a speedboat while she and her friends vacationed on Reeds Lake. She was there for the waterskiing, but her then boyfriend, a boy named John whose last name she couldn't remember, had leapt overboard to escape a mosquito swarm. Carly had intended to lower the throttle but instead gunned it, clipping John's shoulder with the bow. Nothing serious, five stitches, though she hadn't trusted herself then and that went triple now because Jesh's boat was like a NASA spaceship, comparatively.

On top of the marble counter was an old map, little clusters of unpopulated islands circled in red Sharpie and then, later, she assumed, crossed off in black. One island was only circled in red, and hadn't yet been slashed through in dark felt-tip.

It made sense at last. Jesh and his "partners" were searching for something.

The light switches were off to the side of the helm and Carly flipped them one by one. The overheads for the hull. The sidelights. The sternlight. The mastheads. Slowly but surely, shadows went running off the *Star Time* and from this vantage, Carly's paranoia was reinforced. She was all alone.

With one last button left to flick, she hit the under light. The one that set the surrounding ocean ablaze in deep neon purple.

Jesh often sailed into shallows where he'd beg Carly to take a midnight skinny dip. For inspiration. He so badly wanted to glimpse her among marine life. To record her. *"Beauty among beauty"* he'd say. All she could think about was when, and not if, that footage would be leaked to the Internet.

Carly rose to her haunches and looked down at the water. The under light's purple glow was muted from behind the window glass. Carly brushed her palm against it, thinking it smudged. It wasn't.

She was curious now and went to the door, stepping outside and squinting over the rail. The relief she dared to feel was short-lived and the anxiety came roaring back because it didn't like being doubted.

The under light *was* muted by something. By a spill of dark crimson water that sat atop the surface like oil. In that murk, appendages bobbed like vegetables in soup. Carly stared straight at it until her eyes adjusted.

"Oh, Jesus."

She was looking at a piece of a hand, part of a thigh, and an errant arm that drummed against the hull with a lazy knock.

Carly's eyes glossed and tears began tickling her cheeks. She could only watch that ebbing water, struck by the realization that it was all that remained of the people who had once been passengers aboard the *Star Time*.

The blood thinned at last, ceding ground to the ocean's natural color while restoring also the vibrant under light glow. A shadow glided out from beneath the ship, scraping against the steel hull with a deep rumble that Carly felt in her molars.

She choked on a silent scream. Or maybe it was a gag. It didn't matter. Because Carly was already sinking to her knees, trembling so hard she had to curl into a fetal position in order to stop it.

She squeezed her eyes shut, regretting every decision that had brought her here.

The ship swayed and all Carly could think about were the severed body parts settling onto the ocean floor somewhere beneath her.

PART ONE

THE HUNT

ONE

Maxamed Abir Kaahin stepped off the twin-engine plane in Algeria and had not a moment to reflect on the beauty of the Mediterranean Sea as it lapped against the golden dunes beyond the slim strip of runway.

It wasn't often that he was away from his beloved isle of Madagascar, and whenever he did travel, it was never for pleasure. Just business.

Always business.

The humidity here was such that his forehead grew oily and the curl of his underarm hair began to itch. Across the tarmac, he watched women in flossy bikinis bake beneath the scorching sun and wondered why their men allowed them to expose such gratuitous flesh.

Ten years ago, a country like Algeria held only modest aspirations of transforming into a tourist economy. Now, western influence could not be ignored in an ever-expanding global market. The United States and European Union controlled much of the world and, for now, were worth catering to.

Kaahin laughed when those countries openly protested the intake of refugees, citing claims that such "invaders" would inevitably reshape their cultures. He was mercilessly unsympathetic to that line of thinking, because the poison of the west had been doing the same to his people for as long as he could remember.

Not in the same way, of course. Western degeneracy was worse. Because he could never shield his daughters from it forever. They would inevitably seek university where their minds would corrode. The vilest thing about western education was how it turned children against parents.

Reshape their cultures? he thought. Not soon enough.

"We near the meeting," Alzir said as they reached the tinted sedan parked at the edge of the private runway.

"And the conditions are satisfied?"

"To the letter," Alzir told him.

Kaahin climbed into the sedan and Alzir followed, slipping his Desert Eagle out from beneath the linen doublet once they were removed from the sight of prying tourists.

The driver wasn't theirs, but a local boy on loan from a partner. A guy named Cardiff who owned nightlife up and down this beachfront, and to whom they'd offloaded millions in merchandise over the years.

The young driver watched his passengers settle into the vehicle and flashed a gold-capped smile upon glimpsing Alzir's golden gun.

"The Sundry," Alzir said and flicked his wrist so the boy turned back toward his business. The kid shifted the sedan into drive and stomped the pedal.

He was good, driving erratically in order to weed out any tails, of which there were none. "Is not far," Alzir said. "Ten minutes, further down the beach."

Kaahin stared out at calm emerald waters, thinking about how much more comfortable he was out there.

"Here," the boy said.

The Sundry was easy to spot as the sedan rolled up on a strip of tourist traps. It was a tiered building and each level was shorter and more slanted than the previous. One of its sides was curved in order to make it relentlessly modern.

Western.

Kaahin found it an eyesore, though it seemed a fine place to hold a meeting. The wrong people would stick out like sore thumbs among authentic vacationers.

Whether it was INTERPOL, the CIA, or the other one hundred law enforcement agencies that hunted pirates, they never looked quite right—not when you'd been watching them work your whole life.

Meetings like this required Kevlar. Kaahin's wasn't a profession where people tried arresting you. But he wouldn't wear it today because he was not about to expose his paranoia to a pair of smug western producers. He'd take their money, sure, and tell his story, yes, but only on his terms. And if they betrayed what little trust had been built over the last twelve months of covert correspondences, then Alzir had already been granted permission to cut them down.

Secretly, he wanted Alzir to cut them down.

The sedan stopped in front of the ridiculous structure that would look more natural on Miami Beach. Blue neon lights danced across the clean stucco surface, and Kaahin imagined quite a few local men sneaking in here to get a piece of the western degeneracy they promised their wives they despised.

"You wait here," Alzir told the driver. "Running."

The boy nodded and eyed every bit of foot traffic that got within kilometers of the car. He seemed tense now that it was go time. And that was good. A million things could go wrong.

"The place," Alzir said, and cracked the door to get out.

Kaahin had his doubts about any of this, as always. But the producers had stood up to every bit of scrutiny he could afford. And they had insisted upon holding the meeting in neutral suites arranged by the hotel itself.

Alzir requested the manager once they reached the front desk. The clerk mumbled into his lapel mic, seconds passed, and the manager appeared from around the corner as if he'd been waiting on mark. He smiled, pretending to be comfortable in the presence of an international criminal.

"Please," the manager said and escorted them to a VIP elevator accessible only through his key card swipe.

Then they were on their way up.

The producers were waiting in the suite when they got there. The one called Hudson had hair the color of desert sand and his beard was flecked with white powder. He drank bourbon like it was water and chuffed his nose every thirty seconds.

The second man, Gaffney, appeared ready to do all the talking. "This is an honor," he said, speaking in slow motion. "A Real. Bona fide. Honor."

Kaahin ignored the flattery and took a seat at the table of flushed liquor bottles. Alzir stood at the back of the room like a loaded spring.

"I do not see cameras," Kaahin said.

Gaffney slapped his iPhone down on the table and smiled. "We travel light, my man."

Hudson continued to sniff as they exchanged trivialities. Lovely weather, lovelier women, and what an honor it was to share this space with the one and only Pirate King.

They eased into the business side of things. They planned to shoot the whole conversation today. A series of mostly legible questions were scribbled on a yellow notepad in the center of the table, and a damp ring stain marked the top corner of it.

They discussed particulars. Upon commencement of this arrangement, one hundred thousand US dollars was to be wired into a bank account of Kaahin's choosing. Upon successful transfer of this payout, he would allow these men their twenty questions.

"And, hey," Gaffney said. "Should you want anything extra, we've got, you know, a few beach bodies on call."

"Please," Kaahin shrugged. No, he did not desire one of their Hollywood whores. He'd been around enough sheiks to know the kinds of things Hollywood women did for money. There was no more depraved beast on the planet. "The money for your questions. And that will be all."

"We can respect that," Hudson said, rubbing his nose on the back of his hand. "Thing is, my dude, we would like to do a pre-interview with you and your man back there."

"Impossible."

"Nothing's that," Hudson grinned.

"This is."

"Okay." Gaffney stepped into the mix. "Think of it as... an exploratory conversation so that we know how best to direct our questions."

"Absolutely not," Kaahin said. He despised the thought of sitting here for a second longer than necessary, and tensed now that these cocaine cowboys were stalling for time. "I know the details you want," he added. "You will have more honesty than your American audience can handle."

"Oh, no, no, no. We don't want any of that, big guy." Hudson tapped his chest. "Where the hell are my cigarettes?"

Alzir appeared tableside and opened the briefcase to reveal a remote deposit device. It looked like a laptop with an oversized keypad on the screen, but spoke only in savings account numbers and dollar amounts.

"As soon as payment clears," Kaahin said. "We can get on with it. The questions only."

11

"We... really need that pre-interview," Hudson said. "Standard stuff and believe me, it's mutually beneficial."

"Explain."

"We need to know what's off-limits. Things you'd rather we not discuss. This piece... well, it's important to us that both parties are equally happy with it."

"I think it is maybe a good idea," Kaahin said. Right up front he told them some things were forbidden. They were to know nothing of his wife and children (he referred to them as "details"). They could not ask him to implicate anyone else by name. Not the politicians he greased, or the local law enforcement officers who secretly worked for him.

On the other hand, he was comfortable speaking at length about his upbringing. Time on the police force, and how he started out hunting pirates before realizing he was on the wrong side of business. And that law enforcement was an illusory construct designed to keep people controlled.

"One thing we really want to know more about," Hudson said, trading nervous eyes with Gaffney, "is what happened to the *Blue Planet*?"

The producers watched him then, desperate to know if he knew.

Kaahin did know.

Blue Planet was a tourist ship out of Fort Lauderdale that had made its way into international waters in order to shoot an amateur orgy. An entire ship of westerners. Kaahin and his men were glad to take it. Sailed it to the Port of Jebel Ali and cashed in.

Fourteen girls.

Millions of dollars.

Six years later and no one was wiser. He'd been bankrolling his operation off that bounty ever since. And nobody outside his skeleton crew had known for sure what really happened to that ship.

But these guys seemed to know.

Gaffney perhaps thought they shouldn't have asked. It was too late, though. The room was forever tense. "We just wanted to ask," he said. "You can search fifty different websites and there's fifty different theories on the fate of the *Blue Planet*."

"It is not my problem." It was Kaahin's turn to watch the men. They shifted. Cleared their throats. The tip off was Hudson. The longer Kaahin watched him the more he realized the man's eyes were not remotely dilated. And that he suddenly stopped sniffing entirely.

Gaffney told them the popular theory was that the Pirate King had done it, and so they just had to ask.

Sure, Kaahin thought. But that wasn't it. He'd been careful to pin that job on the Somalis because he knew the abduction of fourteen western girls would be the kind of thing that the United States would initiate nuclear war over. So it was him and four men, the ones he'd known since boyhood, chasing down the party boat on rafts, shooting rifles into the air to startle them into submission.

It hadn't taken much.

But if these men were curious about that, then they were not who they claimed to be. And that evidence was mounting.

"Seriously, brother," Hudson said, his coke gaze all but evaporated. "Tell us what happened to those girls."

"If you want an answer to that question, you'd better fly three thousand miles east. Because you're looking at the Somalis for it."

"Somalia's where we started," Gaffney told him, surfacing from deep cover in order to reveal blazing eyes. "They like you for it."

The rest happened in a matter of seconds.

Hudson's hand blurred and his gun lifted high. Alzir was faster, his Desert Eagle already pointed at the man's head.

Alzir never hesitated. He squeezed the trigger. The shot drilled through Hudson's eye and sent him spiraling to the floor.

Gaffney tried screaming, but Cardiff's men, the hotel employees, kept neutral. And kept out.

But then the sound of machine gun fire erupted in the hallway. Kaahin realized these men were CIA spooks and their pals had just engaged the hotel guard.

Gaffney gave the table a shove. It slammed against Kaahin's ribs as he tried to stand. Bottles toppled, some of them breaking, as Alzir and Gaffney traded rounds.

CIA's thoughts splattered the window in jelly red. Alzir put a hand to his side and grunted. "We must go."

They waited by the door for a break in the gunfire. They swapped expressions of doubt, knowing that Alzir was about to stick his neck into the hall and risk getting his head shot off.

But the bullets never came. Cardiff's men were gut shot and crawling around in puddles of their own blood. One man was barely upright, crouching behind a service cart and huffing adrenaline.

In front of the elevator, four CIA spooks were dead, sprawled and bleeding into the carpet. Two others hugged the walls, screaming for backup.

"The stairs," Alzir grumbled. "But they will be waiting there as well."

They moved as fast as Alzir could, trundling down ten flights and into the lobby. Three CIA spooks stood around the front desk and lifted their guns as soon as their targets spilled into the public square.

No time to worry about them. There were far too many tourists between them to give it any thought.

Kaahin dragged Alzir straight for the revolving doors, where they squeezed into the same compact space and wound their way through.

The sedan was still idling, but the windshield had been punctured with frantic bullet holes and the boy's arm dangled dead against the driver's door, fingertips dripping with fresh blood.

"The beach," Alzir said, breathless and frail. He gave a forceful nudge that must've cost the last of his energy, because he nearly fell, and would've had Kaahin not draped an arm around him to keep him moving forward.

They rounded the curved side of the building toward the mounded sand beyond. Kaahin broke into a run while Alzir steadied himself against the wall and squeezed off a few rounds meant to discourage pursuit.

That was all it took to get the public screaming. Panicked bodies rushing in all directions, seemingly everywhere at once. Chaos as Kaahin rushed straight for the water.

Speedboats on the horizon. One began moving inland. For a moment, Kaahin thought the CIA wasn't taking any chances and was determined to cut him off by land, sea, and perhaps even air. He turned back and saw Alzir stumbling for the shallows, blood spilling into the sand around him.

And behind Alzir, the CIA lobby spooks struggled to take aim in between the rushing bodies.

Alzir fired off a few shots. His bullets struck passersby and sent them down into red sand. The spooks, now provoked, returned fire with equal recklessness, sending even more tourists crashing to the ground. Some of them flailing, crying in fear and disbelief, but many more of them permanently stiff.

Adding to the commotion was two uniformed men who came sprinting onto the scene from the other side of the street. Local law enforcement, clearly ignorant of the shadow op in their backyard, no idea who was who.

They trained their guns on the men firing into the crowd, dropping the Langley spooks with surprising precision.

Kaahin waded into the warm Mediterranean right up to his knees and kept going. Behind him, Alzir screamed, "Get to the boat!"

A gunshot cracked the sky and Alzir's next order was severed mid-sentence. This as the boat came slicing through the chop, swerving to its side.

"Poppa!" the driver cried. "To me!"

Kaahin had won the name Poppa from islanders who recognized his work. He didn't particularly like the authority or responsibility it carried, but had learned to live with it. He launched into a full-blown breaststroke as he pushed hard to close the distance to the boat.

Hands reached down and helped him aboard. Kaahin caught a glimpse of Alzir floating face down in red water.

The boat zipped away from the chaos. Kaahin sat with his head in his hands in case any more bullets found him. What he really wondered was how he could've been so stupid. Was it hubris or sheer desperation that made him trust westerners?

"We are taking you home, Poppa," one of the men said.

Kaahin did not recognize them in the slightest, but men did not call him Poppa unless they were islanders eager to be employed.

He tried to relax as he watched Algeria shrink into a line on the horizon. He did not like feeling this way, knowing he had barely escaped with his life. The hunters would never stop. Tomorrow there would be two more to take the place of the fallen.

He turned his attention back the other way, watching the distance through a squint. How eager he was to see Madagascar grow before him.

TWO

At the start of the second full day of her honeymoon, Sara Mosby knew there was a problem with her husband.

He was missing.

Missing, at least, in that he had left this morning without telling her where he was going. Only that he "had to take care of a few things."

On the first day, Sara had suspected Blake might have a few more surprises in store and would be skipping out for an hour or two. He'd hinted as much during the flight. But it was after sunset when he returned, drenched and filthy and refusing to say anything more about it. Only that she was going to love it, just wait and see.

Sara stretched across the plastic pool chair, marinating beneath the scorching African sun. On the small table beside her stood a plastic cup stained with the sticky remnants of whatever tropical drink she was on today. Her stomach had begun to reject the infusion of sugar and liquor.

In college, she took Jack Daniels straight. That was in the years before Blake. Blake couldn't handle anything that wasn't served with an umbrella. She might've adapted but those old habits... they were screaming to be set free.

Pools of sweat slid down her stomach like melted ice. She thought about going back to the room in order to get out of this heat, but she'd just come from there. All-inclusive resorts had ways of blurring time like that. Minutes bled into hours. Hours bled into days.

And the last couple of those were an absolute mystery. Blake's uncharacteristic behavior twisted her guts into knots as she came to realize one simple truth.

I messed up.

Two white guys floated down the pool's lazy river, double-fisting whiskey shots each time they glided past the bar. Sara ignored them during their first few passes, but was having a hard time overlooking their admiring eyes now.

Not that she would ever admit that. Four days ago, she stood at the altar at St. Balthazar's, rambling off hand-written vows while the priest kept having to remind her, "Louder, louder for the grannies in the cheap seats."

And now she was suddenly open to the idea of flirting with other men...

This was the first time since landing on Madagascar that her heart drummed with any excitement at all.

Blake had grown distant in a relatively short amount of time. They had eaten dinner last night at a faux Mexican restaurant, then stayed up late to catch a black Elvis impersonator before going back to their room where she expected to screw so loudly that the couple in the next suite would have no choice but to listen.

Only that didn't happen. Blake climbed beneath the sheets and was snoring by the time she stepped from the bathroom in her lacy white lingerie.

A terrible start to their honeymoon, made worse today by Blake's second disappearance. Sara had pressed him for information before he left, but he would only say that he was trying to surprise her.

It worked. She was surprised.

Sara clammed up while eyeing the newly minted rock on her finger.

Splashes as the guys lifted their torsos up and out of the pool, leaning heavy on contoured forearms. They were tanned and cut and every bit of their flesh glistened beneath shimmering water.

They gave her body a leering once-over.

Sara smiled and glanced away before her attention could be interpreted as interest. A twinge of mischief tickled her stomach. Her ring finger was suddenly heavier than a boulder. She looked again and caught their gazes. "Aw crap," she sighed.

The potential suitors hoisted themselves in unison. Their arms bulged and glistened like their bodies had been oiled. The poolside's sandstone got drenched as they strode over. They flashed hungry smiles and wore eager eyes that gave careful admiration to Sara's dark brown skin.

Sara slid her Ray Bans down to the bulb of her nose and made no bones about admiring her view, especially the way their soaked bathing suits molded around certain shapes.

She was fine with being shameless about it since this was all a game. One she feared she wasn't nearly drunk enough to play.

"My friend says that you have a man hiding around here somewhere." The accent was thick French, and the way it rendered English made Sara's eyes flutter to the back of her head. A sound like pure sex.

"Oui," she giggled.

The other man's English wasn't as refined. Not that Sara would judge when she couldn't speak a syllable of anything beyond her native tongue.

"I see him," he said. "He is, how you say, a ghost." He made a point of looking around the pool area, as if Blake was hanging back somewhere, just out of view.

"Maybe he likes to stay in his room," Sara said. "Keep to himself."

"Impossible," the first man fired back. He wore the perfect amount of stubble on his face and Sara didn't think she could tire of looking into his brown eyes that were mixed with swirls of frozen gray. Good bodies were nice, really nice, but faces, the eyes and smiles, were everything. "A beauty such as yourself should never be alone."

"Who comes to a couple's resort without their significant others?" Sara challenged.

"We are a couple," the first man told her. He pointed to the man standing on the other side of her. "He is Jean-Philippe. I am Guillaume. And we would very much like to spend the afternoon with you."

"Shit," Sara said. "I'm sorry, I didn't mean to insult—"

"Is fine." Jean-Philippe waved his hand dismissively.

"Okay," Sara said, repeating, "Sorry. But... why would you want to spend time with me?"

Guillaume ran a hand through his hair, nearly posing as he enjoyed Sara's gaze. "We like interesting company. And I do not see your man anywhere. That in and of itself is interesting."

These guys were cut from marble, but Sara wasn't so eager to explain herself to a couple of shower time fantasies. The sharpest glistening abs in the world couldn't make up for their invasiveness. So she shuffled her body and sighed and turned her head away from their hungry eyes before answering, "I'm flattered. But tired."

"We just think it's a shame that someone brings a goddess to paradise and abandons her for wild zebras."

Goddess? Sara laughed. Oh damn, nothing good would come from this. "Nice meeting you both," she said and rose, gathering her things as they stepped away to afford her space. There was no real threat here.

Just persistence.

Guillaume and Jean-Philippe were not done thirsting. They gave gentle chase in the form of a hasty walk as Sara hurried down one of the twirling stone paths toward the building. They caught up to her just inside the lobby.

"Mademoiselle, please," Jean Philippe said.

Sara shifted from one leg to the next. Cool air dried her suntan lotion-lathered skin, making it feel like crusted, used sandpaper.

"We are sorry if we offended you," Guillaume said.

"Takes a little more than that," Sara sighed. This was getting lame.

"We only wish to buy you a drink."

"And talk," Jean-Philippe added.

"Drinks are free," Sara said. "Sort of an empty gesture at a resort."

"Don't you tip?" Guillaume grinned. "I keep a handful of USD in my pocket at all times. Goes a long way here. Assuages my white guilt."

"Right," Sara said. "Don't have much of that." They laughed but she knew what he'd meant.

"Just a drink," Guillaume said.

"Here's why I'm thinking *nah*," Sara said. "You just told me y'all a couple. I'm married too, so this isn't going to be any kind of a hook up."

"Of course not," Guillaume said.

"Oh, of course not." Sara crossed her arms and smirked when he appeared to be stumped.

"We would like to know you," Guillaume said. "A memento of our trip, and yours. Friendly faces who would never have come into each other's lives otherwise."

20

"And you look bored," Jean-Philippe said with a shrug. "Almost as much as I am."

Guillaume perked up over this, but decided to leave his husband's comment unchallenged.

"What if I like being bored?" Sara asked.

"Then we'll talk about the weather," Guillaume said.

Sara chewed her lip to prevent the smile.

"So... drinks all around?" Guillaume was confident that Sara was on the hook. His eyes told her there was never any doubt.

She didn't like arrogance in men. But since she didn't have to like Guillaume, she nodded. Said, "Okay, but not until I shower." She wouldn't keep any of this from Blake. If anything, this was a warning shot across his bow. Her husband was up to something, but he wasn't talking. That enraged her.

"Let me get changed," Sara told them.

"We could go with you, have bottles sent right up and—"

Sara pointed to the bar. "Meet me in there in an hour."

The men smiled like the wolves they were.

Sara was already starting off for the elevators, determined to hop inside one before they could follow. "See you soon, boys."

THREE

The narrow tributary that wound inland toward Madagascar proper was stained the color of blood.

Lines of grazing pelicans and pirogues lined the river. Farmers drove cattle across the shallows, pointing the way to makeshift markets. If you didn't happen to see these drives on your walk, you could at least follow their tracks toward commerce.

The bazaar was an informal marketplace where the locals converged to sell and trade their goods: A robust selection of white and paddy rice, corn, pistachio nuts, fish, and shrimp. There was sometimes also a man called Chingh who paid top dollar for sea cucumbers.

Which is why Mosi often went. He was sent by Nosy Berafia, a tiny island off the northwest side of Madagascar. Today, he had made a fortune selling sea cucumbers to the Chinese man.

That was all Mosi cared about.

His people earned their living farming the shallows for sea cucumbers. They worked in seven-hour shifts daily to harvest as many of the spindly echinoderms as could be gathered. There was seemingly no end to their reproduction, meaning their sliver of the world was a resource to be protected.

The goal each day was to gather one hundred. The men and able-bodied boys did this, and then prepared their cache for transport to the informal markets.

Today's visit had been brief. Mosi waded through the bloody water, thigh-high and with a burlap sack of grains and produce slung over his shoulder.

He hated the sight of this river. Hated wading through. He was one of the few from Nosy Berafia who would do it. Most others preferred to go around, and that meant wasting the entire day.

Mosi had spoken to those from inland cities who promised the water was nothing to worry about. They claimed the coloration was from a salt-loving algae called Dunaliella Salina. It produced a red pigment that absorbed the energy of the sun in order to create more energy. Mosi thought that might've been true, but did not care. He only knew that the sight filled him with dread. Made him trudge hurriedly on, eager to cross to the other side.

And he got there at last, dropping the sack into his boat and wiping his brow. There were older moored boats sitting beside his, perched high and dry with sun-beaten hulls. The curved wood beginning to warp from perpetual un-use. Mosi did not know to whom these belonged, only that they had been here forever, and the island was too superstitious to clear them.

From here, Nosy Berafia seemed to bob on ocean waves. He stared at it from across the way. Thirty minutes to reach by rowboat.

One last push, and then you rest for the day, Mosi thought. He was one of the island's best harvesters. But his people had been willing to lose his labor because he travelled faster than anyone. And he was stronger. Which meant he could carry more resources back.

Mosi un-moored his boat and the hull slipped into emerald green water. He waded in up to his hips and then swung over the side, hopping aboard and reaching for the paddle.

"It will not get you," he whispered.

He began to paddle, flexing as the oar slapped the water, pushing the boat along with as much speed as he could give it. The sun was heavy and made the water sparkle. Mosi wouldn't stop until he reached Nosy Berafia's shallows. He wouldn't be safe until then.

"Hey! Hey! My friend."

A long piece of driftwood rocked atop the ocean a few hundred kilometers away. Underneath the blazing sun, Mosi could only see a silhouette lift up onto its forearms and wave a hand around.

"Please!" The voice was male. Possibly American. His hand reached out, stretching toward Mosi.

"Are you hurt?" Mosi called.

"Been floating for a day," he said. "I can... barely remember..."

Mosi paddled harder, veering wide to get closer. "Where did you come from?"

A long pause. Mosi felt the stranger thinking, straining to remember. "...fishing trip... leaky boat..."

Mosi cleared some of the space between them, but the sun refused to let him see the man with any more clarity. Even when Mosi cupped a hand over his forehead, the drifter was still just a floating shadow.

"Actually, it didn't spring a leak," the man said, beginning to laugh. "You will not believe me."

Mosi was close enough now to see him. He stopped paddling. The man was sun-beaten, his face full of broken blisters.

"Came right out of the ocean."

"What did?" Mosi asked, beginning to resume his course to Nosy Berafia.

"Dunno," he said, stretching his arm as if he were close enough to reach Mosi. "Please, friend, get me to land."

Mosi held the paddle still as he considered the plea. This as he watched a splotch of discolored water grow beneath the man's plank. Mosi rowed backward, pushing hard as the man receded and became a silhouette beneath the sun. The shape growing beneath the water was the size of a cabin cruiser. It continued growing and then broke the surface. The force of pelting water was great enough to drown him.

Mosi squinted. The water was like refracting crystal. Shimmers everywhere. The sun cooked his eyes even beneath squinting eyelids.

The man on the drift screamed. Mosi thrust his paddle into the water, forcing his boat away from the scene, away from the man who'd been abruptly silenced.

Mosi paddled hard. He should've kept his eyes on Nosy Berafia's shore, even as the water behind him began to stir. One glance over his shoulder and the stern of his rowboat exploded into fragments, a rushing caudal fin cleaving it into oblivion. The oversized shadow glided through the murk beneath him, and by then it was already too late.

The hull was half gone and the bow was unstable, knocking him off balance. He slipped and his back hit the water where he began to splash.

His world went dark. His ribcage exploded beneath incredible pressure, as if squeezed by a vice. His jaw fell open and water rushed his throat, but by then it hardly mattered.

Mosi was long dead.

FOUR

Blake Jovish was at least forty miles away, riding shotgun in a jeep that barreled inland through thick swabs of jungle terrain.

Large green leaves wound back and flung in, leaving his arms lashed with surface cuts. The driver, a dark-skinned guide from the coast named Kahega, gripped the wheel so hard his knuckles glowed white as he swerved around several would-be collisions, laughing like a boy playing Xbox.

His English was about as smooth as broken glass, but he spoke it. And each time he looked at his passenger, the joy drained from his face. "Stop shaking, Little Sticks," Kahega said. "Ima get you there in one piece, just like you paid for."

Blake was 'Little Sticks' because his arms were like campfire twigs and the guide laughed each time he said it. Most of the for-hire guys were bulked from hard days of manual labor. There wasn't much cubicle work on this continent outside the cities.

Kahega cranked the cassette radio so hard the speakers sang with distortion. "King of Wishful Thinking" by Go West. Blake had never heard the song before and the admission made Kahega indignant.

"What kind of American are you?" he said, trying to get Blake to pick up the song's chorus and run with it.

"One born in 1994."

"You want us to pick up some Justin Bieber at market?" The guide laughed and laughed and somehow that sound was louder than the blaring speaker static.

Sadder still was that Blake had spent most of his honeymoon with this man. And even worse? He somehow felt more relaxed around him.

When Blake got back to his life later today, there would be nothing but tension. Most of it because he was lying to Sara.

Blake didn't have that with Kahega. Their relationship was transactional. Pay the daily fee in crisp USD, and you bought yourself enough loyalty to last till sunset. It was all so depressingly mercenary. But he figured it was also the same principle as any 9-to-5 gig, and more honest to boot.

The jeep sped on, the two of them ducking leaves and branches that seemed determined to reach into the cab and coldcock them. Every near miss prompted another deep-rumbling belly laugh from Kahega. They probably heard it on the summit of Mount Maromokotro.

The next song was "We Close Our Eyes" and Blake thought he might've heard that one somewhere before, though he was too nervous to concern himself with Kahega's dated musical tastes.

He was busy stressing over the fact that he was nearly out of money.

Their Maine wedding had been done on a relatively small scale. It was immediate family, mostly Sara's, along with close friends. Their money lived in a joint account and most of it had been squirreled away for this very trip.

It had taken the better part of a year to warm Sara to the idea of honeymooning in Madagascar.

"This better not be some racist, 'because you're black shit,'" she'd said, jokingly. It was almost preferable she think that, because Blake couldn't bring himself to own the truth. Not when it sounded so ridiculous. He'd spent the last twelve months practicing the speech, trying to find a way to blunt the absurdity of it, and never once managing to get there.

Sara didn't know that as soon as they were pronounced man and wife, Blake had made one last withdrawal from their joint checking account—halving the down payment on their dream home in order to bankroll this endeavor.

Kahega had almost the entire thing, and if this gamble fizzled out, Blake was in a world of hurt and headed down the highway to divorce.

All in record time.

Treasure hunting on the down low wasn't easy.

The jeep cut hard right and plowed to a harder stop. The guide reached between the seat cushions and whipped a gigantic revolver out, pointing it toward the tree line while the jeep's overworked engine clacked and cooled.

Kahega eyed the treetops like something up there watched them.

"What's the matter?" Blake said.

Kahega twisted the radio knob down and raised his free hand to signal silence. The gun went from one treetop to the next.

They sat frozen like that for a long time. Until he hopped from the jeep without warning, saying, "We walk from here."

"Do I get to know where here is?" Blake said, sliding his backpack loops around his shoulders.

"Would you know if I told you, Little Sticks?"

"Fair."

"This way."

Blake thought trekking through the jungle should've been easier on his exhaustion. Here, the sun was almost entirely blotted by the drooping mangroves, but the foliage retained heat like an afghan on a summer's afternoon. His scalp itched and dirty sweat tickled his eyes.

Kahega trudged on ahead, keeping just enough distance to know where Blake was. This was his move in case of danger. Not everyone in this part of the world was happy to see a western man. And some got downright hostile when Blake started asking questions about local history and folklore.

"Far enough," a voice ghosted through the trees.

Blake looked up and found bodies in the branches, peering out from behind trunks. Armed men who'd been expecting them. Rifles hovered like angry specters ready to spit bullets.

The guide fired back in Malagasy—a language Blake didn't understand. It became a volley of words fighting for supremacy. Chaos threatened to escalate and Blake began to fear just how much loyalty his money bought him.

"Tell me what it is you are doing here." The voice boomed, this time in English. There was no speaker attached that either of them could see.

"I have someone here who wants something," Kahega said.

"A white man," the voice spat.

"Every man pays," Kahega said. "This one better than most."

Sure, Blake thought. Better than most.

This was the end of the line.

Blake felt the fear of death. Sara never flashed before his mind, though. He worried instead about missing his chance. He thought of the pages, safe and secure at the resort. He had studied them so often over the last twelve months that every detail lived inside his head.

He was closer than anyone had ever come. There was just one question on his mind today. And if he could get that answer, everything would be different. If not—

A man appeared in the clearing before them and the row of machine guns stood at ease. For a second, Blake thought he might be able to breathe. Until the leader tore a six-shooter from his holster and pushed it against Kahega's temple.

The guide barely flinched.

"I should kill you for bringing this white man here," the leader said.

"He cannot find his way out of the resort without me," Kahega assured him.

The leader took one look at Blake, noticed his cargo shorts, Old Navy tee, and Crocs before concluding that Kahega was correct. "Talk fast."

Kahega gestured to his pocket. The leader nodded and Kahega took that as permission. His fingers slid into his shorts and lifted a wad of Blake's money into the air.

The leader counted the flopping bills and then snatched them. "Where is he from?"

"Maine," Kahega told him.

"Maine is close to Canada," the leader said.

"He does not speak French," Kahega assured. "And he does not come looking for diamonds."

"What else could be so important?" the leader wondered.

"We are here to discuss that very matter with you," Kahega said.

The leader looked intrigued, stealing delight from Blake's discomfort. Then he holstered his gun and waved them to follow, turning back toward the trees. "Let's talk."

The invitation brought them further into the forest. The leader's grin was an awful, lopsided sneer. He pointed to a small trail and guided them along it until they reached a row of huts arced around a skinny mine adit.

"The Canadians have claimed this mine," the leader said. "And the diamonds that are allegedly inside of it." They entered the nearest hut and he poured himself a glass of whiskey without offering his guests the overspill.

The leader sat atop the corner desk with the gun in one hand and a drink in the other. His eyes were like fried eggs.

Blake despised looking at him.

"The money you pay is enough for me to hear your question," the leader said.

Blake looked at Kahega, passing an unspoken question with his eyes. Was this the right time to take the warlord up on his offer? The guide gave a slow nod.

"I am looking for Zanahary's tongue," Blake said.

The warlord knocked his glass back and laughed, a bellow somehow deeper than Kahega's. "Zanahary's tongue," he said. "Is nothing any white man should ever say." He rose, crossed the room and stood nose-to-nose with Blake. His cheeks puffed. "Who told it to you?"

"An old man," Blake said, words wavering. "My father." That was a complete lie.

"What business had your father here?"

"He visited. Decades ago. Met a woman and shared her company on what he could only say was the island's hook. The locals say that can only mean Zanahary's tongue, the northernmost point on the island. But there is nothing there."

"Who was this woman?" the leader asked.

"Someone my father loved very much."

"If he loved her so much, then why—"

"Why'd he leave?" Blake said. "I know. It's a question my father asked himself every day. This was 1986... civil war had made this place unstable and she was determined to stay and fix her homeland. By the time things calmed and he returned, she was missing."

The leader watched his face for signs of the lie. Blake should've cracked, but needed this more than anything. Without it, he was nothing. His life was nothing. If he failed, he'd spend the rest of it wondering about that damn tongue. Dreaming about the life he could've had.

What he could've given Sara.

"Zanahary is from Malagasy orature," the leader said. "True, some of it has been written in books, but the tongue you speak of can only be one place. If you approach from land then you will not see it, because it refers to the rock face that judges Antsiranana Bay." He looked to Kahega, eyeing the porter like he was a charlatan. "You do not know any of this?"

Kahega shrugged.

"You should," the leader growled.

The guide averted his eyes and nodded again, faster this time. Eager agreement.

Blake looked at the floor. Truth was, Zanahary wasn't anywhere in those pages. Instead, it was given to them by an elder merchant on the island of Nose Be who thought perhaps one line of the riddle corresponded with Malagasy lore.

It begins on the hook where you are the bait. Reach the throat and tip the tongue.

The elder they questioned said they would need to travel far into the underworld in order to get that answer, because it was smugglers and warlords who knew best the old names.

So Kahega brought him here.

"If you approach the northern tip from the coast," the leader said, "Zanahary's tongue is the name pirates use to describe the sunken jetty that sprawls across the ocean floor, but also rises up and connects to the rock face."

"Thank you," Blake said.

"Go," the leader told them. "Back to your jeep and away from here. I see you again, white man, all the allies in Madagascar will not save you."

They started to go. Kahega had the hut flap pulled aside when the warlord called after them. "Wait."

They froze.

The warlord had the fistful of bills in hand, waving them around with mockery. "The information you just bought comes with a price."

"It's worth it," Blake said.

"Not the money." The warlord grinned. "Lives."

Blake's glassy eyes were uncomprehending.

"This money goes toward better weapons. Those rifles that greeted you, they are old. Always jamming. Slow rates of fire." He waved the cash back and forth. "This upgrades me to a few fully automatic Russian rifles. We are going to wait here for the Canadians, kill them as soon as they arrive. When you stand on Zanahary's tongue, thinking about that nice moment from your white father's life, you will do so knowing that you've bankrolled the slaughter of trespassers."

"You were going to kill them anyway."

The warlord smiled, delighted by the coldness of Blake's response. "But, without your help."

Blake thought on that, tried to find some kind of conscience for the deaths of men he'd never know. Men who'd be just as dead by different guns if he'd never come here. "They shouldn't be here," he said.

The warlord nodded. "Same will be said of you."

Kahega intervened with a hard squeeze of Blake's shoulder. "Let's go," he whispered.

And they left.

FIVE

Sara walked into the resort lounge and found her afternoon dates sitting at a back booth, facing the entrance. Vape smoke puffed past Jean-Philippe's pursed lips and Guillaume waved to her from the haze.

Sara paused, catching her reflection in the wall mirror. What a mistake, she knew. The dark dress stretched over her curves like spandex, an outfit once intended to tease her husband over Italian in the resort's swankiest restaurant, the one that required reservations three nights in advance.

Prowling eyes crawled her from other darkened tables as she walked. On some level, the attention felt good.

Eager aftershave sifted through Sara's nostrils as she approached. She flashed a polite smile and sat facing them. Guillaume's hair was slicked back, still wet from a quick shower. The black button-down was only fastened halfway, revealing a hint of the clean-shaven chest that had glistened poolside. That he was off limits, allegedly, made him more attractive.

"Still don't know why I came," Sara said.

"No reason needed," Guillaume's smile sparkled with just a hint of game. "We are guests here at the same moment in time. Let that be enough."

The Frenchmen were drinking Cognac, which was an immediate invitation to go hard. Sara ordered a whiskey double, glad for a second that Blake wasn't around to judge. He handled his liquor the way a toddler would, and harbored resentment because she could knock it back with the best of the last callers.

And it beat the steady diet of tropical sugar bombs so sweet her stomach now had cavities.

"What should we drink to?" Jean-Philippe said.

"Paradise," Guillaume said. "May we always find it, wherever we are."

They turned out to be good company. Afternoon conversation was preferable to more lonely hours by the pool. She was glad for the distraction, because right now the mere thought of Blake Jovish tightened her jaw like a wrench.

Jean-Philippe was often distracted, watching the crowd and audibly sighing whenever Sara and Guillaume got off on too long a jag. He referred to Sara as "mademoiselle," and she ignored the passive-aggressiveness of it. She'd retained enough college French to know it meant "unmarried woman."

She felt like a pawn in some married couple's game, but didn't care. Didn't have to understand. Certainly didn't judge. She liked their company, mostly Guillaume's, kinks and all, and thought it funny that in this moment she knew them better than she knew her husband.

The men managed an antique shop right outside of Paris and were occasionally bankrolled into the field whenever their boss needed an opinion on the authenticity of recovered goods.

Sara asked what made their opinion so special, and Guillaume revealed he held an advanced degree in archeology.

"Some Indiana Jones stuff," Sara said.

"Indiana Jones was a professor," Guillaume said. "I couldn't wait to leave university. Besides, I am better looking."

Sara cocked her head. "Than young Harrison Ford? Please."

Jean-Philippe laughed at this, chiming in to talk about how he handled the day-to-day affairs of the antique shop.

"That's a fantasy life," Sara said and couldn't square it. They earned their living completely outside the rat race. Nothing was more enviable than that.

"Plenty of rats," Jean-Philippe told her. "If you're not working for yourself, you're making somebody richer."

Guillaume was interested in Sara's employment as a marine biologist, an unwelcome topic in her mind. She'd rather hear about the exotic corners of the world they'd seen, but he continued to insist on tales of the nautical life.

She sighed. Told them her job title was "Fishery Observer" and that meant she collected catch and bycatch data from U.S. commercial fishing vessels. Her job was to measure what these vessels were taking out of the ocean, what they were tossing back, and the type of equipment and gear used to do it.

It guaranteed adherence to regulations and ensured the sustainability of our marine resources.

It also kept baker's hours. Sara was up and on the road well before dawn, usually 3 am, in order to be at the port before departure. Sometimes she was gone for the day, other times she'd be at sea for a week or even two. She liked the way her schedule shifted because it meant keeping things interesting. Last thing she wanted was to sit in front of spreadsheets all day.

Which is what the job was slowly becoming.

Used to be that she'd compile her data at sea to be debriefed in port, handing over her spreadsheets for independent correlation. But like all things, number crunchers figured out they could save money by cutting loose that middle man, and now Sara debriefed herself by writing up reports on her own data.

Excel nightmares haunted her dreams every couple of nights.

"Excel," Jean-Philippe said.

"Oh, do not start," Guillaume groaned.

"Au contraire," Sara laughed. "I can't resist a good spreadsheet war story. What good is drinking if you can't drown a few sorrows?"

"If he starts on this song," Guillaume warned, "he will sing it all night."

"Warm up that throat," Sara told Jean-Philippe and then slapped the table with enthusiasm. "Because I feel you."

"Inventory reports and profit margins. I'm living to manage someone else's fortune." Jean-Philippe downed his drink and coughed. "Just tiresome, is all."

"And here I thought your lives sounded pretty hot." Sara cocked an eyebrow, caught a flash of Guillaume's seething eyes that he tried to hide.

Jean-Philippe ordered another round for the table. "My job is customer service for a niche that has more money than it knows what to do with. Our boss says we are a full-service outfit and sometimes that makes me more of a slave."

Guillaume rolled his eyes and nudged his partner. Jean-Philippe fell silent, placing the e-cigarette back between his lips. "Sara, how you can say for certain what is taken out of the ocean when there are other countries who do not cooperate with your bureaucracy?"

"It's estimated," Sara said. "Data points are shared among the participating countries while percentages of piracy are factored into the data."

"But what happens when—"

"It's my turn to ask y'all something," Sara said.

The shimmering sun gave Guillaume's dark complexion a bronzed sheen as he lifted a single finger. His grin was winter fresh. He had a model's looks and knew it. "What do you do for fun around here, Sara? Once everyone has gone back to their rooms for the evening, I mean."

"Don't be lame." Sara flashed her ring. "We were doing good. You smiling all cool and shit. Think I don't know where this is headed?"

"Where is that?" Guillaume could barely contain his smile. Next to him, Jean-Philippe blew a rush of vape smoke across the table, enshrouding her.

Sara didn't like games, given that Blake was off playing one without her. "I'm about to finish this drink and wish you a good rest of your vacation."

Guillaume clicked his tongue. "That would be hasty," he grinned. "Let us back up. We three are world travelers. Accustomed to more than just our ports of call. Is that fair to say?"

"Fair to say," Sara said.

"Look," Jean-Philippe put his hand on top of his husband's and held it there with a slight squeeze. "This is not what you think it is."

"Oh no?" Sara said. "You came over to me at the pool like dogs in heat because you wanted to be all intellectual?"

"Sort of," Guillaume confessed. "There is a whole beautiful island here, yet all you have seen is this resort."

"Charity then?" Sara laughed.

"Of course not. You are an interesting woman."

"Who's getting bored fast..."

"Why'd you wear that dress?" Jean-Philippe said, tiring of this dance.

"I'm on my honeymoon," Sara growled. "Didn't pack for a single's night."

"Tomorrow," Guillaume said, "I propose our own adventure."

"Forget it."

"More poolside drinks in your future?" Guillaume said.

A sigh. "What've you got?"

"Diego Suarez is near one of the most amazing sights the world has to offer. The Tsingy Forest. Ever see it?"

"Where the hell is Diego Suarez?" she said.

"I'm sorry." Guillaume cleared his throat. "You know it as Antsiranana. The locals call this city Diego Suarez because that is its founded name. But the Tsingy Forest is something special. In Malagasy it translates to 'where one cannot walk barefoot.' You have never seen such a place. You will feel like you're on Mars."

"Why do you want to take me on a tour?"

"We have been honest with you," Guillaume said. "Here is a woman with a passion for these things. A prisoner to tourism. It's there in your eyes."

"You couldn't see my eyes by the pool," she said. "I was wearing sunglasses."

Guillaume ignored her. "If you crave a more nautical setting, then we look to Antsiranana Bay, which is so imperceptible from the ocean that smugglers once built an entire port inside it."

Sara's bullshit detector was running out of batteries. The longer she spoke to them, the more comfortable she felt. Even if the back of her mind was loaded with suspicion.

Guillaume slipped her a business card for something called LE VASE CASSÉ and told her to drop him a line next time she was in France, as if she went over there every couple of weeks.

"Give that card to the front desk," he told her. "Tell them who you are with. You can also tell the US embassy you are taking the trip. Give them our names, of course. Both are on that card. You would be smart to do these things, Sara. We would not consider it rude, because if you were to lend us the pleasure of your company, I would want your mind at ease."

"This is our first vacation in years," Jean-Philippe said. "We enjoy meeting interesting people from corners of the world other than our own."

Their invitation intrigued her, but Guillaume's spiel sounded rehearsed. Yes, it might set her mind at ease, but it was exactly the kind of thing a grifter might say. Besides, this was her honeymoon, and here she was making plans to see the continent with strange men. Men who were not her husband.

Wherever the hell Blake is, Sara thought, suddenly feeling ill about it.

"Well, at least think about it," Guillaume said. "We will leave from the lobby tomorrow around nine."

Sara chewed on it. "I'll let you know," she said and stood to leave. And then hurried for the elevators because the tears were coming faster than she realized.

SIX

"If I did not give them money, they would have killed us both," Kahega said.

"That's not my problem," Blake shot back. His heart raced harder now than it had in the presence of that warlord. His guide had used all the money to get them out of those crosshairs. Now he wanted more.

"Consider it," Kahega said.

"Appreciate the advice," Blake said. "But I'll take my chances."

"You don't have a chance," Kahega said. "You'll be gunned down where you stand."

"What do you want?"

"To get paid," the guide said, arms outstretched. "Every dime I earned from the last two days was taken from me. For us." The guide reached between the seats and lifted a machete in his fist. The tip of the blade stung cold against Blake's neck.

"This is what they'll do," he said.

"You took me to a warlord."

"The only man on this island who would have known."

"You put a price on my head."

"I should have gone alone? Doomed myself?"

"I didn't say that."

"We are both back to square one, yes? It does not take an accountant to know you are nearly out of money. How will you advance if not without my help?"

As of right now, Blake didn't have an answer to that question.

"Took me a minute," Kahega said. "You were coy from the start, but I should've known what you were really after. People always come here thinking they're gonna find that pirate's stash."

"What?"

"Do not lie to me," Kahega said. "There is a man from Italy who is out here every summer. Spends months at a time hunting it and he has been doing it since Roger Moore was 007." He laughed at his own joke. "Many have tried, no one has succeeded. So at first I laughed at you and thought I would take your money."

Blake put his fingers to the blade and eased it away, a gesture that prompted Kahega to laugh.

"At least you do not deny it," Kahega said.

Blake weighed his options. This was a race against time. He imagined Sara in there, sitting with her eyes on the clock. Waiting for him to return. She had a temper like C4 and when she blew, there'd be nothing left of them but a crater. "What kind of assurance do I have?" Blake asked. "That I can trust you?"

"None," Kahega said.

Blake felt helpless as the jeep idled. His beard itched. He caught sight of himself in the side mirror and lamented that he couldn't even get a tan. His pasty flesh went straight to sunburnt.

The resort walls were six feet from him. It was as far as the porter could drive. No unofficial transportation was allowed past the gates, because vacationers were apparently to be insulated from the island regulars at all times.

"You did not think this through, Little Sticks," Kahega told him.

"I did," Blake said. "That's why it's frustrating. I thought everything through. Cost me thousands to get here, and now I need more to finish, but I have nothing left."

"We did more than buy information back there. We bought our lives."

"I'm ruined if I go in there now," Blake said. "I'll lose everything."

"I can get you the rest of the way," Kahega said. "No longer as your employee, but a partner."

Blake stewed.

The guide gave him a moment. He turned up the radio and watched a tourist bus depart through the gates for the island sunset tour.

What was the alternative? Blake wondered. Go inside now, like this, and 'fess to Sara that they were twenty grand in the hole because he'd gone all Allan Quartermain without her knowledge? She'd find a way to annul their marriage on the flight home.

Kahega understood this as well, sitting with his arms folded, grinning like the future was bright.

"What do you want?" Blake said.

"I'm reasonable. Thirty percent."

"Thirty?"

"If you find it, you are going to have one heck of a time taking treasure out of this country. Our government will pull out every stop to prevent you from leaving with a single coin. That is what I offer. I'll get us a ship. A small crew paid from my end. And then we both live out the rest of our lives in peace."

Blake gnawed the inside of his cheek. "Partners, huh?"

Kahega stuck out his hand.

Blake shook it.

"We leave tomorrow," the guide said. "Perhaps now is the time to tell your wife everything. Because we may have to leave in a hurry."

Blake swallowed hard. This wasn't going to be pretty, but it needed to be done.

SEVEN

Sara had gone back to her room and decided to call her parents, eager to hear a few friendly and familiar voices. Dad was out, and Mom sounded annoyed that she had to be the one to talk to her.

"Look who finally decides to call," she said.

"Flight was good, Mom, thanks."

"Everything okay?"

"I guess?"

Mom didn't hear the reluctance. Or didn't have time to hear it. "Good. Lookit, baby, I'm in the middle of interviews. Hiring a new manager for James' campaign and we're down to just two finalists. I like the girl 'cause she's not afraid of a street fight, and that's what politics is these days. But your father and brother—"

"Listen to them," Sara said.

With a clucking tongue, "You always take their side."

"It's James' campaign," Sara said. "Just don't forget that."

"Forget? Been working twenty-four seven on it for the last two years. Only one who's forgetting anything is the girl currently halfway around the world. One who—"

"On her honeymoon!" Sara screamed and Mom ignored it, continued.

"One who can't help her brother because she feels like she needs to make her own mark in the world."

"Oh, I'm sorry, Mom. I'd like my own life. Is that unreasonable?"

"You gotta make sacrifices. The Mosby name is what's important. One day we'll be gone and that will be all that matters."

"You've made that real clear," Sara said. "A million times."

"I'll tell Dad you send your love. He'll be relieved you called." Mom didn't give her a chance to respond. There was a click, and then she was gone, leaving Sara standing alone inside the darkened room.

She stood frozen for so long, the line clicked over and a voice from reception said, "Emerald Tides front desk. How may I help you, Miss Jovish?"

Sara slammed the phone down and stepped away from it as if it'd bitten her. Her eyes settled on Blake's suitcase. Reminders all around. No, she couldn't stay here.

Her first thought was to go back down to guest services and see what the resort had on the agenda for tonight. But she spotted Guillaume and Jean-Philippe in the lounge. They'd moved up to the actual bar and were deep in conversation with a young Hispanic couple. She hurried out into the humidity.

She passed the pool, tennis courts, and even the beachfront cabanas. The beach was unique, a long jetty that reached out through the ocean like an arm, capped by a balled fist. A bar and rounded patio sat on that fist, overlooking the bay.

The beach was filled with couples. Sara goose-stepped them and twisted her shoulders around the waiters who made endless return trips, bringing frozen drinks to patrons who scarcely tipped. She noted Guillaume's advice and wished she had someone to share it with.

She found a patch of sand that was mostly clear, and she got close enough to the water so that she could keep her ankles submerged, thinking that would cool her off while she closed her eyes and tried to sort her thoughts.

It was there among the pleasant and ambient beach chatter that Sara closed her eyes and slept.

***

She awoke to a scream. A dozen screams, really. Sara sprung up into a sitting position and rubbed the gooseflesh on her forearms while she fought to recover her bearings.

It was dark now. The beach had thinned considerably. What little crowd remained stood gathered in the shallows, shrieking over whatever commotion was happening beyond them.

Another scream. The on-lookers scattered, jumping clear of something. The sudden motion startled Sara into standing.

The shadow of a woman wobbled down the center of the jetty. Her feet scraped through sand as she walked. Two crooked lines were engraved on beach behind her. As she neared the bar, the ambient light there found her, brought her body into detail.

The woman was nude, two-toned. Dark skin with blacker bruises across her chest and stomach. She spoke in deep wheezes and little spittles of blood rained into the sand. She continued to shamble as the people on the patio began scattering in panic, some even diving into the water.

She reached the ocean and the resort light lost her. The night swallowed her whole. As she vanished, an indecipherable cry in her native tongue united the beach in stunned silence.

They stood listening to the sound of a gentle breaststroke that carried the woman from the shallows. Every so often, they heard her scream. A repeated phrase that made Sara wish like hell she spoke Malagasy.

People on the jetty tried to figure out who got touched by the woman's spittle, and the denials were growing desperately angry. Sara was getting ready to retreat when the worst scream she'd ever heard plunged the whole place back into silence.

Complete terror rushed in off the winds, swooping through the souls of every tourist. That horrible noise somehow continued even though nobody's lungs could hold that much air. The scream was wet and swirled with madness because there was laughter in it too. Relief. It seemed to go on forever, until it didn't, leaving everyone there listening to the benign sound of ebbing water lapping somewhere in the dark beyond.

***

Sara got back to her room three hours later, opened the door and found Blake sitting there, hat in hand, looking ready to give an apology for the ages.

She rolled her eyes at the sight. Of course he'd show up now. After she spent the last two hours talking to authorities. Everyone's story was in sync: A woman from the village who suffered from respiratory plague had slipped past the resort gates and marched straight for the water.

Given her disease, nobody had wanted to stop her.

Because of that, sixty people were in quarantine. Sara would've been number sixty-one, except that security cameras showed her far enough away from the action the entire time. Couldn't have been in contact with the woman's highly contagious spittle.

Nobody knew why this woman would carelessly risk the lives of so many innocent people, though everyone agreed on what had been her final word. The twisted way in which she'd said it.

"Angatra."

"I heard what happened," Blake said, bringing her back to an equally depressing reality.

The hairs on the back of Sara's neck tingled. Her first instinct was to go to him, throw herself around his shoulders and cry. For the horrible sight she'd witnessed. For all the stress he'd given her. She needed release, but as she watched him stare at her toes, unable or unwilling to lift his eyes any higher, her needs folded into anger.

"Nice talk, husband," she growled.

"I screwed up." His gaze landed on the whiskey glass atop the bed table and he had the balls, the actual balls, to look indignant about it.

"Tell me how," Sara said. "How'd you screw up?"

Blake didn't want to tell her. He tried sidestepping the topic by asking about tonight's chaos.

Sara refused. She stood her ground and dressed him down to the bone.

"This made sense in my head," Blake said. "Now, as I try and articulate it..."

"You've been gone for two days."

A crowd rolled past their door, moving down the hallway in a stampede. Somebody threw an elbow against the door. The group laughed hysterically, chanting, "Shots! Shots! Shots!"

Blake lunged for Sara, trying to throw his arms around her as if he could simply hug his way out of this. She shoved him back with a growl so ferocious it surprised even her. "Not until you tell me where you've been. You owe me that."

Blake's attention went back to her feet. "I was afraid to hear no," he said.

"You're gearing up to hear fuck off."

45

Blake accepted that bitter pill with a grave nod. "If you had said no straight away," he said, "I wouldn't have been able to refrain from at least trying."

It hurt Sara to hear this. Her husband had secrets because he had no confidence in his partner.

"I'll tell you," Blake said. "Please sit down with me and you'll hear every word."

"If I don't like it, you can sleep in the bar for all I care. That's the condition."

"Fair."

Sara went to the whiskey and poured a glass, slammed it back and lifted an eyebrow that dared him to say anything about it.

Blake ignored the bait. "The burning man," he said, and then got to his knees, professional groveler that he was. He watched Sara pour a second drink and sip the glass.

He was a frightened dog and he'd better have a good goddamn reason for playing this card. Because the night in question, the night of the burning man, had been bad.

She'd never seen anyone more broken than he'd been then.

She found him sitting at the kitchen table in the early hours, a zombie at the tail end of a twelve-hour shift. His eyes glistened like gasoline-soaked charcoal and he stared out at the treetops visible through their dining room window.

The world around them had been silent, save for the ticking wall clock. She counted the ticks out of discomfort and got well over one thousand before he spoke.

When he did, his words were so soft she might've imagined them.

"Saw a man die tonight."

That wasn't unusual for an EMT, but his one-thousand-yard stare suggested this was different. When he finally worked up the courage to turn his head, streaks of tears had cut a clean swath straight down through his soot-stained face.

The story was horrific. His unit had responded to a call where somebody had lapsed into unconsciousness. It was a hot summer night and the air was humid enough to stick to your skin. A large amount of brownouts lined the Maine seaboard

46

because everyone and their neighbor had air conditioners blasting.

Blake and his partner trudged up four flights of stairs in pitch darkness, and as they neared the apartment in question, the air became gas station bitter. The front door was ajar and inside they found a man rocking in a recliner, soaked to the bone in gasoline and trying to light matches by striking them against wooden teeth that so far had failed to catch.

A dead man lay crumpled at his feet, two fresh smoked bullet holes drilled through his brain. A six-shot revolver lay discarded on the floor, tossed aside because it had served its purpose.

"Looking," the laughing man told Blake. "But not finding." In his free hand were several pages of yellow parchment. "Let it burn."

Something about the man compelled Blake forward. He snatched the papers from the jaws of annihilation as the laughing man's match caught, transforming him into a human bonfire.

And while Blake didn't know what had possessed him to risk everything in that moment, Sara knew now what a fool she'd been to pretend he hadn't been searching for answers this entire time.

All those nights he'd wake up screaming, visions of molten flesh staining his eyes. All the ways Sara tried to soothe his mind. All of those struggles, and Blake Jovish had been working the angles without her.

"You bastard," Sara said.

Blake ignored it. He reached underneath the bed and slid a small cloth wrap out from underneath it. "I'm chasing it," he said and unfurled several piss yellow papers, displaying them on top of the bed comforter like sacred texts. "I should've told you, but thought I could get it done faster on my own."

"You thought you could come to a foreign country and, what? Follow a treasure map to a pot of gold?"

"It's not exactly a map, but I got close, Sara."

"Sounds like you came up empty."

"For now," he said. "But I'm still close."

"You said that."

"A few more days, baby. Shit, I never meant to deceive you."

Sara's laughter was so aggressive it startled him into silence. A sense of humor straight up emboldened by the whiskey sloshing around inside her head. At last, it made sense. Here was the real reason for his silence, humility, and trembling hands.

"Lemme guess," she said. "Guy you're working with is out there cruising around with our down payment. That's why you've got shame in your eyes."

"If I'm right about this, none of that will matter."

"Pretty big if," Sara said.

Blake couldn't afford to get into the weeds with her. He lifted the largest of four documents, dangling it in her face like the answer was obvious.

"I'm going to find this," he said.

It would've been easier to swallow her husband having an affair with some island native, because this was bullshit. "I don't know what that is," she said.

"It's what the burning man died for that night," he said, and his face winced at the memory. "We're going to have a home on the coast in every state." Blake took a deep breath. Then he took another and held it there for good measure before giving her the spiel. Oddly rehearsed. One she didn't care to hear.

Her husband was persistent, but the details of the story incensed her. Pirate gold. Lost loves. Hidden treasure. This is the crap that had occupied his thoughts?

She had to give it to Blake. He was right. She would've shot this down with the quickness, because who believed in buried treasure anymore?

She wondered what Guillaume and Jean-Philippe might say about this. Their sudden appearance in her thoughts turned her blood to ice.

"Who else knows you're here?" she asked.

"The guide I've been paying to take me around the island. Why?"

"And all the people you've been asking along the way?"

"Yes," Blake said. "I guess."

Sara swallowed the whiskey. "Word's getting around."

"Shit, Sara," he said. "In my head, this was going to be my gift to you. I was going to deliver something that nobody in modern history can give. To be able to come through that door and tell you this day truly was the beginning of the rest of your life."

"We just got married," Sara said. "That was the first day of the rest of my life. It was four days ago."

Blake waved that away because he was eager to reach the end of this rainbow. "This is different," he said. "This is a life where we don't have to suffer at the hands of the system. We can have beach houses, fast cars, give our children the future most people only dream about. The whole thing. We deserve that."

There was a knock at the door. Blake turned from salesman to scarecrow.

Sara turned and knew she had to answer it. Knew who was there before she looked.

Guillaume. A spirit conjured by mere thought. He haunted the peephole with a grim smile. Her first instinct was to hush Blake, but he hadn't said anything since the knock. He hadn't even moved.

Sara thought about opening the door to the end of its bolted chain. This timing wasn't coincidental. Guillaume and Jean-Philippe weren't interested in cheering her up any more than getting her in the sack.

Stupid Sara, she thought. You're not this naïve.

"I see your shadow in front of the hole, you know," Guillaume said. Gone was the flirtatious attitude and pleasant softness in his face. At this angle, the light sharpened his jutting cheekbones into knives.

"I think you're a little early," Sara told him.

Blake took point beside her. He reached for the knob, twisted it—

And Guillaume flung the door open. The chain braced, leaving the two men glaring.

"Who's this?" Blake said.

"A friend." Guillaume didn't bother to smile. "Who would like very much to come inside."

"It's late," Blake said and started to close the door.

Guillaume's shoe was wedged inside the jamb. "Sara?"

"It's late," she agreed.

Guillaume frowned at the rejection, angled his face so that he could see over their shoulders. "Is there nothing I can say to make you reconsider? Three friends and a bottle of wine at the bar? On me?"

"It's. Late," Sara said.

"Too late, I suppose." Guillaume gave Sara a small frown and walked off.

Blake closed the door and pulled his shirt off, tossing it aside and dropping onto the bed like all was forgiven and this was just another night on vacation.

"I think we'd better go home," Sara said.

"Soon."

"Tomorrow."

"Why don't we get up extra early and pack."

"Good."

"Yeah," he said. "Because we're headed out on the ocean tomorrow." He rolled back over so their eyes could meet. "Sara, I want you out there with me."

"I don't get a say? You've already made the decision."

"My guy, Kahega, is making the arrangements. Will you give me a few days? It's where we've got to go. To finish this."

Sara watched him roll over and bury his face in the pillows. A moment later, he was snoring.

She poured another whiskey, desperate to quell the drumming in her heart.

She wasn't going to sleep tonight.

Too anxious.

She only stared at the door, fearing the man beyond it would be back.

EIGHT

Zane killed the motor and dropped anchor. He stripped and reached for the crumpled diving suit on the floor behind him.

"How long you need?" Lullo slid a plate of body armor over his chest and loaded the AK-47, certain that trouble was coming. Already on edge from it.

"Thirty minutes, I hope." Zane didn't have the heart to tell Lullo that pirates would turn him inside out before he could fire off a single shot. Lullo had fancied himself Zane's protector since they were kids.

The mainland was a black splotch on the horizon line. Zane had never been one for maps, just eyeballs. He stared at the distant landmass and flashed his thumb up, squinting so that his overlong fingernail fit neatly into the rounded dome of Maromokotro's peak.

It wasn't exact, but damn close.

With his gear assembled and his body stuffed inside the constricting body suit, Zane popped his mouth and placed the breathing apparatus inside. He gave Lullo a supportive tap on the back.

Zane balanced himself on the rail and dropped toward the water. The moonlight reached down a few kilometers so dark blue became a gradient of deeper blacks. Soon he was paddling through impenetrable onyx.

He flicked on his light once the world around him grew so dark and weightless that he might've been paddling through space.

A pair of butterfly fish darted through his beam. Zane grinned as wide as he could with the breather in his mouth. Theirs was an important sight and he knew his sense of direction hadn't failed. Butterfly fish fed on coral polyps, and so he knew there was coral here.

Red coral, specifically.

A quick sweep of the floor proved that Zane had already harvested this shelf. It was nothing but nervous fish and uneven terrain. He was the only one who knew about this spot, discovered through a stroke of miserable luck. Most coral hunters stuck to the reefs, picked them clean because the picking there was easy. Zane never bothered with the obvious places unless he happened to catch the regrowth.

Tonight, he was going to have to go deeper.

This was more than just a luxury hunt. Zane needed as much of that red gold as his hands could carry. His daughter was headed off continent to university. His wife gave reminding eyes of that fact every night, weighting their relationship with permanent urgency. When Zane was home for the evening, it wasn't to relax. It was to sit and strategize how he was going to find more coral.

Zane hated the globalized world. The Internet squeezed this planet like a tightened belt. Anybody with a computer could buy every single color of coral. And since the Internet's marketplace was global, the demand was constant. Interested parties scoured every corner of the world for whatever they could sell.

Everyone praised progress without considering how inconvenient convenience was.

Zane swam up on the edge of a cliff that dropped so deep it was impossible to see how far down it went. Overhead, the boat's spotlight resembled a moon.

Flippered feet wobbled against the edge and Zane took a deep pull on his valve, swallowing a burst of bottled air before dropping through the gloom like a brick.

The overhead light became a far off star. His feet touched down and Zane kicked off horizontally, paddling through the murk with his light outstretched. His chances of finding coral receded with every descent. Thing was, the sun could reach this far. It was still possible to find what he needed.

A few healthy patches of it would get him to his goal. How badly he wished his child to have a better life, because this wasn't living.

His light settled on a coral crop across the way. The red kind. The kind that lazed like slow motion brush fire. He kicked for it, thinking of Krill and how much of his life was currently in that sculptor's hands.

Krill lived on the island's north side, just beyond resort row. His high-level gift kiosk saw steady foot traffic. His sculptures were so popular that word traveled. They knew his name on the African mainland, and word of mouth brought plenty of curious customers looking to come away from vacation with an original Krill. He was open all day and night, residing in a little hut just beyond his commercial lean-to. Always working and selling. Perpetual hustle.

Zane couldn't simply relax at home when he knew Krill was carving up coral like the world might suddenly run out. He had to dive. Had to keep the artist supplied with the good stuff, otherwise Krill would start looking elsewhere for a pipeline.

Past the waving red coral, Zane's light hovered on the tips of floating pink. Another triumphant grin from behind his mask. Coral prices were based on color, saturation, and polish. If you managed to harvest red or pink, you got gold. Of course, there was literal gold coral to find, but you had a better chance of seeing Jesus down here helping you look.

The trickiest part of coral was that it was a lot of luck. Zane had recovered some pieces in the past that he thought would put him on easy street, only to have it cleaned and polished and turn out worthless. It all came down to polishing. If you got a piece where the color shimmered through like a jellyfish, you were set.

Krill would pay almost anything for those, because glimmering sculpts caught the eyes of rich tourists, who eyed them like they were blood diamonds. People with bread thought nothing about paying top dollar for extravagance, and Krill was the only sculptor on the island with the talent to get it done.

Zane swam toward his daughter's academic future, reaching toward the coral. He closed his wet-suited hands around the thinnest of pieces, rocking it gently until it snapped and could fit easily inside the sack hitched to his belt.

While he worked at separating them from the floor, he felt a dozen vibrating sensations cross his body at once. A startled, bubbly growl escaped his mouth behind his breather. A large school of small fish raced past, knifing through the gloom toward the safety of further ocean depths.

Zane turned and stared into a cavern surrounded by jagged stones. He hadn't previously noticed this entrance—too distracted by the loot, he supposed. The pink coral he'd spotted from afar was missing suddenly, leaving him to question whether he'd seen it at all.

He was ready to turn back when he saw it up close. His eyes widened and his heart seemed to push against the confines of his wetsuit.

A shark.

It tore through the water with such speed that Zane knew he was dead if it wanted him. He pulled his blade from its sheath, ready to stab the bastard through the eye should it get any ideas.

The fish didn't appear to notice. It darted past Zane like it was in pursuit of those other fish.

Zane took a deep breath and figured that was likely. Then he turned back to the remaining coral. There was enough of it here to take a few days off. All he wanted to do was get home and get a little sleep before sunrise.

The coral broke off in his fists and he had a full bag before he knew it. Now he was starting on the second. He could see Krill's approving eyes now and tried to remind himself this had been worth it.

He sheathed his blade and spun the flashlight around one last time to make sure he hadn't missed anything. Especially that pink coral.

Zane was somehow closer to the cave now. He studied the obstruction, certain it hadn't been here at first. And it wasn't a cave. The stalagmites seemed to widen as the opening moved forward again, closing the distance between them. The fleeing shark made sense then, because Zane realized he was looking into the mouth of a much larger fish.

A fossil.

The open stone mouth enveloped him.

Zane kicked through the water to try and propel himself back through the opening. He rocketed toward it like a torpedo and only got half way.

The stalagmites closed fast. A spring-loaded trap that cleaved him in two. The surrounding water turned to bubbles, a ruby red fizz. Zane floated up over that mist, now level with an eyeball that seemed carved from stone.

Zane's disembodied legs floated past his head, moving toward the surface where Lullo's searchlight might've passed for the promise of an afterlife.

Just before Zane's gaze went forever black, he saw the fish lumber from the gloom, waving its large caudal fin back and forth as it swam up to greet his boat.

NINE

Mr. Reeves sat beneath the lean-to, noshing a papaya while Mr. Davis stood on the shore of Nosy Berafia, surrounded by agitated villagers. He was asking the residents of this jerkwater village if anyone here spoke English.

Mr. Reeves was glad the younger agent had gumption because, hell, someone needed to rub elbows with the undesirables. He wasn't going to get his loafers dirty for this. Bad enough his Hawaiian shirt would get those really awful pit stains that didn't come out, even after a couple of washes.

He didn't give a good goddamn who down there spoke English because it didn't matter. They didn't know anything and you only needed to take one look at this sorry place to get it. Still, someone had to say they asked. They had a government to protect. And friends to avenge. Whatever Mr. Davis thought he was doing over there was nothing but a formality. Too green to know it was anything but a waste of time.

Mr. Reeves finished his papaya and was eyeing the banana on the table beside him when Mr. Davis jogged back.

"They see him or what?" Mr. Reeves asked.

"They don't even think he's on the island."

"Ain't that the way," Mr. Reeves said. "They think we're a couple of rubes."

Mr. Davis was eyeing the banana now, too. "You gonna have that?"

"Yeah," Mr. Reeves said and took it, peeling it down. "This is, what? A hundred calories?" He figured he could choke it down without going over his limit. And if he did, he just wouldn't log it in his phone app.

"I can't believe you just did that," Mr. Davis said.

Mr. Reeves looked at him with a mouthful of banana. "Did what?"

"The nice lady who greeted us put two pieces of fruit out. They weren't both for you. You took the papaya."

"You're the one who had three bowls of Corn Flakes on the flight. Now, quick, tell me how you understood what any of those people had to say."

They were supposed to have a translator/guide, but he hadn't been on site when Reeves and Davis landed. And Mr. Reeves did not like waiting for the locals to get their shit together.

Mr. Davis continued to stare at the half-eaten banana with longing eyes. It wasn't until Mr. Reeves cleared his throat that he remembered he needed to answer. "Oh, right," he said. "One of the youngest there speaks some English. Says the Pirate King has not been seen, but that one of his closest friends is some fugitive warlord, guy called Imani, and that we should find him if we want to know for sure where he's at."

"Oh bullshit," Mr. Reeves said, spewing banana bits all over Mr. Davis, who brushed his thighs with a disgusted tsk. "They're covering for his ass, it's plain as day."

"Not sure I agree," Mr. Davis said. "You want the truth, everyone seems shook because they've got a missing person. Young guy who went to the marketplace yesterday and never returned."

"Right," Mr. Reeves said, watching a small boy piss into the sand a few feet away. "Who would ever abandon this paradise?" He tossed the rest of the banana to the dirt.

"Probably wouldn't have left," Mr. Davis said. "Got friends and family here. And they're all saying he's dead."

Mr. Reeves stood and brushed his hands on the thin bit of fabric that covered the lean-to. "I don't give a shit about them. Know who's dead? Marshall and Roy. Gunned down in some fucking Algerian hotel room. Killed by a fucking animal who calls this place home."

"An animal we've got orders to capture," Mr. Davis said at a whisper.

"Let's go," Mr. Reeves ordered. "We're not going to learn anything off these aborigines."

The two men began to walk off. Mr. Davis turned and gave the villagers a fond smile and a loud wave. Mr. Reeves hurried for the chopper. It was a mile away and he couldn't wait to get back to air conditioning.

TEN

"This is the guy, huh?"

The resort's courtesy cart carried Sara and Blake down the long stretch of twisting pavement where the road was flanked by candy-colored flowers.

The barred entrance gate was swinging inward and Sara spotted a guy who had to be an island guide sitting on the hood of a dumpy green jeep across the street.

"Kahega," Blake said.

Whatever his name, he was the enemy. The son of a bitch who'd fleeced her out of ten grand.

Sara had checked their account balance earlier this morning while her clueless husband snored his way through dreams of fortune and glory. A little more than half their joint bank account was now in this guy's pocket.

Did Sara believe Blake's delusions of grandeur? She wondered. Spent the last few hours thinking on it and decided she didn't know. Maybe that inconclusiveness was because, deep down, she wanted him to be right.

It would be the easiest way through.

The night was on its way out. In the distance, a band of golden rays threatened to overtake the dark horizon.

The guide straightened his posture upon realizing it was his marks who were puttering toward the gate. With a cigarette stuffed into the corner of his mouth, he smirked.

The cart stopped on the sidewalk and a menthol cloud floated across the street to greet them.

Sara hopped off and tipped the driver three singles. She left Blake to drag their baggage over the crosswalk. The guide watched with folded arms and a slightly emboldened smirk. It was the only thing about the guy Sara didn't hate.

"Miss Jovish." Kahega reached for her hand.

Sara snubbed him.

Kahega was not the least bit phased. "I have heard so very much about you. Forgive me if I say you are even more beautiful than your husband describes."

"Ain't heard a damn thing about you." Sara hopped into the rear seat and threw her backpack down on the cushion. At her feet, a few cylindrical alloy steel tubes poked through the choke point of a fabric sack. Rifle barrels.

Jesus, Sara thought and moved her legs away from them. Last summer she'd been maid of honor in her friend's wedding. They'd gone to a rifle range as part of the bachelorette party. Sara had never held a gun before then, and while she had to admit there was something uniquely satisfying about every trigger squeeze, it was more responsibility than she ever wanted to feel.

Kahega turned the ignition while Blake did all the loading. The two men exchanged partner's nods once he settled into the passenger's seat. Neither one bothered to connect their eyes to Sara's.

The guide stomped the gas and did a U-turn without yielding. A few approaching tourist busses scattered to the sound of irritated horns.

Sara kept eyes on the gate, expecting to catch Guillaume and Jean-Philippe tailing them.

"How did these letters get all the way to Maine?" she asked.

Sara's question went unanswered as the jeep zipped along the eastern coastline, offering a postcard view of an ocean that was one long stretch of aquamarine.

A piece of her was excited to get out on the water. So much of her job had been reduced to cubicle life that she was glad for any opportunity to get the ocean beneath her.

She might've been touched by a nautical gesture had Blake thought to spin it. Suddenly he was too dumb for that. In college, he'd prepared two hundred oceanography flash cards during the week of finals—marine life, including every species of fish long extinct. On the day before Sara's exam, he spent the entire afternoon quizzing her until the material was second nature. And he'd done it all while prepping roasted lamb and mint sauce for dinner.

That was the thoughtful man she'd fallen in love with. This guy...

At last, Blake turned, as if remembering she'd asked a question. "We talked about that."

"We?"

Blake lifted his thumb to Kahega. "These letters first became known to the public sometime in 1976. They were found in the basement safe of a private collector after he died."

"Everyone wanted those letters," Kahega said. "I suspect they were smuggled off the island in order to remain hidden."

"By the Burning Man?" Sara asked. "I don't know his real name."

"Milago," Blake said.

"I have asked around," Kahega said. "Between the time you contracted me and your arrival on Madagascar, I spoke to some here who claimed to know this man. Milago fled during the fall of the Barre government sometime in 1986."

"He didn't stay gone though," Blake added.

"Even though he begged you to let it burn," Sara reminded him.

"It consumed his life," Blake said. "He didn't have a pot to piss in at the end. He'd blown every last dime on periodic expeditions back here. He was a contractor for North Central Construction. I checked with them after he died and discovered he made trips here in '92, '99, and '04. Whenever he had enough capital and vacation time banked. He was so sure he was going to find it. Never did."

"Oh, but we will, right?"

"Yes."

Blake's lack of awareness astounded her. She watched him small talk the guide and tried to ignore the sack of weapons at her feet. Tried to forget about the hollowed out bank account. She tried not to cry as hopelessness turned her mind toward annulment.

Kahega cranked the radio so there could be no talking during Patrick Swayze's "She's Like the Wind."

It annoyed her so much, Sara got loud. "It's not the 80s anymore," she said.

"And that is too bad, I think."

"You can't get any new music shipped in from the mainland?"

"Where do you think we are," Kahega said. "I could get a new radio that connects to your iPhone if I wished to spend my money on something so foolish. I do not wish it, and that is beside the point."

"What is the point?" she said.

"The world moves too fast," he said. "We do not even have time to forget things anymore. That to me is all the more reason to remember. To celebrate the world as it once was, lost treasures as valuable as the one we hunt."

"Nobody's getting rich off listening to the *Dirty Dancing* soundtrack."

"It's not always about getting rich, Miss Sara."

"Right," she said. "Can I have my money back then? If you're too woke to take it..."

The men exchanged an indecipherable look and Sara couldn't decide which of them she hated more.

No, actually, it was still Blake.

The jeep brought them to the port of Antalaha. The guide said they were looking to rendezvous with a ship captain. And they would find him inside a bar with no name. This place was one big shantytown. Hard to believe they'd find anything amidst the chaos of wrecked boats and collapsed homes.

"What happened here?" Blake asked.

"A cyclone touched down a few years back," Kahega said.

"No rebuilding efforts?"

"Our government promised to, but..."

"Why am I not surprised?" Blake growled.

They crossed black dirt onto a rickety pier that looked to be made of matchsticks.

"Funny how they leave this lingering destruction off all the tourism sites," Blake said.

Sara braced for another of his impotent spiels about the evils of the west when a child's scream halted them.

They looked around, but the locals didn't so much as stir. On the shoreline, a little boy stood with his feet submerged up to his ankles. The palm of his hand was outstretched to show his mother a bloody gash.

Blake started down the incline and Sara followed. Kahega threw his palm on her shoulder and gave a slight squeeze. She turned to question it and his eyes were gravely cautious. Do not, they said.

Blake approached the shore, a hand buried up to his wrist inside his satchel bag. He produced a cap of Neosporin, tore a strip of gauze, and began dressing the child's wound. The boy's screams intensified, then quickly receded as the ointment soothed him. The mother stood with her arm around her child, listening to Blake's instructions on how to treat the injury moving forward. He left the tube and the gauze roll in the palm of her outstretched hand.

"Onward," Kahega said and they resumed their march.

It was hard to believe this is what passed for civilization one hour from paradise. Destitute faces watched them pass. Hungry eyes roved their thirty-dollar Old Navy shorts. Sara's sleeveless linen top made her feel like a pariah. Whenever she made eye contact, faces smiled back attentively.

"There's no commerce here," she said. "How can anyone afford to run a bar?"

"People here find work on other parts of the island," Kahega said. "Many in the resorts to the north. Some have money. And there are precious few distractions to make them forget about their day."

On the waterfront, everyone was too busy to pay them any mind. The old pier probably hadn't changed much in forty years. The boats seemed that old, but the people manning them moved with all the precision of engrained daily routine. Nets of fish came off the boat, handed to carts that waited on the dock. Once they were filled to capacity, the cart runner moved inland toward one of the many shacks set up to process the day's catches.

"Americans," A voice boomed in perfect English. Sara thought it had to be their ship captain.

"Americans, come here!" A man stepped from the hustling crowd, gripping a machete that dripped with fish guts. Uneven wooden planks bent beneath his feet.

Blake and Sara drew back in unison while Kahega pulled the AK-47 from the sack and lifted it.

Sara's eyes fanned out across the crowd, thinking somebody here would stop this. There wasn't a single head craned their way. They were the ghosts of wayward tourists that only Machete Man could see.

"Lost Americans," Machete Man said with glee.

Kahega barked something in his native tongue. It was enough for Machete Man to slow his approach. But he didn't stop.

"Go," Kahega called. "To the bar."

Blake took Sara's hand and pulled her back the way they came.

Machete Man found their eyes and gave no mind to the man holding a gun on him. A pocket of fishermen moved down the pier and enveloped Kahega for a moment. It was all the time Machete Man needed to dart off between two shacks.

Blake and Sara ran for the bar they couldn't find, catching flashes of the Machete Man moving parallel on the other side of the buildings. His head was craned toward them, eyes blazing with excitement. A greyhound chasing rabbits.

Sara pulled on Blake's hand just as Machete Man disappeared beyond the next building. They had about two seconds to lose him. She steered him into a glut of broken ship wreckages. They weaved in and out of the piles, circling back the way they came.

"There," Sara said and pointed to a building on stilts in the distance. A few rickety chairs pushed up against it said it might be the kind of place that served exhausted fishermen after a long day. They ran toward it with raised knees, Sara getting out in front of Blake who was bogged down by their luggage, a panicked tourist rushing to make a departing flight.

She was nearly to the stilts when Blake yelled out. Machete Man had closed the gap and was nearly upon him, moving like a storm. The blade sliced through the air. Somehow, she had a second to realize nobody around them cared.

"Blake," she cried out.

The blade never connected. Machete Man's shoulder jerked back as thunder cracked across the sky. The next boom corresponded with a second spasm in Machete Man's shoulder. His upper torso twisted as his legs continued to charge, tripping on his own contorted lunge. Splotches of crimson broke out across his chest like fireworks.

It took Sara a second to realize what had happened. Beside her, a swirl of smoke teased her nostrils. Sometimes at sea, captains would fire rifles to keep larger predators off the schools they were counting. Or catching. She'd grown accustomed to that smell, the way it swirled through her headspace now.

"We're not going to want to hang around here, darlin'."

Sara turned and found a man standing behind her with a rifle drawn on his target. A sun-chapped white dude whose off-white linen coat hung unbuttoned to reveal bare-chested strength. He stunk of whiskey and looked like he won bar fights for a living.

The Machete Man lay unmoving in the muck and Blake crawled away from him like a battered dog. He wiped tears and snot from his face and looked at Sara like she was his mother, desperate for the comfort of her lap.

Sara was shaken, too, pins and needles in the tips of her fingers. And still, she nearly scoffed at the pathetic sight of her lover.

Kahega appeared out of the crowd, taking stock of the situation and breathing a huge sigh of relief when he counted Blake and Sara among the survivors.

"Almost lost your meal ticket," Sara called.

Behind her, the white gunman laughed.

Kahega reached down and tugged Blake to his feet. "Sara," he said. "Meet Holloway."

"Captain of the *Frozen Cocktail*," Holloway added.

"Huh?"

"My ship," he said.

"Right," Sara cleared her throat. "Thanks."

"Don't thank me yet," Holloway told her. "We don't know how many friends your buddy down there has. You can bet there's a few more standing among the curious."

At the embankment, a chattering crowd had gathered.

Kahega shouldered most of the luggage this time and Sara helped lighten that burden. All she wanted was to be away from here.

Blake tried to ask if she was okay, but his voice was too wobbly for chivalry and there was no time to acknowledge it.

"I'm right down there," Holloway said, pointing to the water. "Best we go now. And fast."

The captain pointed to a young boy following them by hopping overhead rooftops.

They ran for water, and reached the *Frozen Cocktail* at the end of the pier. The ship itself was somewhere between a small yacht and a personal fishing vessel.

Sara tossed her stuff over the railing and then scaled it herself to get aboard. Kahega followed and Blake brought up the rear as the world's worst Indiana Jones, running like hellfire chapped his ass when the only thing in pursuit was a summer's breeze. Even the little watcher in the sky stayed back, spying from the last building on the pier.

Blake rolled onto his side as he crashed to the deck, sucking air furiously in order to catch his breath.

Holloway and Kahega cast off and the boat began its slow drift away from the dock. Blake remained on his knees, his hands curled tight around the *Frozen Cocktail*'s rail. His head was half-buried as he watched the port fade and become a tiny speck on the horizon.

Only then did he stand up and straighten out his clothes. "You shot somebody," he said. "Straight up murder."

Sara sighed. "Blake—"

"No, Sara," he screamed. "If this gets worse, who do you think is going to go down for that? Him?"

Holloway ignored him entirely. "Good thing I packed the ship this morning." He smirked and extended his hand to Sara.

She shook.

"Les Holloway," he said. "Welcome aboard."

Sara introduced herself and her shell-shocked husband, adding, "Worst vacation I've ever taken."

"Pretty clean port, though," Holloway said. "Could've arranged for us to meet inside one of the tourist traps, but you get too many thirsty eyes there. Too many radars. The ones we're trying to stay off."

Sara thought of Guillaume and Jean-Philippe and realized he was right. He knew his stuff and that set her at ease.

Sara followed Holloway down the thin side deck where the space between the cabin and the rail was tight. "Look," Holloway said. "Is he going to be okay? I need to know who I'm working with."

Blake was the color of milk. He sucked the air like his lungs needed it. The pathetic sight brought Sara's fists to clenches.

It was too late to go back. Holloway might've been a professional, but he wasn't in this for charity. His hands were bloody and all of them together had incurred some debt.

"He'll be okay," Sara said. "But we should probably talk about getting this over with."

"We're partners now," Holloway nodded. He was shameless about looking her body up and down. "So I think that's probably a good idea."

ELEVEN

At dusk, the runner came for him.

A boy no older than ten. Covered in sweat, wearing shorts no more constrictive than loincloth. When he reached the tent, he buckled with his hands on his knees, sucking air.

Kaahin rose from his cot and pulled the flap of his lean-to aside. The humidity had thinned and the breeze that rolled in off the ocean seeped straight into his pores. He only had to shut his eyes and draw a few deep breaths in order to feel at peace.

Beyond the boy, his men patrolled the shoreline with AK-47s at the ready. Steel-eyed sentries with eager trigger fingers. He paid them to kill, never defend. And since the world was out hunting the Pirate King right now, he needed those hair triggers.

His men caught motion in their peripherals and looked to Kaahin with expectation, eager for work. One hand wave told them there was nothing and they resumed their watch. Beside him, the boy's breathing returned to normal.

"Speak," Kaahin said.

"Mabek is killed."

Kaahin did not know Mabek. He had plenty of loyalists, and when the job required more bodies, more bodies were easy to recruit. There were many on Madagascar who promised allegiance to him, but he could no longer afford to pay so many, preferring instead to rouse those bodies only when necessary. In the gaps between, they were free to earn however they could. That also meant they were on their own when things went wrong.

"Shot by a white man," the boy added.

"Tourist?" That did not sound right. More likely, this Mabek had tried breaking into a resort or some other part of the continent that employed whites. But the small boy shook his head and that prompted Kaahin's curiosity. "Tell me, then."

"A boatman. He met two Americans and an islander and took them out on his ship."

Kaahin waited for the young boy to finish and once there was nothing else, he tossed the boy a few ariarys.

The boy folded the bills in his fist and bent toward him in a gesture of deep gratitude.

Kaahin touched the round of his head with a chapped palm and smiled warmly. "Tell no one." Then he watched as the boy sprinted off into fast-approaching darkness.

He waited a moment and then strolled down to the water where the men guarded their dinghies. "We may have work," he said.

The men perked like starved dogs.

"Prepare just one of these," he said of the small boats. "Any more and we will arouse attention." They nodded and the Pirate King left them to get ready.

He cleared the brush and thought of Alzir, who had taken multiple rounds in the back off the coast of Algeria in order to guarantee his escape.

Because of that, Kaahin could not go to his family. They were being watched and if there was so much as a hint that he had made it back to Madagascar, the westerners would do more than spy.

His wife knew what to do when he refused to check-in. He hoped.

This was too important to risk.

TWELVE

Five minutes. That's how long it took for Sara to tire of Blake while aboard the *Frozen Cocktail*.

She found Holloway on deck, huddled alongside Kahega and the three other black men who comprised the captain's crew.

Sara asked if she could have another room and the men laughed.

Except Holloway. He came away from the railing with a wolf's grin. "Take mine, darlin'."

Sara raised her hands so he wouldn't come any further. "No, that's okay."

"I know how it sounds."

"Good."

"I'm not going to be sleeping much."

"Why is that?"

"What happened back in port. Word's all the way around the island by now. Mercs'll be gunning for this ship everywhere we go."

"You had no choice."

"Locals won't be as sympathetic." Holloway started past Sara and flicked his fingers so she followed him below deck. The central hall was so thin it needed to be walked single file. But there was more space down here than one might've suspected. Four staterooms and additional storage compartments.

Blake heard them coming and opened his door, stood in the jamb and watched.

Holloway brushed right by like he wasn't there and reached the last room at the end of the hall, pushing in on the door. "This is the Frozen Bunk and usually, you sail with me, this space sets you back an extra five hundred."

"Is this a fishing vessel or a luxury yacht?" Sara asked, watching as the lights fluttered on, igniting the bed's undercarriage in a deep blue glow.

"Because it doesn't look like much?" Holloway seemed wounded by that insinuation. Sara rolled her eyes and left the comment hanging.

"I can't take your b—"

"Don't be flattered," he said. "If we had other guests, I wouldn't be offering it." That grin again. Infectious enough to spread to her lips. Her muscles had been so firm, her face so miserably dour, that the stretch of her mouth felt good.

"If you're sure," Sara said.

From the hallway, Blake cleared his throat and went right on being ignored.

"Positive." Holloway stood one moment longer than was appropriate. Then he was gone, leaving Sara to listen to his footsteps stalking back above deck.

"Here," Blake said and threw her bags over the threshold. "You want to be rid of me? Be rid of me."

She leapt out of the way as her backpack skidded against her feet.

"All I said is that I needed some space to myself. To think."

"I told you everything," he said. "What's left for you to think about?"

"You really don't know? Or are you just mad because I haven't kissed your forehead and told you all is forgiven?"

He mumbled something beneath his breath. She scooped the yellowed papers in her hand.

"I need to see what you sold our future for," she said.

She headed back inside the Frozen Bunk and clicked the lock. Didn't want him coming in here to make amends.

She tossed the papers onto the bed and stripped, leaving her clothes in a wrinkled trail that led straight to the bathroom. Through the small portal window, the ship nodded up and down while slicing through placid waters.

Sara got beneath the meager shower stream and felt the tension at the small of her back loosen like a shoelace.

Once dry, she took a seat on the cushion and reached for the letters. Each page was clipped to a second, less yellowed sheet. Thumbing through she saw those were the English translations for what must've been Spanish originals.

To You, Stranger:

I do not expect my pleas to be heard, though I must leave behind a record in case I do not make it.

My name is Isabella de Carcena of Aragon and I write as a prisoner on my own island, held in captivity by a man who once claimed to love me, but now thinks of me as treasure.

We met three years ago on Ile Saint Marie. I do not know where my island lies in relation to that bustling port, only that it takes several days to reach by ship and you will see nothing but water for so long that land begins to feel like a dream.

My captor is the pirate, Alejandro Roche. A long time ago, I loved him in good faith. But there is nothing now. What can there be on this island of two? I must face the truth that he has tired of me, just as he tires of his bounties.

We used to venture to Ile Saint Marie on occasion—until Roche became too paranoid to leave his vault unattended. Something I thought was absurd until the last time we were there. I shared a dance with an English port trader named Martine Vernier, who confessed to me after too many flagons of rum that he had come here to hunt Roche's treasure and planned to take it for his own.

For our own. That was his offer. We made love that night, and he promised that he would come for me. That he had heard of the island from the wife of a missing laborer—one of the men Roche had paid to construct our isolated paradise. I must return there with my captor, Vernier said, and promised that my time there would be short.

I do not know how, but Roche learned of my indiscretion and forbade any subsequent departures from our island. So now I walk these beaches alone, feeling the sand between my toes as I watch the horizon and pray to catch sight of Vernier's approaching ship.

Anything to bring resolution, though I do not believe myself that lucky. I think I truly could die here. Though the end of my life does not scare me as much as a wasted one.

For my sanity,

Isabella

Sara's hands trembled as she read it.

The words were a knife to her heart. Isabella de Carcena had lived hundreds of years ago, but might as well be a pen pal for as much common ground as Sara thought they shared.

Sara's jaw tightened as she imagined this woman's life. It was easy to relate.

Could Isabella have made it off the island? Sara guessed not if these were found in someone's private collection in 1976.

But the woman had written more.

My love,

I write so you will not worry. This note will take weeks to reach you, and I only need to say that I am alive. For now.

Yet you simply must hurry. Roche does not let me out of his sight for even a moment now that he suspects my allegiance has shifted. He caught me watching the ocean last night over dinner, and demanded to know why my attention lay on breaking waves. He accused me of rooting against him.

I did not tell him, of course, though I suspect he knows. Because in his ever-increasing madness, Roche tells me he wishes that someone out there would solve his riddles and find our island. He is desperate for competition.

In his isolation, he becomes increasingly bored. The men who constructed this fortress are not allowed to leave, and the traders who arrive from the Far East by rowboat are instructed to come no further than the beach.

Never further. I have to pay them to take my letters, left in secret on the beach in a sack filled with doubloons.

The night after I left you on Ile Saint Marie, we planted the key at Roche's request. He selected two men from port who could hold their breaths for four minutes and ordered them to do it. One went to a watery grave like a drowned rat. Roche shot the other as soon as he surfaced and confirmed the job done. But it's there, waiting for you, my love.

Roche is paranoid beyond usefulness. Each drink I serve, every meal I cook surely must be poisoned. He looks at me with suspicious eyes, as though every move I make is a plot against him. Of course it is, and so now I must once again consider my own role in his madness.

I never wanted this. Any of it. I only want you, my love. Which is why you have to find me. Which is why I supported the plantation of that clue. Roche wishes someone would come.

So come. But do not come alone, for he plans to kill each of you.

I will wait for your arrival, but if I never see you again, just know that you occupy the space between my ears. Roche may have the rest of me, but he cannot get my thoughts.

Those, my love, belong to you.

I

Sara sunk into her chair. How grim to face your mortality at such a young age. There was too much optimism in her tone for the girl to be any older than a teenager.

And for all Sara knew, the stains on this paper were salt from Isabella's tears.

There was more here and Sara felt like knowing all there was to know about the island Blake was looking for. And how it all started with a tongue.

Apparently.

To the Curious:

You are cordially invited to find the estate of Captain Alejandro Roche, for which the English Navy has searched tirelessly for nearly two decades.

It shan't be easy, and many who come looking will not survive. But there would be no challenge in that. To those with the cunning and the patience to succeed, there is so much to await you.

Begin this hunt on the hook. Where you are the bait.

From there, travel along the path of the plate to the glaring twins, who watch the sky in order to see the sign.

Once you are there, have a seat among the red feet.

Use your taste buds to feast forever.

Understand... these words are ghosts. They move across the moonlight; promises as purple fog.

Do not be discouraged. There is a little pirate in everyone.

I

This paper was different. Written on different stock.

And while the handwriting was close enough to Isabella's, there was no doubt that Roche himself had authored this. It was gleeful in its invitation of death. Holding it in her hands, Sara had never felt closer to a monster.

She put the document aside as if holding it any longer might poison her mind. She reread Isabella's pages until the world dimmed and she smelled the candle wax that hardened on the yellow paper in small half bulbs.

They lived hundreds of years apart, on opposite sides of the world, and Isabella would never know Sara Mosby existed. Yet, Sara felt a kinship with her all the same.

Each time she read the girl's words, a little more of the author crept off the page. The terror in her scribbles. The hopelessness of her actions—stuffing a letter inside a cask of pirate wine, slipping Far East traders some extra coin in order to take it the rest of the way, all while hoping for the best.

How horrible that uncertainty must've been.

Sara thought of the pirate and wondered what about him had driven Isabella into his arms. He must've possessed a roguish charm that, when coupled with his considerable wealth, made him impossible to resist. Sara knew it because, if Blake somehow pulled this off, she may very well forgive him.

God, she hated to admit that.

She folded the pages and her thoughts drifted inexplicably to Holloway. The way his steely eyes had roved her like a lion looking at dinner.

Sara slid her torn jean shorts up past her thighs and buttoned them. A dark tee covered her dark breasts and left a hint of midriff exposed. She looked herself over in the floor-to-ceiling mirror and nodded.

I look good, she thought.

She opened the door and hurried past Blake's room without a second thought.

***

Holloway and Kahega were at the bow. The guide had the automatic rifle slung over his shoulder, glaring at open water.

The captain stood beside him and their chatter crumbled away with the sound of her approach. Across the deck, the small crew of the *Frozen Cocktail* performed their jobs with silent efficiency.

"I feel left out," Sara said, crossing her arms and pretending to know what they were looking at.

"We're trying to make it around the island without arousing suspicion," Holloway said.

Kahega snorted. "Which is hard, given the fact that you shot someone."

"Yeah," Holloway said, resuming his watch. "Look, Sara, you really should go back to your room."

"Because it's not safe out here?"

"Safer here than your goddamn house," the captain said.

"So why do I need to stay out of sight?"

The captain shrugged, a look that said, "your funeral." The three of them stood quiet until Holloway excused himself and headed to the stern. Sara was left staring at the back of Kahega's neck.

"You really do not like me," the guide said.

"Blame me?"

Kahega laughed and turned in profile. "I suppose not. But I have done what I was supposed to do."

"Is it really out there? The treasure?"

"I would not have taken your money otherwise."

"Well, then. Case closed."

"You still do not trust."

"Not even a little."

"You should," he said. "Because the wrong man would have slashed your husband's throat. Left him bleeding and taken the map off his corpse."

"You're a real good guy, huh?"

Kahega snickered. "Just an honest one."

"This ship, the people on it—"

"Comes out of my piece," he said. "What else can I say to ease your mind?"

"Nothing, while you're holding that. Guns make me nervous," Sara said.

"They should."

"Not exactly the comfort I was hoping for."

"This is not the coast of Maine." Kahega unslung his weapon and held it out, shaking his fists until she took it.

She held it the way someone holds a newborn baby for the first time. Even though she liked shooting these things, they never settled into her grip the right way. She was always too aware of their potential for destruction.

Kahega put night vision binoculars to his face as the sky around them darkened.

"Take this back," Sara said.

Kahega allowed her request to linger, at last taking the rifle and slinging it back over his shoulder. "You really should relax," he said. "I can show you how to shoot this thing, might help you some."

"I said I don't like them. Didn't say I couldn't shoot one."

Kahega smiled, gave a slow but prideful nod. "Want to know the worst part of this?"

"Being on your honeymoon and finding out your husband looted your bank account to pay some shady-ass tour guide?"

This drew a belly laugh. He shook the smirk off his face. "The villagers will take my jeep, which I can live without. But my tapes..."

"Get us through this and I'll buy you an iPod loaded up with every song the 80s ever produced."

"Even Don Johnson?"

Sara thought maybe she knew that name from The Eagles, but had no desire to ask. Everything was on iTunes these days. "Sure," she said. "Even Don Johnson."

"Fair deal," Kahega laughed. "Tell you what, Sara Mosby, if we find what we're looking for, I'll pay your husband back every cent I took thus far."

"Nah," she said.

"It must happen. I did not realize the circumstances in which he paid me."

She smiled at the gesture, but the topic was too awkward to continue.

The guide craned his neck. Sara followed his line of sight to a figure moving up the mast ladder. It was Holloway, looking through his binoculars and gesturing with increased fervor.

He called down, some of his voice lost to the swirling ocean breeze. It sounded like "horizon!"

"Back to your room," Kahega told her, sliding the weapon off his back. "And tell one of the men to give you a pistol."

Something was coming to kill them. Sara swallowed hard but couldn't bring herself to move. Never had she felt more vulnerable. Blake had driven them out to sea in a floating coffin.

Kahega swatted her away and ran to the bow. Overhead, the captain descended, barking orders at his men to arm up. The three crewmen were everywhere at once, their clicking weapons sounded like clucking tongues.

Before Sara could get below, one of the men stuffed a pistol in her fist and closed her fingers around the handle.

She took it below deck and hurried to her room.

Blake's bunk was still closed tight. Her hand hovered over the knob but even then, she couldn't make herself go in.

So she went instead to the large suite at the end of the hall and locked the door behind her.

THIRTEEN

The Zodiac boat zipped through the shallows on the far side of Nosy Be. Island fires danced across the shoreline there, guiding them toward Madagascar's tip. Toward Antsiranana.

It wasn't the fastest way, but Kaahin knew they would find the least amount of resistance here. Given the Algerian ambush by Langley spooks, he was through taking chances. His feet tapped solid board beneath his feet while stomach acid swam at the back of his throat.

If they had taken him alive, there would've been questions. Where was the *Star Time*? What happened to the people aboard it? Kaahin was not prepared to answer.

That meant they'd imprison him in some CIA black site, conjure his house on satellite feed and threaten to drone strike it. Langley wasn't going to abandon their search for him just yet.

Kaahin's point man lifted the portable searchlight and clicked it. The sky was so dark they appeared to be floating across glass. Only it wasn't glass that Kaahin looked at, but wreckage. The remnants of what had been a fine sea-faring vessel. It was driftwood now, broken into a thousand pieces, bobbing like it was trying to reassemble itself.

The Zodiac boat slowed and puttered through the mess, careful not to damage its propeller on the flotsam. It was everywhere, as far as the searchlight could see.

Somewhere inside the crushing black of night, human cries were louder than the motor. Gibberish at first, but growing into something slightly more coherent the longer their ears stayed open to it.

"Death's head... Death's head... Death's head..."

They found a naked man lying over a bit of curved and broken wood, staring into the water and refusing to lift his head at the sound of their approach.

Kaahin killed the motor and two of his men reached out to grab him. Kaahin listened to the sound of rhythmic drums in the night, finding them all the way out here from the shores of Nosy Be.

They had to grab the man beneath his arms and heaved him through the water. His torso slipped in alongside the floating debris and he screamed so hard his voice turned to scratches. They lugged him over the edge of the inflatable boat and dropped him face down at Kaahin's feet. "Death's head," he slurred. "Death's head!"

His hand bolted up and seized a fistful of Kaahin's pant leg, glaring wild-eyed as if he could see nothing except the gates of hell.

"Death's head!"

Kaahin realized there were body parts floating alongside the debris. Limp and half-eaten hunks that floated face down on relaxed swells. The sole survivor chanted nonsense from the center of their boat. One of this man's legs was missing beneath the knee. The gushing appendage blasted their ankles with a flood of crimson.

Kaahin did not have to ask what these men had been doing. They were poachers, he knew. And did not like it. His fingers closed around the sidearm on the seat beside him. He dropped the hammer. The man was too agitated to notice. His eyes were wider than marbles and he kept screaming those same two words over and over.

"Death's head! Death's head! Death's head."

Superstition rose on the faces of the men. Nervous eyes darted through the water, suddenly tense because they feared the evil waiting just beneath the surface.

The man's voice grew louder still, even more agitated. Kaahin hated it and pulled the trigger. The bullet drilled straight through his forehead, red slush pelting the faces of his soldiers.

"Toss him," Kaahin said.

His men rolled the corpse up onto the rubber wall and pushed him overboard, the body bobbing in the matchstick mess behind them as Kaahin restarted the motor. There was still a ways to go and they could afford no more distractions.

Kaahin glanced back and smiled at the dead body floating there. Whatever madness had taken him would not infect his men.

80

Kaahin thought he saw the body slip beneath the waves. And then a geyser of red bubbles shot up to replace the spot where he'd been.

Rather than question it, Kaahin accelerated. None of the men could bring themselves to look over their shoulders. None wanted to. Instead they checked their weapons and clutched them harder.

Kaahin thought he should give them a word of encouragement. In days gone by, Alzir would've been the one to do that. But the Pirate King had a rule and that was to never lie to his men. While eager bodies were a dime a dozen, loyalty was rare.

And yet there were no words to set their minds at ease. He might've known something about what haunted these waters, but it was nothing to ever speak aloud.

He stayed quiet.

They kept going.

FOURTEEN

Sara sat with Isabella's notes in her lap, trying to shut out the bustling footsteps stomping above deck.

It wasn't working, and by the time Holloway knocked at her door, she was relived for the distraction.

"We're being boarded," he said.

"By who?"

Blake stood behind him. The captain hooked him by the arm and flung him against Sara before pulling the door shut. "Lock it and keep quiet."

Sara did.

Blake moved to starboard portal and squinted through.

"Get away from there," Sara said. "If they see you—"

"We can't let them find the papers." Blake reached for them and—

Sara was faster. She snatched them in her fist and scanned the cabin. Her first thought was to slide them between a few of the old softback books on the shelf beside the bed, but Blake didn't agree.

"First place they'll look."

They went back and forth about where they wouldn't look, still uncertain who *they* were. Sara went for her duffel bag and Blake snapped up her wrist.

"You're joking," he hissed. "They'll think we've got bricks of coke in there."

"We've got limited options."

"Trick is to keep them in the open." Blake stripped down to his boxers and arranged himself into an Indian fold on the bedspread. "Quick," he whispered. "From my room... the notebook."

Sara's heart felt like dynamite as she pulled the door back and peered through the sliver. The boarding party hadn't swept this far down yet. There was still time.

She dashed for their couple's cabin and found Blake's notebook atop the desk, opened to a page where he'd written furiously about their honeymoon. Certain words jumped out at her. Disgust. Ingrate. Didn't have to read it to know exactly what he'd written.

She flung it at Blake once she returned. He ripped a few pages out and placed them among the translated notes.

Above deck, a shouting match erupted between Holloway and the uninvited. Sara braced herself, half expecting to hear gunshots. Through the window, she saw the familiar emblem of home. The insignia of United States Coast Guard blurred past and then she was looking at the ship floating beside the *Frozen Cocktail*.

"Take your clothes off," Blake said, his voice mostly pleading.

She stripped and climbed beneath the covers, stretching out to pretend they'd just exhausted themselves. She wondered if this wasn't an opportunity to get off this ride.

"We love to be where we don't belong," Blake said, never missing an opportunity to pontificate.

"Yeah, that's the takeaway."

"It is, he said. "We're fucking imperialists."

The sound of hustling bodies filled the stairwell, the search turning to the ship's interiors. Military boots landed fast and stomped heavy. If they barged in, how were they going to sell themselves?

"We're on our honeymoon," Blake said. "Remember that. There is nothing but truth here."

Sara nodded. "Saw Holloway's boat and thought it'd be fun to look at the island from the ocean."

"And you're a marine biologist so it checks."

A knock hit their door. They swapped nervous glances and then she rose with the bed sheet wrapped around her. Gooseflesh lined her forearms as she strode to the door, twisting the knob and flinging it wide, giving the soldiers beyond it an unexpected show.

They averted their eyes and apologized for the intrusion, asking if they'd seen anything unusual in their travels. With a soft chuckle, Sara told them they really hadn't been paying much attention.

"Look wherever you'd like," Holloway said. He stood so far to the back of the overstuffed hallway she couldn't even see him.

The coast guard gave their quarters a cursory check and decided there was nothing out of the ordinary.

"Won't be necessary." Sara heard one of the men reply.

They proceeded to open the rest of the doors, checking the other bunks with only slightly more attention. This while Sara left their door wide open and dropped back into bed. She grabbed a paperback off the shelf and pretended to read while the men completed their sweep.

"And the storage compartments," Holloway said, still out of sight. Still in full compliance mode. Laughter boomed as he continued to charm them with anecdotes and jokes Sara couldn't hear.

Once every last body was back on their own ship and pulling away from the *Frozen Cocktail*, Holloway reappeared at the end of the hall.

"You kids rekindling?" He smirked.

"She's my wife," Blake said.

"See plenty of couples in my line of work," Holloway told him. "Don't see too many who opt to stay in different bunks, though."

Sara scoffed, collected her clothes in her arms, and headed into the bathroom to change.

Blake, on the other hand, marched into the hall in his checkered boxer shorts and got in the captain's face. "Mind your business. I won't tell you again."

Sara held her breath, positive that Holloway was about to deck him. She pleaded for mercy with a silent glance and he accepted with a confirmation nod like, s*ure, but only because you asked.*

"What are they doing out here?" Sara asked.

Holloway brushed past Blake, taking her question as an invitation to answer. And enter. He sauntered close, a sleeveless arm brushing against her shoulder blade with a bit too much familiarity. She held her arm in place, taking deep breaths through her nose because his musk was a calming combination of a rugged day's work mixed with salt water.

"You see it from time-to-time," Holloway said. "Preventative steps taken by our government, intended to alleviate situations that could blossom into crises. They bring doctors, scientists, trainers into areas that desperately need them."

Sara thought of the woman who'd gone screaming into the ocean with plague blood dripping off her face, remembered the mother who'd taken Blake's gauze like it was a blank check, and thought maybe they could afford to send a little more support this way.

"They also keep watch for pirates," Holloway said. "This area's got more than a few."

"Have they seen any?"

"Pretty sure they're looking for one," he said.

"How do you know?"

"Went on my share of raids in the service. Compounds where the bad guys stashed weapons, money, all the things needed to fund and support their ops. Orders were always the same. Kill your targets. You remember the faces of your men in those situations. And when these guys came aboard, they had those same eyes. Hard and cold. Killing eyes."

"Pirates," Sara said with an exasperated laugh. "Making this part of the world worse since the beginning of time."

Out of the corner of his mouth, Blake smiled.

FIFTEEN

They made camp on an uninhabited island off the coast of Nosy Be. A jagged circle of sand and dirt no larger than the size of a parking lot. Enough space for five men to steal some sleep.

Kaahin assured them there was nothing to fear in these waters. That superstition plagued the shadows of their collective mind, and that such fear was a prison.

His four men had nodded like they understood, then went to sleep. Each of them tossed and turned well into the morning.

The more time Kaahin had to reflect, the worse he felt about the waters around Madagascar. There had always been whispers. Growing up, he'd heard them. Things glimpsed off the coast. Boats gone missing without explanation. The Malagasy people talked about the evil beneath the surface. Deep down, Kaahin had always wondered when he might see this for himself.

You went a remarkably long time, he thought.

He sat in sand, knees to his collarbone, staring at the undertow that continued pushing out eager tide. He felt a deep, nesting shiver as his thoughts tried to forget about whatever was out there.

This was his career and he'd grown accustomed to the uncertainty. In every man's life, there came a time to quit. And it was up to every man to figure out for himself when that time was. Were the fates screaming at him to do exactly that? How many more close calls could he afford?

Kaahin clenched his jaw. He narrowed his eyes and glared at the water, blacker than tar. The dark and shifting body lifted and fell like it was alive and breathing.

"Not yet," he whispered, glancing over the rising and falling breaths of his slumbering men.

SIXTEEN

"They're not moving," Sara said. It was her one contribution to the conversation.

Everyone aboard the *Frozen Cocktail* stood against the curved bow, watching as they approached a floating yacht that looked more like a spaceship. They couldn't see the ship so much as the neon strobes flashing across the hull, lighting the water around it.

Hot pink, bright purple, electric blue. Even at this distance, the wind carried excited laughter and thumping bass right to them.

"Everyone out there's smashed," Blake repeated, throwing a dismissive hand.

Holloway stood quiet beside him, his cheeks flaring as he considered the variables.

Isabella's words echoed in Sara's mind. As much as she wanted to liberate the poor girl's memory, there were louder thoughts weighing heavily. Mainly, she didn't trust anyone aboard this ship to not rob them blind.

The party yacht was precisely where they needed to go: A little further inland. There were sixty eyewitnesses on that boat who would wonder what in the hell the crew of the *Frozen Cocktail* were doing.

"That boat go out every night?" Holloway looked at Sara to answer.

"Every other," she said. "We were going to do it."

"Again," Blake said. "Who cares about a bunch of drunks?"

"The people who need to get that boat back to dock for the night aren't drunk, pal. And they already know we're here."

The *Frozen Cocktail's* bowsprit pointed toward Madagascar's shallows in the distance beyond the party yacht. It pointed to the jutting pylons that lifted out of the Indian Ocean like fangs.

Zanahary's teeth. Under which they were going to find a tongue.

The next conversation was how they were going to go about finding it.

"We're going down there," Blake said. "Kahega and I."

The guide nodded slowly and handed his rifle back to Sara. She took it this time, allowing its weight to distribute through her.

"Ya'll have talked this through, huh?" Holloway said.

Blake and Kahega swapped nods.

The *Frozen Cocktail* sliced water until the party yacht thumped just a few hundred feet off the portside.

"How do you know what you're even looking for?" Sara said.

Blake and Kahega stared back like the answer was obvious. They were halfway into their wetsuits before either of them answered.

"That is the mouth," Kahega said, referring to the stones poking out of the shallows in the distance. "The tongue will be directly beneath."

"That leaves us, darlin'." Holloway grinned. "We're gonna radio our friends over yonder and sell them a woe is me story about how you missed that boat and just had to see the island from the water anyway."

"What good does that do?" Sara said.

"Make them stop wondering before they even start. Tell them I'll take fifteen percent off the trip if you really are a guest. Make them check. Then your identity's confirmed and we're legit."

The divers finished gearing up and positioned themselves on the ship's ledge.

Sara tried to think of a time when she'd seen her husband dive and couldn't even recall a moment where he'd even swam.

"Hey," she said, approaching and taking his rubbery hands in her palms. "Stay safe, okay?"

Blake pulled the diving mask over his eyes and dropped backwards into the water. He might've winked, might've smirked, it was too hard to tell because of all the gear blocking his face. But all she'd wanted was some verbal confirmation that they were the same people. Because this sure as hell didn't feel like their life.

Sara watched the rippling black water disappear them as she swallowed a ball of stress. In that moment, she knew.

She was never going to see them again.

SEVENTEEN

Blake kicked into the gloom and the world around him was in tunnel vision.

Kahega had cautioned against paddling too fast through the dark, but Blake was close to it now and eager to finish. He felt Sara's trepidation overhead. Her contempt, a ticking clock that set him paddling with haste. Anything to finish.

Their lamplights sliced the murk, finding a jagged ledge growing out of the void before them. They had to swim up to reach it, shining their lights down past their flippers as they went. The ocean there was an impenetrable sprawl of dark green. Once they scaled the ledge their bodies went horizontal, floating over little cityscapes of coral.

Kahega flicked his light off and on to grab Blake's attention. The guide swam a few body lengths ahead, schools of fish breaking around him. He unsheathed his diver's blade as a jellyfish darted forward, though the creature had second thoughts and went cresting overhead.

Blake swam for Kahega's beam, angled down on the ocean floor, resting over a natural formation between the bases of two stone pylons. Here were the "teeth" in question. Moss sprouted out along the rock face, mimicking the fleshiest part of a human tongue, though it was roughly the size of an airport's tarmac.

Blake lifted his own blade in hand and kicked down on the tongue. His fingers brushed the soft surface as he checked for obvious points of entry. The men broke there, with Blake swimming back in the direction of the *Frozen Cocktail* while Kahega drifted further inland.

The tongue narrowed into a thin tip just a few feet away from the cliff's edge. A small recession on the other side of the rock face ran directly beneath the tongue.

Had to be it.

Blake attempted to signal Kahega. A few clicks of the beam went straight up. But the guide was out of sight. No way of knowing if he'd seen it. Blake pressed his face against the entrance. It opened into a wider space he figured could accommodate him.

He thought about the hatred in Sara's eyes. The disgust she had for him these last few days. He'd leveraged everything and couldn't come up short now. So as much as he didn't want to squeeze through this space that was roughly the size of a manhole, he'd rather die than climb back aboard that ship a failure.

Blake floated in. The dark here was even more oppressive. Like waking up in the middle of the night with your head wrapped in blankets. Blake clicked the light and realized it was already on.

No place to go but down. His claustrophobia tightened as he paddled blind through space that began to squeeze. All he could imagine was getting stuck down here. No guarantee that anyone would find him.

Blake tried to remind himself that somebody had come this far. Two people, according to Isabella's letters. And one of them had survived the ascent back up without the benefit of a diving tank. It could be done.

Blake's shoulders scraped the tunnel. His flippers got caught on some debris as he kicked, wrestling one of them off his foot. He kept going, thinking he'd snag it on the way back if he was lucky.

Not that there'd been much of that going around lately. He thought back to holding Sara's smooth hands inside his as they exchanged vows underneath that pavilion. In awe of the way her gorgeous dark skin contrasted against the soft ruffles of her angelic wedding dress. He wanted to get back to the way she'd looked at him that day. And knew the only way was to keep diving.

But the cave refused to widen, even as the dead end loomed. His arm was stuck in a charging position, holding the light out in front of him. This cavern was no wider than a torpedo tube. He wouldn't be turning around to swim out.

He was going to have to do it in reverse.

A red ruby lay inside a nest of seaweed at the very bottom. Beside it, the remnants of a human arm, broken bones at both ends—picked clean by a host of creatures throughout the years.

Blake reached for the ruby and closed his fist around it, feeling the adrenaline pump through him. He used his free hand to ebb backward, awkward, given his position.

This was a reverse climb. His body bounced around, scuba tank scraping the cavern's ceiling as panic bubbles erupted around his breather.

He kept pushing, sliding, moving one inch at a time. No way of knowing how long it had taken him to get this far. Kahega had said the tanks would last about 45-60 minutes but it had been longer than that, hadn't it? Was he about to run out?

The irony, of course, would be to die now that he had the key. Every instinct inside of him wanted him to thrash, to fight against the reality of his location. Blake was too scared, too eager to ease his way out. His lungs burned and his throat was swollen.

His arms dangled down the slope like Superman. He used the bottoms of his wrists to push back toward freedom as his legs ebbed freely, taunting anything that might have followed him inside.

Shit, don't think like that, he chided himself.

He continued to ease his way up, slow and certain. He shut his eyes to find a groove, but the panic was so great that his entire body was in danger of shutting down. His mind ran to a dozen defeated corners, projecting possible fatalities. How he'd rip his wet suit and drown. How he'd puncture his scuba tank and rocket back down, doing a header into the dead end. Did tanks even work like that, or did movies lie?

Blake kept moving but only because he was too terrified to do anything else.

Beating that bastard Roche when nobody else could was everything. Blake inexplicably thought about the Canadian men the warlord had promised would die in exchange for this information and, even in his darkest moment, decided he didn't care. Because every inch back up this incline meant he was closer to freedom.

His feet wiggled free at last. One final push of his wrists and his body was out. Blake gasped at the sight of freedom and did not dare procrastinate, pushing off the rocks and knifing straight back up to the tongue where he scanned the ocean murk for his partner.

But Kahega was nowhere to be found.

Blake ascended higher and threw the beam down, searching for his friend who wasn't there.

He swam inland, clicking the light with increased urgency. Surely Kahega would catch sight of that.

Only stillness greeted him back.

It unnerved him like nothing else. Maybe Kahega had thought the same of Blake and returned to the ship. Besides, his tank had to be close to empty by now.

Blake squeezed the gemstone tight in his fist. It was the only thing that mattered.

He frowned at the sprawling emptiness and began paddling back the way he came, eager to reach the *Frozen Cocktail*.

EIGHTEEN

"Gonna be down there a while," Holloway said, watching them slip beneath the surface. "How about a game of cards?"

Sara leaned against the rails and watched the space where her husband had disappeared, wishing like hell she could stop worrying.

Worse, it was getting easier to imagine life without him.

Holloway's forearms rested on the rail, a cigar nestled between clenched teeth. His company was better than no company, though Sara didn't have the heart to tell him she hated the smell of those disgusting things.

"What do you suggest?" she asked.

Holloway stared at the resort party boat in the distance. "I radioed and told them I had you aboard. They offered to swing over and pick you up, but I declined."

"Do you always need an excuse to be out here?" Sara asked.

"Maybe some people have questioned the intentions of my boat in the past," Holloway said.

"Oh, Jesus."

"Nothing like that, darlin'. I just like to make sure my Is are dotted and my Ts are crossed."

"That's what a criminal would say," Sara said, to which the captain only laughed.

The wind shifted as the music from the party boat haunted the sky around them. "Celebration" by Kool and the Gang, straight off some 1970s ghost barge.

"You really are an unwilling participant in all of this?" Holloway asked.

"Jesus," Sara said. "Even treasure hunters gossip like secretaries."

"Everyone gossips like secretaries."

True. All throughout Sara's time at sea, everyone aboard commercial vessels, from ship captains to deck hands, got off on speculating above their stations. Whenever people said men didn't gossip, Sara had a hundred old sea dogs to cite as evidence to the contrary.

"Have a drink with me," Holloway said.

"Nah."

"We're locked in place until our boys surface."

"I know that," Sara said. "But I don't trust you."

"You shouldn't." Holloway used his finger to signal one minute and hurried off, leaving Sara alone with the cheeseball disco track that Kahega would've enjoyed.

Her eyes drifted back to the placid waters and her heart leapt at the thought of him.

Any number of things could go wrong down there. A dozen horror stories gleaned from listening to those same gossipy sea dogs: equipment malfunction, oxygen toxicity, or the bends.

For Blake, she worried most about a panic attack or nitrogen narcosis, both of which could cause him to become disoriented and lose his sense of direction. Hopefully Kahega would prevent that, but that was a lot of trust for a rogue who, frankly, deserved none.

"Shit," she mumbled. She was thinking about Blake again. Her fingers curled the ship's rail, giving the metal a frustrated squeeze.

Holloway returned with a bottle of J & B. "Told my men to shoot me if I get out of line." The closest crewman waved and lifted his rifle overhead, as if to reaffirm the order. "So there you go," Holloway said. "My best behavior. Now down the hatch."

Sara gripped the bottleneck and set fire to her throat.

"Trust me yet?" The captain grinned.

"Oh hell no."

"Aw."

"I'm not stupid, captain."

"I'd be over there talking to my man if you were."

That same close by deck hand turned and threw a high wave that prompted Sara to laugh and return the gesture.

Holloway told him to keep watch for their divers, and then led Sara below deck. There was a small sitting nook just behind the entry ladder. She was wound tighter than a snake as she sat across from him. He maintained a gentleman's distance as he divided the rest of the scotch between two plastic cups.

Sara was more than a little embarrassed by how much of her backstory Holloway knew. Kahega had of course filled him in on the immediacy of the situation—potentially volatile clients in a bind because her husband had pillaged their bank account.

She was glad when the topic passed, giving way to lighter and easier conversation. A couple of laughs. A way to forget her insides were twisted into a mass of worried knots.

Sara relished the opportunity to think about anything else and kind of hated how well they got along, happy to keep their chemistry separated by a table's length.

"Kinda curious about you," she said.

Holloway grinned. "Whatever you want to know."

"White boy does tours off Madagascar. Don't take it the wrong way, but that's... interesting."

"Came for vacation one year. Couldn't leave."

"Weak."

"What is?"

"Your story."

"Heck of a way to talk about my life."

"You're hiding."

"What is it you think I did?"

"No idea. I just know that nobody works out of that port unless they've got no choice."

"I work out of many ports."

"Even shadier."

"So I'm shady now?" Holloway polished off his glass like it was water. After some silence, he said, "It's a weird life. Remember when you were in high school and you'd have to see your guidance counselor and tell him what you wanted to do."

"Always wanted to be in fish."

That sounded wrong and they laughed about it.

"I was in the Gulf War," he continued. "There's no story there. Life's a lot duller than that. After two tours, I still didn't know what I wanted. Just knew it wasn't that. So I got out and spent some time in that part of the world—Middle East."

"How was that?"

"A learning experience," he said. "More I talked to the rest of the world, the more I realized how much I empathized with them. Don't get me wrong, there's bad, bad people there, but the folks who live there, man they're just like the ones back home. Trying to raise families, practice their faiths, hell, they're just caught up in the shit. To them, we're invaders. And we can't think of it that way 'cause we weren't trained to think of it that way. I don't know about you, but I was raised to believe we're the good guys. But then you see a history of wars we're waging all over the world and... well, I get the resentment."

"Find me a perfect government," Sara said.

Holloway lifted his empty glass and grinned proudly. "A patriot. Okay."

"My dad was military. Didn't come out with your perspective."

"My problem ain't with the men and women in uniform, but with fuckin' Uniparty that sends 'em out to die for nothing."

"My dad would hear that."

"But you don't?"

"I think life's too complicated for the 21st century. Maybe I agree with some of that, and maybe I think that's too simplistic a worldview. I keep all of it to myself most days because there's always someone eager to tell me how wrong I am otherwise."

"Knew I liked you," Holloway said and refilled his glass. "Anyway, I didn't have much of a life back home. No family left living. No girl to keep me tethered. No belongings to speak of. Thought it'd be easier to just... stay gone."

"See the world?"

"See the world."

They drank to that. Sara crossed her legs and rubbed her thighs and felt a tingle as the captain checked her out. They both grinned as if fessing to wandering minds.

Holloway cleared his throat. "I could've set up shop in the Mediterranean, but a dollar goes a lot further here and the weather's just as good most days."

"You caught enough fish to buy a yacht?"

"Won this ship in a card game."

"Shut up, Han Solo."

"Scout's honor."

She laughed again. Some people's lives were ridiculous. Her own included.

"Hey," she said. "Another question."

"Shoot, darlin'."

"You really believe in it? The treasure?"

"More than God."

"And harder to find."

"Maybe," Holloway laughed. "And it's none of my business but... I wouldn't be too hard on your husband. Idiot's a lot closer than anyone's ever come. No offense about the idiot thing."

"I'm too worried to care," she said.

"Well, it shouldn't be long now. I'd better get back." Holloway rose and headed topside.

Sara watched him go, swallowed the rest of her scotch and took a few heavy breaths. Her face was hot and other parts of her were just as heated.

"Jesus," she said beneath her breath.

She thought about taking a cold shower but decided she didn't trust herself to be naked right now. If the captain came back...

"Would you quit it?" she scolded herself and then followed Holloway above deck.

A familiar voice screamed out. Indecipherable commotion.

Sara scurried toward open air in a graceless climb, reaching the deck on her hands and knees as her husband's high pitch screams catapulted up from the ocean below.

"He's dead," Blake screamed. "Kahega's dead."

NINETEEN

"What say you, king?"

Kaahin sat at the rickety table inside the shack off the beach, staring at the night sky through planked wood. The moon stared back, leaving even darker slats across his dark face.

Imani stood in the doorway. His fingers nervously scraped the bamboo jamb as he eyed the pirate's men spreading across the beachfront, weapons in hand. An outsider would mistake this as a meeting between warring tribes, not old friends.

The warlord repeated his question, pretending not to be intimidated. "What can I do for you?"

"Some westerners make for the tip of Antisiranana."

Imani shrugged, but could not entirely chase the guilt from his features. This was insulting, given their history. Imani was a former despot, ousted from Zimbabwe during a revolt where the citizens tired of election rigging and forced the prime minister's resignation.

Kaahin had brought Imani and his men to the island for a price and the two had been in business ever since.

Kaahin stared. Too often men betrayed their intentions with unnecessary words, and he had long since learned to hold his tongue. He preferred silence because others often rushed to fill it.

"I saw the western man," Imani said at last.

"There is more than one."

"This one came to me with a guide from the coast. Paid for information."

"Who are they?"

"No threat to you."

"I decide that."

"The white man is a coward," Imani said.

"They make for Antisiranana's tip with another white man, a ship captain. I have heard of this man, and he is no coward."

"They mean to find Roche."

Kaahin smiled. People always came here looking for Roche. And Kaahin was always glad to find them when they did. They brought the best equipment on the most expensive boats. Westerners were often bold enough to bring their women, too, arrogant enough to believe such business could double as vacation.

He used to take those women as a gesture of loyalty to his men. And once those needs were served, the bitches were sold to the Saudis for big, big dollars. Couldn't do that anymore. The world was always watching now.

Imani turned and took a presumptive step toward the table. Kaahin's best man brought his pistol forward and cocked the hammer. The warlord raised his hands and said nothing.

It was too hot for this. Every man here wore sweat like jewelry. Underarms soaked as perspiration rushed from their pores.

The warlord stared at the Pirate King from beyond the gun. Uncertainty in his eyes, wondering if desperate times hadn't gone beyond desperation.

Kaahin half-smirked. "I allow you the inland mines, do I not?" That was a pretty good way to make a living. Too much attention for Kaahin, though he was glad to take a cut in exchange for brokering certain protections. The warlord only needed to be honest about his profits.

"Of course, old friend."

"You have helped them," Kaahin said. "That treasure, if it exists, belongs to me."

"If it exists," Imani said. "Nobody has ever found it. If the Americans manage it, they will not make it out of here alive."

"A risk."

"No," Imani said. "The Malagasy Navy knows they are out there."

Kaahin sighed. It was not the Malagasy Navy that concerned him, but the United States envoys currently assisting them with maritime conditions. As had always been the case, Americans loved to meddle where they did not belong.

That was one of the reasons Kaahin needed to be careful. Of more concern to him was what he'd seen on the eastern shore just hours before. The wreckage. The bodies. Screams of

"Death's head, death's head!" Fresh memories that haunted him and his men.

Kaahin waved Imani to the table and reassured his man that it was okay to holster the weapon and leave.

"I saw it tonight," Kaahin whispered once they were alone.

"What exactly did you see?" Imani asked.

"A boat that was all splinters."

Imani looked back through the door, to the beach beyond. He moved his seat out of view as if the ocean spied on them. His voice was barely a whisper now. "At last you know."

Kaahin clicked his tongue in disgust. "What can you know about the sea?" In Roache's day, they would have called Imani *landlubber*. Kaahin did not wish to hear any such thoughts on what lived beneath the waves.

"I listen when people speak, Kaahin."

"What they speak of is superstition."

"And yet just now you confess to seeing it. With fear in your eyes you confess."

Kaahin learned long ago to never fool oneself. There was no benefit to it. He'd survived long on that philosophy. But after seeing a poacher swallowed by something in the sea, something he lacked the words to describe, it had become clear that the unthinkable was true. The thing his countrymen feared was real.

He could ignore it, but at what cost?

There was suddenly much more to be done, and that thought made him tired. This little voyage might have begun as a blood hunt, a means to resupply while the governments of the world had eyes on him.

Now it was something else.

Kaahin couldn't recall off hand the last time he'd seen his family. In order to ensure their safety, they did not live anywhere near here. He communicated with them through VPNs when it was safe to do, and while most of his profits had gone to them, he wasn't certain he'd made the right choice in abandoning them. What kind of man leaves his loved ones to the fates?

Too late to turn back. The world hunted pirates because there was not a single country on earth that wished to abandon tourist dollars to such a nuisance.

The problem in Kaahin's mind was that whatever he'd seen tonight was responsible for more disappearances than his two decades on the Indian Ocean.

Now Kaahin sat at the table, looking up at the full moon and wondering why his ancestors had waited so long to show him the truth.

He knew better than to spread this news to his men. It might alleviate some of the long-term damage to morale, but at too great an expense. People spoke of how Kaahin allowed his crew to die in order to feed himself. How his voyages were cursed. That he should not have slaughtered all those supply ships that had been trying to reach the Middle East back then. He needed to reclaim his reputation. And he wouldn't be able to do that if his men were too scared of the water to help him succeed.

"So what will you do, my friend?" Imani asked.

Kaahin tapped his fingers on the desk. Chewed it over. "We'll use the boat."

"The boat? It is the last asset you have. You would spend it so foolishly?"

"There is nothing foolish about why I am here."

"You are serious about the hunt?"

"Nothing can be accomplished if that thing is to remain out there."

"There are other ways."

"There are not." Kaahin stood, walked to the door and looked at the water.

"If you choose to confront Madagascar's past, you will die," Imani said. "But I see that your mind is made up."

"Just tell me you have what I need."

"I do," Imani confirmed. "My men supply yours as we speak."

"The RPG?"

"If you are going after the devil, you will need more than an RPG, but yes."

Kaahin took one last look at his friend and then hurried toward the boats beached on the sand.

TWENTY

Holloway's cheeks pulsed as he watched Blake shimmy gracelessly from the top half of his wetsuit. The entire crew surrounded him, demanding answers.

Sara couldn't defend him. That was the worst part. The path forward would've been, "My husband's no liar," only that didn't fly anymore, because that's exactly what he'd become.

And they were made. Strangers knew their situation. So it was impossible to make any serious claims about the integrity of Blake's word and have it mean anything other than shit. Sara would have an easier time convincing the captain that she was Santa Claus.

Blake wasn't about to wait for his wife's defense. "I came up out of the cave and Kahega was gone," he said, breathlessly. "No sign of him anywhere."

"How hard did you look?" Holloway pressed.

"My tank was practically on empty," Blake said, sucking air like he'd never taken a breath before. "I barely made it up."

The captain had no choice but to take his word. He seethed, losses suddenly greater than what he'd been willing to incur. Hadn't once stopped to consider anything on this trip could be so devastating.

That spoke volumes about him. This had been rushed and sloppy from the beginning, the entire hunt born from a lie. Blake was no diver. That hadn't concerned anyone. Their only worry was finding whatever down there passed for a demon's tongue.

"Suit up," Holloway told them. "Everyone goes in." He smashed his hands together and roared so loud the Emerald Tides party ship might've heard them. "Move your asses!"

The men hurried below deck to their gear lockers as Holloway continued to glare, fantasizing violence. Sara slid an arm around her husband. She helped him to his bunk. Her fingertips only hovered around his shoulder.

Once they were safely out of earshot she asked, "You okay?"

"One minute he was there..."

"I know."

"Then..."

"It's not your fault."

"Just say you believe me."

"Yes," Sara said. "Yes, of course I do."

Blake's feet scuffed the floor as she brought him straight to bed.

Sara tugged his floppy wetsuit the rest of the way off. It snapped like broken elastic and she flung it into the corner with a frustrated growl.

Blake's head was cradled in his trembling hands. He took deep breaths but couldn't hold back the emotion. "All for this," his voice wobbled, overturning his hand to reveal a muted red jewel the size of a baby tomato. The corners of his mouth tried to turn up, but the gravity of the evening made sure his frown stayed anchored.

Sara's heart lurched. She didn't fight it. You couldn't stop caring for someone the first time they betrayed you. No matter how bad it was, the soul wasn't wired that way. Even when your brain argued it was for the best. God, this would be so much easier if she had the power to shut Blake out.

She got to her knees and closed her palms around Blake's wrists, gently parting his hands so that she could see his eyes.

"What happened down there?"

Blake wouldn't talk about it. Said that if he tried to tell it, the panic would come back and finish him. He knew nothing of Kahega's fate, he swore. And that she believed.

"You need to sleep," Sara said.

"I should help them." He started to get up and her hands were on his shoulders to prevent that from happening.

"You can't," she said. "Just sleep. I'll wake you when there's news."

She used a towel to dry his hair. Got him to lie down. She slid a blanket over his shivers and brought a bottle of Perrier from the fridge. Put it on the bed table and took the jewel in her fist, promising to keep it safe while he slept.

"A few minutes of rest." Blake repeated her suggestion like it was an inspired idea. He put up no further resistance and she left.

Holloway remained on the deck. His clenched fists gripped a scoped automatic rifle. He squinted through it, watching the night.

Sara stopped short of approaching, leery of getting any closer to a defeated man. If he was the lashing out type, he could blame her for everything.

He knew she was there and turned to reveal grief-stricken features, sullen and sunken. "He's gone."

"Blake isn't lying," Sara insisted. "I know what you'll say, but he isn't."

"I know."

"It's not his f—"

"Just told you I know it ain't."

She lifted her arms to feign surrender, gnawing her inside cheek to prevent the mean-spirited smile. Since grade school, Sara had never been able to stop herself from laughing at the most inopportune times. Some people processed grief and awkwardness this way, and it was a bitch.

And this was funny. From a certain point of view, it was downright comedic. Somber cowboys who blazed across the ocean, cocked and loaded, ready to kill for their dreams, only to suffer humiliated silence once those dreams wised up. If you couldn't laugh at that, then what?

Sara had no stomach for this, but as far as she could tell, she was the only one not pretending.

Silence was the name of this game. She and Holloway played it for an hour. Not a single word passed between them. The divers began returning in groups of two, and all their reports were the same: Kahega was a memory.

Sara stared at the ocean like it was a murderer. All the horror stories she'd heard from seamen while on cataloguing runs and there was nothing more terrifying than a man who straight up vanished. The calm water lapped the ship's hull the same way a guilty dog licks its master's hand to apologize for shredding couch pillows.

Sara had seen stuff in her line of work, but this was the first time that the ocean's beauty felt completely sinister.

She shouldn't be surprised. On one of Sara's past voyages, the men had described the discovery of a corpse on the ocean floor, trapped beneath rocks. Turned out to be a missing spring breaker in a wet suit. Crabs had gnawed the flesh away from his exposed skin. He was little more than a meaty torso when they discovered him, a skull face and skeletal limbs picked so clean its bones nearly glowed.

Holloway ordered most of his men to their bunks. One would take navigation duty and another would keep watch in the crow's nest. But it was sleep for everyone else while the captain figured out next steps.

Holloway was all slouched shoulders and quiet anger. He shambled below deck and pulled a bottle of Stoli from storage. Sara followed at a distance.

"You going to call this off?" she asked with rising optimism.

The captain tossed the vodka's bottle cap in the trash and took a parched swig. Wiped his mouth with the back of his hand and shook his head. "Can't, darlin'."

His face wasn't all that weak. Sara studied it and saw determination carved into his age lines.

"Mind if I drink with you?" she asked.

Sara led the way to her stateroom. His bunk, really. She locked the door as Holloway entered. She eyed the bed with a trundling heart. God, it'd be nice to feel something good tonight. One of these nights. At her back, the captain continued to go at the vodka like it was water.

"Best guy I ever knew," he said.

"Kahega?"

A smile passed through his features, warming his eyes for just a moment before vanishing like a ghost. "I was at Stanley's one night... that's a lousy dive right outside Toliara. A few ship captains there got word I was intending to compete for the affections of area tourists. Wanted to know why I needed to be here, of all places, and shouldn't I fuck off back to the states?"

"How territorial."

"Humans are like every other kind of animal."

"Animals don't usually take things personally."

"Okay, professor," Holloway said. "I'm staring down the barrel of a bunch of switchblades and machetes and it's like those old westerns where the bartender disappears because there's about to be trouble."

"Knew you were shady," Sara said.

"Anyway, Kahega, a guy I never met beyond a few quick exchanges at port, appears out of nowhere and tells them they cannot harass his cousin. And you wouldn't think that'd work, right? Everyone in the place looks at us like, bullshit. He starts in on this story about how their fathers were brothers and how my daddy made me promise to come back to Africa and do right by it... just enough detail to sell the lie."

"No offense, but why'd he do that?"

"Thanks."

"I'm glad he did, but what prompted him to stick his neck out for a stranger?"

"Asked him that," Holloway said. "He had no answer. Just thought we needed to be better. As a species."

"God," Sara said, thinking of the way she'd dogged him all the way to the coast. It'd been justified, of course, but as she told Holloway before, humans were too complex to be viewed in simple terms of good and evil.

"You're glad he did, ay?"

Sara gave a weak smile. "Very glad."

Holloway put the vodka down and leaned in. His breath was 80 proof and he looked at her like she was a snack.

Sara closed her eyes as their noses touched, pushing in so her lips could reciprocate. They kissed. The simple touch was electric, energy that discharged across their bodies.

Her fingers reached for the bottom of his shirt and lifted it. He helped wrestle it overhead and then her hands roved his carved physique, fingers tracing the contours of his muscles. She moaned while his hands cupped her breasts, squeezing them together while his mouth worked on her neck. He lifted her shirt so her breasts spilled free. She moaned softly, thinking of her husband asleep in the next room.

This was wrong, and that excited her. Brain chemistry was a traitor. She dug her nails into his back and he growled excitedly. But then she pushed him off so their foreheads touched.

She shook her head no and then Holloway nodded in agreement.

"Sorry," he said and rolled over to face the wall.

Sara stood and the heat flushed from her body. She was so worked up she thought she might've gone through with it if he'd wanted. Just two people desperate to escape the pain. And to think, it was the roguish ship captain who backed away.

"Nothing to apologize for," Sara said.

"Oh, I've got plenty."

"You want to feel something other than pain."

"If you say so," he said.

"If you want to talk, I—"

"Look," Holloway said. "I shouldn't have tried to take advantage of you. That's on me. And since I'm already the bad guy, let me get one more thing off my chest."

"Can't wait to hear this."

Holloway was leaning up on one elbow now, neck craned to face her. "You're a thousand times better than the schmuck you married, no offense. That's not me coming on to you. It's me saying that you deserve a lot better than being stuck in the middle of the ocean in a bunk with some barnacle twice your age."

"I could be offended by that," Sara said. "But I think I'm gonna read it as a compliment in your own socially inept way."

"Read it any way you like, darlin'." Holloway dropped back onto his side and scrunched the pillow up beneath his head.

And before Sara could continue the conversation, he was already snoring.

TWENTY-ONE

There was no walk of shame for Holloway.

He didn't have the ability to skulk back to his own bunk since this was technically it. He lay on his back with his arms stretched against the headboard, snoring like a pig.

Sara showered, scrubbing away the guilt that came with infidelity. No, it wasn't sex, but she'd wanted it. And for everything that Blake had put her through, those vows... well, they'd meant something to her. At one point not that long ago, they'd meant something.

She brushed her teeth twice and slid into white shorts topped off by a grey tee that hung loose off her shoulders. Cotton wouldn't stick or itch and she needed every edge in this godforsaken climate.

Because she wasn't staying in here.

Isabella's notes sat folded on the chair. She scooped them up and hurried out, standing with an elbow against the wall as she caught her breath. Behind her, dueling snores from the two men she'd given herself to. Sara hurried on, eager to escape the noise.

The only spot aboard the *Frozen Cocktail* that afforded any privacy was Holloway's little drinking nook. She settled there. The floor space was clean and if she concentrated hard, she could pretend she was alone.

When she was at sea, she did her best work inside the engine room where the electric hums were so loud that every other distraction got tamped down.

Sara spread Isabella's pages out around her in a semi-circle. "What happened to you?" she whispered, touching the original notepaper with her fingertips, as if the answer might be absorbed through osmosis. She drifted back through time, moving through the corridors of Roche's keep where the air was stale and flickering torchlight made everything smell of scorched wood. She imagined that place sitting out there somewhere, just waiting for the right person to rediscover it.

Would it really be them? Could a band of misfits ever be so lucky?

"Why do you think she was so vague?"

Blake stood in the hallway, his palms tapping the stair treads nervously. He was unable to make eye contact.

"You should be sleeping," Sara said.

Blake ignored the advice. "I, uh, looked for you in your room. Found him." He wasn't being confrontational, but self-reflexive. "I shouldn't have brought us here."

That was the damn truth, but funny he needed to lose his dignity in order to realize it.

"I want to find her," Sara said.

He looked at her finally. "Really?"

With a shrug, she added, "Someone should."

"We're going to," he said and fought the smile that threatened to twist his face. He wasn't out of the woods yet, not by a long shot, and knew it.

"I want to give her closure," Sara added. "These notes, the life she lived... she deserves that much."

"Her life on that island was a death sentence. I think she wrote those letters hoping that someone would help."

Sara tapped the pages splayed around her. "These were written specifically and altruistically. These first two entries, at least. She wanted her true love to find her. This guy, what's his name... Martine Vernier."

"Think they were really in love?" Blake asked.

Sara thought on that, figured the likelihood wasn't so great. For some reason, she couldn't say that, though. "I guess we'll never know."

Did it matter? The girl stood around waiting for someone to save her. People always looked at history through an excusatory lens and with stupid rationalizations like, "it was a different time then." So what? A girl ran off with the wrong guy. It happened every day in every part of the world.

It was happening now.

She pictured herself in Isabella's shoes. Imagined standing on the shore of some hidden beach, fingers tugging her bodice collar without realizing that the suffocation was coming from inside. Riled waves served as the world's most unflappable jailor. What could you do? Wish the appearance of a rescuer on the horizon? And then die a little each day when he never showed?

Maybe there was nothing to do. Maybe Isabella had died trying.

"Back to bed," Sara said, realizing Blake was still standing in place, looking glad to be on speaking terms. She flicked her wrist back toward his bunk. "Go."

"I'm not—"

"Look, I need a minute."

"Yeah, okay." She could almost feel his slumped shoulders and defeated posture while listening to his scuffing feet scrape sadly toward his room.

Sara turned the gemstone over in her hand and wondered if its discovery was intended to be proof of concept for explorers who needed a little certainty at this point in the hunt.

The next hint was even more baffling.

Travel along the path of the plate to the glaring twins, who watch the sky in order to see the sign.

Sara's fourth grade teacher, Mrs. Zimmer, would kick off lunchtime with a riddle. The winner got a few pieces of candy, and then burned off their sugar rush on the playground.

Sara was the only kid to go the entire year without answering a single one. It wasn't that she overthought things. It was more like her brain would simply sputter and refuse to catch, like a failing engine. And to this day she had nothing but disdain for minds that were quick enough to find those answers.

"Not going to let you beat me, Roche," she whispered and lifted the page an inch from her eyes. Who even knew if this had been translated properly?

Sara put the pages back into the protective sleeve and decided she needed a walk. A warm breeze gusted across the deck. She looked overboard as the hull continued to slice through placid waters. Even the fizzing whitecaps were dark tonight.

Whatever time it was, and Sara wasn't keeping track, the Emerald Tides' party barge had gone quiet. They must've gone back to port until her eyes adjusted enough in the dark to see a large, yacht-shaped silhouette bobbing up and down in the distance, further away than it had been, but still unmistakably there.

"Anyone else see that?" Sara said. One of Holloway's men stood at the helm, and one other circled the deck with an automatic weapon in hand. Neither responded to her.

Sara leaned against the wall and slid down, stretching her legs and throwing her neck back in order to watch the stars. This expanse was the same one that Isabella had watched, and somewhere up there was a sign that was going to lead them right to her.

On the path of the plate.

Whatever that meant.

TWENTY-TWO

Blake never got back to sleep. He watched the ceiling and tortured himself over all the ways this had gone bad.

People always said to forget the past because it cannot be changed. Those people hadn't made his mistakes. He counted errors like sheep until his forehead began to roast in the sunlight reaching through the port window.

Then it was time to get up.

He dressed in whatever was nearby, reaching for any twisted wrinkle of clothing. It didn't matter. Anything so long as it got him out of this room.

Sara and Holloway were nowhere to be found. He was glad for that.

Breakfast was a granola bar that had been stuffed inside the pocket of his linen shirt. He reached the deck and stayed aft of everyone else, watching mild green water lap the hull. The chatter coming from the bow was either agitated or excited, and given what happened last night, probably a little of both.

Without Kahega here to keep things balanced, Blake wondered what kind of double-cross the son of a bitch captain was fixing to pull.

He's already got your wife and that's your fault.

Blake was defeated. The treasure was everything, even though he'd lost the person he wanted it for. It was sort of meaningless now that Sara was a stranger. He watched her from a distance, speaking to Holloway with the familiarity of old friends and probably more. He wondered how many times they'd fucked last night as he felt a swell of shameful arousal pass through him.

None of that was rational, Blake knew, but he didn't care. Every bit of trust they'd built steadily over seven years was extinct. He'd done that. But he resented Sara for letting it all go to hell without a fight.

"Shit," he grumbled.

Shrieks sprang into the sky like fireworks. Everyone aboard rushed to the port rail in one mass, gasping at something he couldn't see. Blake followed their line of sight and found a speck rising on lazy waves in the distance.

Holloway ordered the helmsman to bring them around and the *Frozen Cocktail* cut sharp through the water. There was a capsizing ship growing fast on the horizon. They closed the distance and caught sight of the Emerald Tides branding just as the logo slipped beneath the sea.

Last night, this barge had been so full of life that there had been ecstatic screams and DJ booms from a couple hundred feet away. It was almost impossible to believe this was the same ship.

"Life boats were dispatched," Holloway said, pointing to empty hooks. "Must've hit trouble out here and abandoned ship."

"Wouldn't they have come to us?" Blake asked.

The captain didn't answer. He squinted toward the wreckage. The one side of the hull they could see looked like Swiss cheese.

Horror overtook Blake. He felt sick, knowing that something out there had done this. The same something that took Kahega, he knew. "Whatever's down there is after us."

Holloway glared.

Sara didn't look at him at all, almost is if there was a physical barrier between them.

Good, Blake thought. Let the guilt of what you did eat you alive.

The *Frozen Cocktail* floated close enough to the barge for them to reach out and touch it. Except nobody wanted to. The walls were stained by erratic splotches of blood so dark it was nearly tar.

The people that had spent last night grinding against sweaty and scantily clad bodies were a memory, and Blake knew that if they were to call the resort and check to see if any had made it back, the answer would be no.

"Coast Guard will be back this way before long," Holloway said. "Looking for whatever caused this mess."

"Ocean's about to get a lot smaller," Blake said.

Holloway barely acknowledged him. He raced to the *Frozen Cocktail's* bow at the sight of a second ship suddenly materializing in the distance. The captain screamed "incoming" and brought his rifle to aim.

It was a yacht, far bigger than the *Frozen Cocktail*. It moved with purpose, and Blake thought he knew what had the captain so concerned.

It was headed straight for them.

The helmsman above saw this too and brought their boat full throttle. Holloway's men took defensive positions with weapons ready. Orders and strategies were exchanged, some of the shouts lost beneath the fury of whipping wind and agitated water.

The sky overhead dimmed as if someone had turned down the lights. In the distance, the horizon cracked with blinding white light as thunder rumbled in stereo surround.

"Kill them all before they get close," Holloway shouted. "Or they'll do the same to you."

Blake and Sara were side-by-side, strangers at a bus stop. Whatever death they faced was nothing compared to the trial by fire that had singed his soul last night. Down there, his life had flashed before his eyes. Up here, they had enough firepower to take Madagascar by force if necessary. He hadn't gone through all that to die.

The yacht was close now and everyone saw the solitary figure standing at the tip of the bow. A blonde woman in a bikini that was closer to dental floss. She waved her arms back and forth, desperate to be noticed.

Everyone aboard the *Frozen Cocktail* held their fire as the approaching yacht eased off its throttle. A second thunder crack tore a hole in the sky and one of Holloway's men on the starboard side dropped his gun on the deck, spinning like a top. Half his head was gone, blown into the sea, leaving streams of gore to splatter like a lawn sprinkler.

On the opposing ship, the blonde Trojan horse screamed at the sight and hit the deck, falling prone as a second shot tore off. The man nearest Holloway leapt back, propelled through the air as a hole the size of a cannonball was blown through his back.

Then all hell broke loose.

Holloway returned fire, shooting at nothing because there was nothing to see. Other men did the same while some took cover behind whatever they could manage.

Small boats appeared aft of the enemy yacht, zipping at them with alarming bursts of speed. The men onboard brandished machine guns that spat bullets like dragon fire.

"Sink those fucking things," Holloway screamed. "Then shoot them like fish in a barrel."

But the barrels had already fanned out. The crew of the *Frozen Cocktail* divided their attention between breaches, opening fire on the invaders as barking sniper fire coming from the center of the yacht continued to dwindle their ranks.

Blake dove for a discarded rifle smeared with blood. He scooped it and tugged at Sara who had taken a handgun off the deck in much the same way. They fell back toward the rear of the ship so the sniper fire couldn't easily reach them.

Holloway and two stragglers were falling back in a similar fashion. The rest of the crew already decimated.

The survivors regrouped aft, hiding behind the cabin wall. They had inadvertently made life easier for the sniper because now there was only two thin planks of deck to watch.

"We should go below," Blake said.

"They'll sink us," Sara screamed.

"If we're lucky," Holloway said.

A portable ladder lifted up from the ocean and hooked onto the railing. Blake called it out and Holloway barked that a second one had appeared on his side. In a moment, dark faces appeared level with the railings. Holloway and his men shot them, rappelling the boarding efforts.

"They're going to keep climbing," the captain said.

They killed the next two faces just like the first. And as soon as that appeared to be a losing strategy for the pirates, the yacht began to rumble and float around to the port side, only it couldn't get as close as it wanted due to the capsizing resort barge floating between the vessels.

"Only so many places a sharpshooter can be," Holloway said. His men were crouched in cover looking through scoped rifles, fixing to take the sniper out before he could do any more damage.

Sara moved below deck, sighting one of the siege ladders while under the benefit of cover. Nobody else tried to board. Across from her, one of Holloway's crewmen covered the starboard ladder wrung.

Visibility was dropping fast. The swirling storm turned the world into shadows.

"The windows," Holloway said.

Blake's heart smashed like a hammer against an anvil. If the sniper was parked in a window, Blake couldn't see him. He slid the scope across the deck and found the blonde woman, thinking she deserved death for her part in this. The way she'd flagged them down, hoping they'd lower their defenses. He spied her ankle jutting out from behind some diving equipment and felt a great deal of power as he thought about amputating it.

Blake sighted those toes.

His sweaty finger started to squeeze the trigger—

And a gunshot exploded in his ear. Blake lowered the rifle and pushed on his eardrum, stumbling inside as the gun fell from his hands and dropped below deck. Sara spun and said something, her words lost beneath the high-pitch ringing.

Blake balanced himself in the jamb and squinted to see a black man stumbling around on the deck of the opposing ship, blood pumping from his throat with such force it looked like an exaggerated movie effect.

And the blonde woman was back on her feet, waving again, screaming in what Blake's ears interpreted as tinnitus rings.

By the time Blake saw what she was pointing at, it was already too late.

Two pirates stood aft of the *Frozen Cocktail*, having just cleared the boarding ladder. They charged the small group of holdouts with raised machetes. It was the captain who opened fire and cut them down.

The *Frozen Cocktail* rocked on increasingly agitated water, leaving the two corpses to slide around in a thin puddle of blood.

One of Holloway's crewmen rushed the ladder and unhooked it from the railing, dropping it back into the ocean.

"The other ladders," Holloway screamed. "Now that the sniper's down, get the other ladders!" He pushed one of his men along the portside and then shoved Blake against the starboard rail.

Blake and the crewman rushed up like they were racing. The crewman reached his ladder first and stuck his gun barrel overboard in a display of caution. No need to fire. He lifted the top metal wrung and let the ladder fall away from the hull.

Blake got to his ladder next and reached overboard. A machete blade lunged forward and sliced his neck with the speed of a striking cobra. He tried to scream but his voice was already a ghost. He tumbled back with wide eyes, powerless to watch as the large man came aboard with frightening speed. The pirate lifted the machete and swung it again. The blade struck Blake's shoulder. His nerves cried out louder than his voice, which had been reduced to a pathetic and near-silent rasp.

Beyond his murderer, another pirate hopped over the rail and opened fire on the port crewman sprinting now to assist Blake. That body hit the deck and a puddle of blood rushed beneath Blake's feet.

The machete went high. Blake could only stare into the eyes of the madman who swung it. The eyes weren't angry, but tired. And as two more invading men hopped the rail and moved aft across Blake's peripheral, the blade came down into his skull one final time with a fatal crack that echoed in eternity.

Blake's body smashed to the ground like a bag of bricks and all he saw at the end of his life was the bare feet of the man who'd murdered him.

The sky overhead split. A torrential rain fell like God himself was pissing on him.

It was the last thought Blake had before everything went permanently black.

PART TWO

THE GLARING TWINS

TWENTY-THREE

Kaahin strode across the deck of his latest acquisition, bare feet splashing through thin streams of watery blood. The rifle in his hands trembled. He needed to keep this display of weakness from his men. They were busy corralling the survivors below deck, and he needed to steady his nerves before joining them.

The blonde woman standing on the *Star Time's* bow wore disgust on her face. Kaahin threw her a patronizing wave and she turned away.

You are still my slave, he thought and took great satisfaction in the way her posture slouched.

Her sobs were silent at this distance and looked more like dry heaves.

Kaahin grinned at the sight.

He went below and found the *Frozen Cocktail's* three survivors on their knees and wearing the blood of their friends and lovers. The dark skinned woman wept openly for the mutilated white boy they had just tossed overboard. This incensed him.

"Silence." His voice was a whip crack of English that reduced her sobs to whispers.

Through the nearest portal, Kaahin watched the sunken resort vessel at last surrender to the cresting waves. The busted hull drifted into watery oblivion.

He drew a sharp breath as he realized what it meant. Death's Head was beneath them. The battle for this ship had thinned Kaahin's ranks beyond comfort, but the fresh corpses would make good bait.

He rushed topside where discarded bodies floated through the whitecaps, staining the fizzy water cherry red. The corpses fanned out, becoming driftwood on the horizon.

Death's Head had already decided to ignore the bait. Whatever hunted them wouldn't be lured out by something so obvious. This creature was a hunter and it desired sport.

Kaahin's other ship, the *Star Time* ran parallel to the *Frozen Cocktail*. He wanted nothing more than to shoot the blonde woman through her million-dollar face, but knew he could not. He was going to need all the leverage he could get.

"Bring her," Kaahin commanded as he looked across the water. "And bring the rest of them up."

The *Star Time* closed the gap between ships. One of Kaahin's men across the way put a pistol to the blonde's head and motioned for her to jump.

She hesitated and caught a pistol whip against the back of her head for that insubordination. She shrieked and hopped the railing, balancing her back against it before leaping.

The chasm between ships was insignificant. She made the jump down because of the height differential between decks. She came crashing aboard on her shoulder, sliding across the deck like an animal carcass, eventually looking up with a battered face.

Kaahin's men dragged her across the deck and tossed her against the knees of his other prisoners.

The only captive that concerned him was the white man. He was of comparable age to Kaahin. Of the two males they had taken prisoner, only the American projected any sense of danger. It was the unpredictable glare in his eyes. The sort of crazy that promised he'd sink this fucking ship and ride it to the ocean floor before handing it over.

Kaahin needed to humble him quickly. "Put your crew to work," he told him. "Clean this deck as if this ship still belonged to you."

The American grinned. He stared over Kaahin's head in protest. Quiet showmanship to prove to his crew he was not happy to comply, but would. Then he began giving orders, inaudibly at first but soon much louder.

The white woman groveled in a puddle of blood that receded steadily in pouring rain. She curled into the tightest fetal position she could make. Kaahin allowed her to lie there shivering for now. She had one use and this was not it.

The American handed out cleaning supplies like weapons and the prisoners went to work on cleaning the bloodstains that had spilled below deck. They scrubbed the ship of hardened splatter, some of it clinging stubbornly even in the face of constantly lashing rain, removing as much trace evidence as possible.

All corpses got tossed, regardless of affiliation and Kaahin watched for signs of Death's Head, desperate to see the cursed thing. What fish refused even the freshest bait?

It took a little more than an hour to sweep the *Frozen Cocktail* clean. The prisoners were stored below deck, all of them in the same quarters. All but the white woman, who hadn't moved from her cat-curled position.

Kaahin stepped over her and ordered his ships to deeper waters, knowing Death's Head would follow.

They headed north, eager to distance his makeshift fleet from the resort wreckage. People would come looking for that.

The sky refused to let up as they sailed. The decks were permanently slick beneath sheets of rainwater. The ships rocked harder and the men used the rails to traverse, clinging to the metal for fear of falling overboard.

Kaahin went below deck to the prisoners' room. He pointed to the dark-skinned woman and waited in the hall for his men to untie her.

She came out glaring. That temperament took him by surprise. He thought of the blonde waiting above deck, more whimpering animal than woman, and assumed any western bitch would crumble that way. Usually, they could not even look him in the eye. Not this one, though. He admired her strength.

Kaahin hated speaking English, but it was a necessity when it came to ignorant Americans. Over the years he'd learned not to waste time asking if they knew another tongue.

"Your husband was looking for Roche's resting place," he told her.

She said nothing.

"Turn over your materials to me."

"You're going to kill me anyway."

"I'm going to give you a choice."

"What choice?"

"I'm sorry," he said. "I meant to say chance."

They reached the end of the hall and he stepped aside so she could climb above deck first. One of Kaahin's men greeted her there with an automatic rifle to the face.

"All you can do is decide not to die," Kaahin said.

She took a plastic bag out from beneath her waistline. He knew it was there from the way her shirt outlined the square shape of its contents, but he was glad to see her cooperating. He liked to know how far people were willing to go. How smart they were.

"All I got," she said.

He picked it up and leafed through the sheets. Tears poured down her face. Her tummy stuttered and she gagged, certain she had just handed over her only bargaining chip.

Kaahin hooked his elbow around her neck and flexed. He patted her down with his free hand and felt a bulge in her pocket. His hands dove into the fabric and retrieved a sparkling ruby.

The sky flashed blinding white. He released her and she spun to face him. They stayed like that for a split second.

Kaahin found he had seething contempt for her. She mourned a white man. She was young, attractive, and willingly gave her genes to western weakness.

He shoved her. Really shoved her and the slickness of the deck did the rest of the work for him. The girl's eyes went wide. Whatever she'd been expecting, it hadn't been that. She stumbled and hit the rail, took it so fast she flipped over and went face-first toward the water. Crashing and disappearing into the rising emerald waves.

The storm roared, but Kaahin heard her panicked splashes over it. This is the plan now, Kaahin thought. He stormed toward the bow and tore at the lifeless blonde woman cowering beneath the life preservers bolted to the wall.

Her blue eyes fluttered and then snapped open as he dug under her shoulders and dragged. Kaahin had a choice to make, keep her in case the Coast Guard boarded them, which wouldn't fool anyone, or add a second helping of live bait to the waters behind them.

Suddenly, he needed to rid himself of this eye sore. He spat in her movie star face and smacked her across the eyes with his knuckles. Again and again. Taking the time to make sure she bled first.

She twisted her lip up in a defiant smirk while his phlegm dribbled off her cheek.

Kaahin didn't care.

He threw her overboard.

TWENTY-FOUR

Sara slipped beneath the waves. The current flung her against the *Frozen Cocktail's* hull. She rang it like a bell.

She was off-kilter. If she swam, there'd be no way of knowing which direction she was going. And if she surfaced, they'd shoot her to pieces.

She paddled through the gloom with eyes wide, water stinging.

The *Frozen Cocktail's* hull stretched above her no matter the direction she swam.

A long thin stream of fizzy water caught her attention. Golden hair formed a crude yellow halo around a dark shadow. A body straightened and fished toward her with the grace of a mermaid. She kicked past Sara without noting her at all.

Sara twisted around and followed the pale body. The blonde who still had her bearings because her skull hadn't been smashed on the way down. Sara's lungs were getting raw, her chest tight. Her eyeballs felt like they suffered bee stings. She couldn't last much longer.

The blonde arched her back and paddled up. Sara followed and they broke the surface together, gasping and scratching for air and safety. They had reached the other side of the second ship.

Still, the blonde refused to acknowledge Sara. She thrashed around and went aft to the swimmer's platform. Above it, a ladder led up to the deck.

Just as the blonde reached the platform, Sara caught sight of a pirate scrambling to the edge of the deck high above, pistol in hand.

The blonde was determined to risk it. She scaled the platform and leapt for the ladder with a surprising show of speed. She caught the deck railing just as the shooter fired wide.

The girl reached up overhead and closed a fist around his pants. She tugged him forward and then dropped all her weight so that he flipped the rail and went careening onto the swimmer's platform.

Sara heard the wet crack from here. Two bodies crashing and wrestling. The pistol slipped from the pirate's fist and disappeared beneath rising waves. Sara scrambled onto the surface herself, joining the scuffle just as the blonde tried to separate herself from the action. She slipped and fell back gracelessly, knocking the three of them into the drink.

The ocean lifted them on angry swells that seemed determined to throw them back. All three of them reached for the platform. The pirate's hand fell over Sara's head, grabbing a clump of her hair. The blonde hooked an arm around the man's neck and scaled his back, squeezing his windpipe while his face puffed.

Sara brought her knees up against her belly, feet finding traction against the pirate's abdomen. She pushed off and left a bloody tuft of her hair in the palm of his hand.

The blonde continued squeezing his neck from the v of her elbow, pulling her wrist with her other hand as if she might wrestle his head right off.

Sara paddled backward, watching and hoping the blonde wouldn't need her help. Behind the blonde, a pile of rubble floated toward the struggle. Storm debris, Sara guessed.

Except it was worse than that. It was a weathered piece of earth, floating stone somehow.

The debris rose from the ocean like a nightmare, some kind of inanimate object that was at first impossible to comprehend. You'd call it a fish, only it was about the size of a school bus and with a body that seemed cut from pure stone.

The blonde sensed the monster at her back and slipped beneath the waves, leaving the pirate floating atop the water. Sara locked eyes with him for one final moment, and his face flashed helpless. The gigantic fish was behind him, its grinding jaws cleaved him to pieces, slicing through his body like deli meat.

The creature continued forward unsated, as if the food that headed to its belly didn't register. Its mouth rose and fell in seeming automation. Its massive head glided along, gnawing indifferently on air. Its teeth weren't teeth at all, but extensions of its stone face. They reached down from its beak and up from the bottom of its jaw. As it approached the yacht, Sara heard the sharpening sound these "teeth" made as the top and bottom rows scraped together.

Sara reached the diving platform and pulled herself up as the fish slipped beneath the waves. Gone as fast as it had appeared.

The blonde broke the surface next, scurrying to the platform and then passing Sara by for the ladder, ascending.

"Jesus Christ, hurry!" she screamed and thrust a hand down at Sara.

Sara couldn't get up that ladder fast enough.

TWENTY-FIVE

Kaahin watched the fish swallow his man and disappear.

Again.

The awe and wonder of its appearance turned very quickly to horror as he and his men realized in unison that the fish had two choices.

It was going to come for one of these ships.

The American and his one surviving man took off below deck. Kaahin started to lift his weapon and thought better of it. They were going to need every bit of ammunition to kill that demon.

And even then, it would probably not be enough. Imani was right, after all.

"Now you'll come," Kaahin mumbled. "Won't you?"

As soon as he finished speaking, the fish lifted out of the water and charged straight for the *Frozen Cocktail's* hull.

TWENTY-SIX

"Where's the gun?"

Before Sara could interpret that question, the blonde seized her by the shoulders and shoved her against the cabin wall. A vanity sculpture that was bolted into it drilled against the small of Sara's back, bringing tears to her eyes.

"Where is the fucking gun?" the blonde repeated.

Sara couldn't remember. She was petrified by the thing that had popped out of the water back there. Trauma that followed Blake being hacked to death, and of course the warzone on the deck of the *Frozen Cocktail*.

The blonde continued to demand answers Sara couldn't give. Sara only shrugged along, hoping it might take some of the heat off.

It did.

The blonde let her go, mouthing "fuck" while she zipped around the room searching out a weapon. "There's at least one man left aboard this boat," she said. "We've got to kill him."

Sara dropped to her knees and retched. Projectile nerves splattered onto marble finish. Even in panic, Sara understood why. The man aboard this ship was probably already coming for them.

When the blonde's search was unsuccessful, she returned to Sara, sidestepping the pooling vomit in order to help her up. "We have to keep moving." Her voice was gentler now that the adrenaline was beginning to drain. "If they catch us, they will rape us until we're dead."

Sara might've been lost and miserable, mostly hysterical, but she couldn't bring herself to give up. There would be time to mourn Blake later. But as she thought on that, she realized there was nothing for her back home anymore. Emptiness grew in the pit of her stomach, a stretch of darkness she didn't think she could weather.

It was just easier to keep moving for now.

So they moved. Quiet steps on bare feet through the entertainment area, where carpet bolstered their stealth. A winding stairwell up to the staterooms. To the one pirate who was surely steering this ship. The blonde took a corkscrew opener in her fist and held it like brass knuckles. Her breathing was raw and shallow.

"Arm yourself," she ordered.

Sara was distracted again. Only this time it had little to do with the situation that surrounded them. It was instead about the décor of this living space. A large antique globe of the Indian Ocean was straightened and spread across the wall, encased in Plexiglas and surrounded by sea fearing trinkets. Antiques bolted into place to form a loose border.

Sara stumbled toward them, entranced, while somewhere behind her, the blonde sighed and stalked off.

But Sara knew she couldn't leave her fate to chance. For all they knew the helmsman was already steering them right back toward the *Frozen Cocktail*.

She wondered briefly if Holloway and his mate were still alive, realizing that she would probably never know.

Another thought to push off as she turned and hurried to catch the blonde, pausing once more to yank a fire axe off the stairwell wall.

Sara caught up to the woman standing against an entry space. The blonde noticed what Sara had clenched in her hands and gave a quick smile. "He's never going to come out of there," she said. "They need this boat."

Sara eyed the door with the axe heavy in her fist, wondering if they could "Here's Johnny" him to death. But it was metal so that was a no go.

The ship continued to traverse storm waves, rising and falling. The women steadied themselves in the constricted hall space searching each other's war faces for signs of trust. Something in the blonde's cool eyes was centering. Words weren't necessary. They understood the only path forward.

These men were cowards who attacked without warning. They could be beaten.

The blonde crept into the kitchen and moved low behind the granite counter while Sara broke away and headed down the hall, toward the door that led into the whipping wind. She passed through and was lashed by constant streams of splashing water. The deck was slippery and that went double for the rail, which wouldn't prevent her from crashing down onto the main deck below if she took a spill.

Machine gun fire popped in the distance. She hadn't realized until now the *Frozen Cocktail* was probably still nearby. A ladder led straight to the helm, and each metal rung felt slathered in bacon grease. Sara hooked an elbow around each as she scaled it.

The hull was glass on three sides. Rain sloshed against it. The interior lights were dim, filling the cab with impenetrable darkness. Sara stayed low and kept her distance from the door because the next time lightning lit the sky, she'd be center spotlight.

She wondered if it hadn't been a mistake to leave the blonde. They'd been safer together.

The long-awaited lightning set fire to the sky and Sara caught shifting motion in her peripheral. A black man knelt among supplies spread across the upper deck, just a few feet away. He'd been there the entire time, rising now and lifting a shotgun away from his chest.

Sara swung for him, her blade scraping the steel gun barrel. It batted the weapon away from the pirate's hands.

He knew this was life or death and charged like a bull, head pointed at the floor. His arms clamped around her waist and flung her against the half-rail. The small of her back smacked for a second time, sparking her nerves and making her howl.

She unleashed a flurry of fingernails in response, clawing his face and peeling little curls of flesh away like woodcarvings. The pirate barely recoiled.

The helm's lights clicked on as the blonde appeared in the doorway. Sara watched her silent stride. She glided forward, rain dripping like she was fresh from the shower.

The pirate pulled a blade from a belt sheath and spun toward her, sensing her approach. He slashed through her ankle, drawing a line of blood. The blonde shrieked and fell and the corkscrew hit the floor with a clang, instantly lost beneath sluicing water.

Everybody was on the ground now, flailing and grabbing and punching and screaming. The pirate repelled their awkward fists with thrashing legs. Each of their efforts bought surface slashes on their ankles and forearms.

131

But the pirate also knew he couldn't afford to stand. Not until the blade landed inside one of their bodies and bought him the necessary time.

The knife lifted high, its glint nuclear white while caught inside the glow of the motion lamp above. Nothing in this world could prevent it from landing, Sara knew.

And it did. It delivered a brutally cold slice that cut her belly and retreated just as fast. She could only watch as the blade scaled the sky once more.

The blonde crawled behind them, going for the gun, the axe, the corkscrew, whatever. No way she'd get to any of them in time...

"You want the treasure, right?" Sara's voice sounded shrill and full of terror.

The pirate grinned gold. His tongue rested on his lips like a contented animal.

"Treasure." Sara threw her forearms over her face. X marks the spot. "Kill me and you'll never get it."

The pirate lowered the knife just a smidge. Not in retreat. But to instead stick the blonde, whose arm was stretching for the gun barrel. The blade broke through the back of her hand and pinned her fingers in place. The blonde howled like a wolf caught in a snare.

Sara and the pirate had the same idea. They both got to their feet. She was slower and caught a punch to the nose. Then he was squeezing the life from her throat.

"Show me, bitch," he snarled, and then yanked the blade from the blonde's hand.

TWENTY-SEVEN

The cumulonimbus clouds above Kaahin were bleak and pulsing with bolts of lightning that threatened to strike them where they stood.

Below, a creature beyond anything he'd ever seen had declared war. It rammed their hull, rocking the ship with violence, and then swam out to sea and repeated the process like it knew exactly what it was doing. Like it had taken more than a few of these things down.

His men fired at it upon approach. The shots that hit had no effect in slowing it down.

It's keeping us off-kilter, he thought as he went below deck to the hogtied prisoners. The American's glare was no more threatening than a zoo animal. He was alone with the exception of a single remaining crewman, both at his mercy.

"Help me kill the fish," Kaahin said.

"What fish?"

"You have heard of Death's Head."

On the far side of the bed, the American's man, an island native, began a panicked chant. A Malagasy prayer begging the forgiveness of his ancestors. He was too far-gone to negotiate with. The American would decide both their fates.

"He has heard of it," Kaahin said.

"It's a fish," the American said.

"Some say it is more than that."

The American flashed a shit-eating smile and Kaahin had never wanted to slash any throat more. He leashed his temper, though, because the conflict aboard this ship was the last thing that mattered.

"I'll take my chances," the American said.

Kaahin reached down and sliced through his hogtie. The American sighed and scrambled into a sitting position, rubbing his rope-burned limbs.

Kaahin tossed the blade at his feet. "Free your friend and join us on deck," he said. "You help me, I'll put you on a dinghy and send you away from here."

"Bullshit," the American snarled.

"Believe what you wish," Kaahin replied. "Once you see that thing, you will wish I killed you already."

He left, eager to rejoin his men and the sounds of gunfire that raged above deck.

TWENTY-EIGHT

Sara's cheeks were scorched. Panic twisted her guts into knots she feared would take years to untangle.

The pirate had refused to kill the blonde. Sara thought she knew why, and the motive made her shudder. He had left the woman high above deck, her bikini stripped away in order to bind her to the rail. To ensure she remained neutralized, the pirate had tossed the fire axe and corkscrew overboard.

Sara moved through the yacht's sprawling interior with cautious steps, shuffling to the entertainment deck while the pirate breathed down her neck. Whenever she moved too fast, he'd slap the back of her head and shout something in his native tongue.

She moved with molasses and when she got too slow, he shoved her along with hands that caressed her buttocks.

She led him back to the map wall without really knowing why.

The pirate gripped the blade with anticipation. He was torn between sticking the steel through her flesh and sticking himself inside of her.

Sara's finger daubed the Plexiglas. "It's there," she said. "Don't you see?"

The pirate stared gape-mouthed, eyes panning over the map and then falling out of focus.

"Look at the currents on the map," she said, trying to keep panic from infecting her voice. "If you—"

His hand shot up to her neck, squeezing. The hysteria she'd been keeping at bay broke through. She begged. Cried. Didn't want to die here. She saw Blake screaming as a machete hacked his head away from his neck, cutting away his vocal cords so that the pitch of his scream rose to an inhuman shriek before the abrupt silence. Sara, abandoned in bloodshed on her honeymoon.

Life couldn't end now. Not for her. Not like this.

Flashpoints in her mind: Parents she'd never again see, an older brother preparing a run for state rep, and the family she had always wanted, was so close to getting, but would never have. Not with Blake. All due to a few sudden bursts of thoughtless violence.

Then Sara saw the body dropping into view on the yacht's open deck, appearing just outside the open sliding door. The silhouette moved inward and shadows scurried off the blonde's naked body. She stalked forward, soaking wet but somehow gliding with almost impossible stealth. Storm water had cleansed her body, though her stab wound continued dripping little red patters like a runny sink.

The pirate caught shifting light in the corner of his eye, began to turn...

The blonde brought the shotgun out from behind her back with her best *Terminator 2*, throwing the pump with one hard jerk of her shoulder. She tossed it an inch into the air and grabbed the stock before it got too high, sliding her finger around the trigger and lifting the barrel outward.

Sara shoved the distracted pirate away, knowing she needed to clear the incoming spread and uncertain that the blonde with crazed ice chips for eyes would care at all about collateral damage. She was surprised the woman seemed to anticipate this, dragging the gun barrel outward to where the pirate had stumbled.

The crack was louder than hell. The pirate's head blasted to pieces like shattered glass. The body went sliding across the floor on a red slip and slide, pumping more blood out of its neck cavity than Sara thought could've been inside the human body.

The blonde threw the gun down at once and then fell to her knees, struggling to catch her breath.

"Thanks," Sara said in complete disbelief. She planted down beside her. Her beating heart was loud enough for them both to hear.

"Yeah," the blonde said.

A long stretch of silence, probably close to six or seven minutes' worth. "I, uh, just realized where I know you from," Sara said.

"Not going to ask for an autograph are you?"

Forced laughter followed by more long pauses.

"My brother used to have a poster of you," Sara said. She left out the part about it being tacked up over his bed.

The blonde allowed a quick smile as she remembered scenes from her previous life. Then she extended a limp hand. "Carly Grayson. Guess you already know that."

"Sara." She hadn't been Sara Jovish for a whole week yet. Hadn't started the process of changing it over legally, and didn't know now that she would. She could've just introduced herself as Sara Mosby, but for some reason she didn't. Something about her mother's lecture on the surname mattering more than the person who wore it. And she didn't feel like getting into that, either, so she kept it as Sara and left it there.

Carly didn't seem to notice or care. "They destroyed all forms of communication aboard this thing. Smashed the radios and tossed the phones overboard. So that's out. Don't suppose you know how to use the navigation equipment?"

"It's a long shot," Sara said. She thought about all the little lessons she'd been taught on all the different vessels she'd worked on, barely more than anecdotal asides, and realized she probably didn't know the first thing about navigation. "But I might be able to figure something out."

Sara was thinking there probably was some kind of autopilot. But a yacht's autopilot was closer in function to a car's cruise control feature, meaning she and Carly would have to take turns sitting up there and steering the ship. The only thing that autopilot actually managed was propeller speed. Not much help if they didn't know in which direction to go.

"Hey," Carly said with a faint sigh of relief. "I'll gladly take might after all this."

Sara helped the actress to her feet. Carly stood with her back arched, stretching her nude body like it was no big thing. And maybe it wasn't. Sara thought about the small handful of Carly's movies she'd seen and remembered how often she'd been nude in them.

"What day is it?" Carly asked.

"June thirtieth."

"No," the blonde sighed. "It's been two months."

It was weird for the actress to be so well groomed and kept.

Carly noticed that question in her eyes. "They were going to auction me off," she said. "Demanded I kept body hair at bay 'cause god forbid you remind men that you've got any."

"I'm sorry."

The actress shrugged. "I'm alive. The one in charge wouldn't allow them to rape me, so I only spent the last two months worrying that they'd try. Each time he wasn't here, I'd lay awake with my heart pounding."

"What do you mean, auction you?"

"Happens out here all the time. To people all over the world. I guess the one in charge changed his mind when he decided to use us as live bait."

"What was that thing out there?" She asked this as if Carly might have the answer.

"Tell you the truth, I sorta hoped you hadn't seen it."

"Shit," Sara said. "Same here."

"Been telling myself I've been out here too long. That I'm long off my meds so my eyes are beginning to play tricks."

"Sorry to disappoint."

"Que será, sera... Sara."

Sara was back to staring at the map décor on the wall, but really at the trinkets bordering it. In college, she'd taken a course on oceanography in order to satisfy an elective. Because of it, she was certain now that she knew what Isabella and Roche had meant by *the path of the plate*.

Of course, she thought. It all fits. The tool. The time period... Isabella had crafted a riddle that had grown more difficult to solve with the passage of time. "I hear you, girl," she whispered.

Carly didn't question the way Sara's fingers stoked the golden trinket fastened to the far corner border of the Plexiglas.

There was an ancient gold astrolabe there. Sara jiggled it with gnarled fingers until it snapped out of its cradle. The thick gold disc turned over in her hands, bringing with it an awesome sense of history. Who were the sailors who had used this very device to find their way along the stars? she wondered. What were their stories? Lost now to time?

To the layman, the astrolabe *was* a plate. A golden, disc-shaped inclinometer that, for all intents and purposes, enabled the user to hold the universe in the palm of their hand. It was used in the old world by astronomers and navigators to measure the position of a celestial body, day or night.

"This is it," Sara said, triumph in her voice.

Atop the disc was a smaller ring that allowed for the user to hang it eye level in order to look through it while on a ship's deck. The disc had a pen-tip sized hole at its center and a line passed straight through that, representing the horizon line.

Sara recalled the short, stocky Middle Eastern professor, Dr. Paul, who had taught the class, and had brought them an astrolabe from his private collection in order to illustrate its many uses. Across the disc, or "plate" as Isabella had described it, was a series of pointers that each signified a particular star in the sky. Depending on location, the astrolabe would swap out plates with different navigational engravings.

The back of the disc had a small ruler fastened to it, with tiny sights on both ends that could be used to tell time by dangling the astrolabe and pointing the ruler toward the sun, keeping the palm of your hand flat beneath it so that the sunlight would pool there.

"Are you... looking for something?" Carly asked. "Because I might know a little about that."

It never occurred to Sara that Carly would've been in on this hunt.

"My boyfriend brought me out here," she said. "And I was stupid enough to think it was going to be a week at sea... just the two of us. Instead it was a group of men I'd never seen before. That fish out there got them all and the only clue I had about any of it was a single document clipped to an old map of the ocean."

"They were looking for Roche, too."

"Roche?"

"Can I see that map? And the document?"

Carly pointed to the plate. "Tell me what that is first."

"An ancient calculator, I guess. Used to identify stars or planets. Or to determine local latitude."

All of this energized Sara. Holding the ancient device in her hand was the only distraction, and the possibility of finding Isabella loomed large once more.

"Help me with this," Carly said. "Once we clean up, I'll take you up to check the map."

They dragged the headless pirate by the arms. A trail of blood, closer to grape jelly, followed them onto the deck where they struggled to get him up over the railing and overboard.

The storm made the sky blacker than a burnt match. And while they weren't exactly far away from the *Frozen Cocktail,* the weather had disappeared the other vessel entirely.

Carly stretched again and allowed the rainwater to rinse her blood once more.

They swept the ship for weapons next and rounded up a single handgun stuffed with a magazine of five shots, one Swiss army knife in the draw of a passenger bunk, and a rusted machete brought aboard by one of the pirates. As Carly had told her, the radio room was all smashed equipment and there was no way to leverage any of it.

Sara asked again to see the map and Carly begged first for a quick shower. "Won't be able to think straight until I get the chill out of my bones."

Sara was about to say that was none of her business when the actress added a caveat. "You mind waiting with me? Once I stick my hand under a hot stream, it'll be sheer luck if I don't pass out."

Sara kind of did mind, but followed her into the bathroom anyway while Carly got the water piping. The blonde slipped inside the standup shower where the curves of her outline were perfectly amplified by patterned glass.

Sara watched the oppressive blackness outside the portal window. It was as if they'd sailed beyond civilization to an uncharted world.

She wondered if on some level the actress wasn't simply scared to be alone after all this time. The way Carly kept turning her head toward the glass to ensure Sara was still out there. Sara understood that. Carly was just as glad to be in the comfort of someone else who wanted to get out of this mess.

The actress stepped out and wrapped a towel around her body, flashing her damaged hand that continued to dribble thin red streams down her wrist and forearm. "Can you bandage this? And my ankle?"

Sara rummaged through the first aid box and popped the peroxide cap, then doused the wounds. The blonde's bones tensed and her muscles flexed.

"Hurts," Carly sighed.

"Could be worse." Sara wrapped the gauze tight and clipped it into place.

"Feels better," Carly said and lifted her leg atop the sink. The gash there was deep but somehow dry. Her body was in impossibly good shape. Sara guessed Carly Grayson was probably fifteen to twenty years older, though her stomach was somehow tighter.

Sara wondered how she could notice minutiae amidst a crisis, though she was beginning to understand that superfluous details are often what keep people from going insane.

Once the blonde was bandaged up, she slipped a black summer dress over her head and took the pistol from Sara. "Now you. Get clean and don't worry, I'm staying right here."

Sara stripped reluctantly and Carly averted her eyes, checking the gun's magazine. She handled it with certainty, the way most people held cell phones.

Sara got beneath the stream and soaped up. "You were pretty good with that shotgun," she called over the water.

"Did a couple of movies where I had to make it convincing," Carly called back. "I sorta kept up with it. Surprisingly relaxing."

"Thought you weren't allowed to like guns in Hollywood."

"Thing about Hollywood... nobody there says what they really think."

Sara washed and noticed the wedding band on her finger. A cruel reminder of the life she thought she'd been signing up for after saying "I do."

She got a few tears out, careful to cry in silence.

Blake often talked about how quickly someone's life could change. He saw examples of it each time he went to work. Someone glances at his cell phone while driving just as a child steps into the street and in a flash everything's different.

Sara's hair was still soaked when she slipped back into the humidity. Carly handed her the semi-damp towel and stole a quick glance at her naked body while she dried off.

Sara slipped her clothes back on and they went to the helm together.

"There's another problem," Carly said. "We're almost out of fuel."

"How close?"

"Won't get back to make Madagascar," she said. "But here's the thing. They kept this boat hidden in an island cluster somewhere close by. They needed somewhere to hold us tight while the pirates searched out a buyer. The islands had almost no traffic. A group of fishermen came near one time and the pirates shot guns at them until they took off."

"What good does it do us to make for an uninhabited island?" Sara asked. The right play was to get back to port, away from the sickos that hunted them. But if they couldn't do that...

The pirates had tossed them into the ocean as bait for that thing. Sara thought again of the creature and was at a total loss to describe it. It was so surreal that she knew in a few days she'd be able to deny it had happened at all.

Carly was already trying to make that a reality and Sara couldn't blame her.

"Do we make for Madagascar and see how far we get?" Carly said.

"I think that's the play," Sara agreed.

Carly attempted to steer the ship around while Sara checked over the navigation tools. The Gyrocompass said they'd been moving northeast. The radar had no pings for land or any other ships. It was like the *Frozen Cocktail* had disappeared entirely.

"If we can point this thing southwest, we should be in decent shape."

"Until we run out of fuel," Carly said.

"There is that."

"I'll try and be more optimistic."

"Why don't I look it over while you go and get those documents. Please, Carly. I need to see what you have. I think I'm close to finding it."

"I still don't know what it is..."

Blinding halogen flooded the helm. Electric white beamed through the cab's windows. Sara lifted her fingers to try and blot it out, but it was everywhere at once, growing brighter with every passing moment.

Carly flung the door wide, gun in hand, and took aim at the sky. Sara ran for her, eager to yank her back toward the safety of the cab, but found herself staring up at whirring helicopter blades.

For a split second, everything seemed fine. Like all the hopeless strategizing they'd just done was all for nothing. Because here was the Coast Guard. Had to be.

And not a moment too soon.

"Prepare to be boarded," a voice thundered from overhead. God himself calling down. The order froze the women where they stood.

TWENTY-NINE

Each time the fish rammed the hull, it felt as though the *Frozen Cocktail* was running aground. The sides of the ship creaked like worn floorboards as the creature continued its barrage.

It moved like a tank, slower than any predator Kaahin had ever seen. Its trudge so sluggish that any ship should've been able to lose it on open water. And yet, each time it collided, the world felt ready to shatter. The men cowered and whimpered and looked to Kaahin for reinforcement, nothing of which he could muster. Because he was certain they were going to die out here.

"Anybody got eyes on it?" Kaahin screamed, his voice competing with the storm. Waves of rainwater rushed the deck, watery walls that crested fast and crashed hard. They soaked the floor and sent the men sliding across it.

Visibility was next to nothing. Kaahin always caught fractured glimpses of the fish just seconds before impact. The world seemed to slow to a crawl with each sighting, his brain unable to process the otherworldliness of the thing. It looked wrong. Looked... impossible.

"Goddamn thing's going to puncture us," the American screamed from across the starboard side. "If we go down right here, it just picks us off as we swim."

They were already down another man. One whose name Kaahin had never taken the time to learn had gone overboard in the last swell, vanishing as soon as he hit the water—as if the Death's Head had been right there waiting.

This is no fish, Kaahin thought, furious for continuing to label it that way. It is a demon. A demon that had learned to hunt man. Knew how to beat them at their own game. Everything Kaahin had thrown at it had failed.

He thought it would take the women. Live bait. Their terrified splashes summoned it like a dinner bell. And yet, the demon had decided to turn its attention on him. And that was good. At first, Kaahin had been excited. Because they had enough firepower to blast it to hell.

A lot of good any of that had done them. They hadn't been able to hit it with anything more than a few AK-47 bursts. 7.62 x 39 rounds sunk through its hindquarters, where its armor did not appear to extend. But if the demon bled at all, they couldn't see it.

Kaahin had also lost sight of his prize yacht. The women had made it aboard, and he hoped that Babek had taken them. Only Babek had neglected to fire off a signal flare, meaning the struggle remained in flux.

"We should make for deeper waters," Kaahin called to the American. "Tire it out, make it work for its dinner."

"Move away from land?" the American said. He had ropes tied around one wrist and one ankle. Buntline knots attached to unoccupied brackets on the cabin's exterior wall—a safeguard against going overboard if the swells happened to catch him just right. "You crazy, pal? We need to get closer to shore before that thing takes this ship down."

That couldn't happen. The longer this creature swam these seas, the more unwelcome attention this part of the world would attract. The Malagasy had spoken of this demon in whispers for years, but it was agitated now. Striking everywhere. Constantly. If Kaahin did not stop it here, he would lose these seas above and below. Given all that he was hoping to accomplish back home, Death's Head needed a quick death.

"We're sinking," the American said, louder this time.

"It will take hours to sink."

"One hour. Maybe two."

"Best to kill it fast, then."

"Shooting gallery's not doing shit," the American said. "I've put round after round into that thing and it hasn't bled a drop."

If it bleeds at all, Kaahin thought. If he could get the demon's head and drag it back home and force the whole island to see what they feared, they would know then their land was safe. And even more importantly, they would come to recognize Kaahin as a godkiller.

Here was immortality. He only needed to take it.

"Bring the cannisters," Kaahin ordered.

145

The American began to protest, saw the anger in Kaahin's eyes and thought better of it. The American pulled a knife from the scabbard fastened to his shoulder, and the gesture made Kaahin take a step back and lift his weapon.

The American sliced himself free of the ropes. He disappeared below deck and returned with two jerry cans. Once all the reserves had been brought up, he told Kaahin, "Water's up to my knees down there. We're dropping fast."

Kaahin's men had lugged these on board in order to refuel the *Frozen Cocktail*. When Kaahin raided, he needed to ensure there was enough fuel on hand in order to get their bounty to wherever it was going.

Carrying gas on raids was risky, one errant shot would turn your dinghy into a fireball. But if you gambled with the lives of your men then you owed it to them to mitigate risks. Dying came with the job. Running out of gas after you'd taken losses was something else entirely.

"Drop anchor," Kaahin ordered.

"Listen, pal," the American said. "If you're fixing to send us up in flames, let me and my guy swim for it."

"The demon will take you before you can swim two kilometers."

The American thought about that. He looked out across the roaring ocean and suddenly had fire in his eyes. He pointed to the helm controls. "An idea, but I gotta go up there to do it."

"Go."

"I will. Just don't want your men shooting me in the back."

"Just go."

The American did. And within a moment the *Frozen Cocktail* sputtered and then slept, leaving it floating on raucous waves. The American had killed the motor.

Kaahin knew why and his next order was simple: Everyone take a canister and wait for the fish.

Soaked, uncertain faces did as they were told. The American took two gas cans and hurried to the bow. His one remaining man followed. Kaahin's men fanned out with the rest of the canisters.

From the crow's nest above, another of Kaahin's men kept close watch with the RPG ready. Once the water around them caught fire and burned away some of this night, he'd be able to see the fish wherever it surfaced. And blast it to pieces.

Yeah, Kaahin thought. Right. His heart began to push. Wide eyes stared down at excited water. Around him, shivering bodies braced for the inevitable.

These last ten minutes had been the longest break between attacks so far. It wasn't for nothing.

Kaahin hurried around the boat and handed each man a flare. "Once the gasoline is poured, light and drop."

The deck was a bit closer to the water now. The American was right. They'd be swimming soon.

The storm was loud and cold and Kaahin's face felt chapped. His fingertips rubbed the bulb of his nose and he felt a fuzzy numbness there.

The water flung the ship high and then dropped it back down. Their stomachs lurched with it.

A raw scream from the stern. Kaahin started toward it, bracing against the constantly sluicing water.

He signaled for the men to begin the gasoline pour, but aft cries were louder than even the howling wind and he wasn't sure how many had even heard his command.

He edged around the cabin where the deck was thinner. One of his men blocked the path forward, face twisted into a plea for help.

Kaahin thought at first the ship had gone up on another large swell. Or that the hull had taken on too much water and was beginning its final descent. But Kaahin turned and saw the bow pointing straight up at the moon as if the bowsprit was looking to stake it.

Then his feet began to slide and his back crashed against deck and he was vertical, gliding down. His bare feet connected with his man's chest, pummeling him and sending him hurtling toward the demon that's mouth was wedged around the entire stern.

Kaahin saw it up close as he fell toward it.

Its head was massive. Unblinking eyes were permanently widened and completely dead. Jaws moved up and down as if it wasn't a mouth at all, but a wood chipper. Its bite shredded the *Frozen Cocktail's* stern, reducing it to instant driftwood.

Kaahin's man slammed against the demon's mouth just as Kaahin managed to grab hold of some errant netting that prevented him from following. The relief on his man's face said he thought for a moment he'd missed the fish's opening, but it was instead an instant where the fish's mouth happened to be closed. Those jaws sprung wide again like a loaded bear trap and the man slipped inside and was gone.

Overhead, the one with the RPG went tumbling from the crow's nest with a scream, crashing headfirst into the waves and taking the RPG with him.

At least one of Kaahin's men had managed to light the water on fire. A small lick of flames danced portside. Because of it, Kaahin saw the demon's eyes even better. What he'd thought had been a permanently wide glare was instead some kind of armor piece that shielded its real eye. That area was wide and niched, rough like the outer shell that encased the demon's entire head. Its blazing eye sat beneath a cross-shaped divot.

The fish continued to chomp, barely acknowledging Kaahin. The top half of its body was sheathed inside that protective bone, making it nearly impossible to breech.

No wonder so few of their shots had landed.

Against all odds, the men had done their jobs. Hissing flares popped and glowed. White-hot phosphorus dropped to the sea like a spilt basket of hungry snakes. Kaahin's hands squeezed the rope net as the ocean caught fire and encircled the ship.

The fish began to sway, building the necessary momentum to escape the heat. Each motion made the boat whine a little louder as Kaahin saw his last chance begin to fade away. Nobody would ever have this opportunity again.

So he unsheathed his machete, thought for a moment of his children and country and how none would ever know what happened to him. But he was beyond that.

A quick prayer passed through his mind and then he let go of the net and rode the deck straight toward those bony jaws.

Kaahin slashed at the creature and the blade bounced off its mouth like he was hacking stone. He slammed the machete down again and again, determined to break through. Desperate to see just a smidge of blood.

Just to know it could die.

The fish continued to flop around in an effort to dislodge itself from the *Frozen Cocktail's* stern. The idea of escape made Kaahin swing harder. The blade snapped but at last a thin trickle of blood dribbled from a tiny gash.

The pirate lifted the jagged blade and stuffed it straight down through the wound, pushing it further in, embedding it there. More blood bubbled up around the sunken blade as the creature's eye glowed with something approaching fury.

Pain, Kaahin knew. It has not felt such for a very long time.

He was waist deep in water now, fumbling to get the pistol from his submerged holster. He did and the shot went off, sinking straight into the gash. The next shot drilled away a bit of its fossil flesh right beneath the eye.

That did not deter the demon from glaring. It managed to snap free and at last embrace the ocean. Just as the fire caught up to it and surrounded the ship in a perfect ring of roaring flames. A sizzling trail climbed across the creature's back.

The demon slipped immediately beneath the waves, leaving a darker splotch of blood resting atop the fiery ocean.

The pirate dropped his shoulders beneath the rising water and began to swim. The American still clung to the bow alongside one of Kaahin's men. The American didn't give it a second thought. He shot Kaahin's man through the eye, splattering his brains into the Indian Ocean.

Then he dropped into deeper water and drew down on Kaahin. "You never had a chance, pal," he shouted.

Kaahin stared up at the barrel. He would never beg for his life. Hard to think it could end this way, but many through history went to their graves struggling to believe the same.

"I know the girl gave you those journal pages before you killed her. I want them."

"You will never find that treasure," Kaahin snarled. No westerner must ever find it.

"Just take us in. Land ho, asshole."

Kaahin watched the gun. Best not to tempt fate. "There are more dangers than just that fish," he said.

The American thought about that. Looked around. The wall of fire continued to burn, though was already dying. They couldn't face that creature again. Maybe Kaahin had managed to injure it, but they'd lost everything to do that. And they hadn't killed it.

"I don't care about those," the American said finally.

There was no other option, so Kaahin dove beneath the waves and paddled hard to escape.

THIRTY

As the helicopter glided over the yacht's bow, two rappel ropes appeared, dancing in the sky. Two hulking bodies appeared on the chopper's landing skid and surveyed the scene as a searchlight swept the deck. Then they slid down, boarding.

Armored soldiers who knew just where to go.

"Do not resist," said the booming voice from overhead.

The troopers began their ascent up the helm ladder. Carly leaned over the ledge and sighted one. Sara yanked her by the elbow, jerking her back inside the shelter.

"They'll kill you, Carly!"

Next came shouting Sara couldn't understand. Equipment boxes glided down the same rappel lines. They fell like blocks of cement and the helicopter swerved as a wall of water broke across the ship. The boxes skidded around in the flood, spreading out across the wide-open deck.

The first of the two men had goggled eyes that glowed military green. He appeared outside the helm and drew down on Carly with an automatic weapon that would cut her to pieces if she did anything other than disarm. He passed through the entrance wearing so much armor he barely fit inside.

"Throw it down, Carly," Sara told her. "Now."

Before the blonde had a chance to react, Glowing Green Eyes snatched the shotgun, barrel-first. He tossed it behind him and pointed the submachine gun at her heart.

The second man entered and sighted Sara with an equally eager weapon. The voice behind his facemask was muffled, asking, "The ship clear?"

Sara nodded fast and the trooper lifted the night goggles away from his helmet and pulled the facemask off his head.

"Nice to see you again, Sara."

Guillaume. The man standing directly over his shoulder was Jean-Philippe.

The helicopter lights swerved again to avoid a second breaking wave. It glided away from the deck, dipping toward the ocean where it began to flounder, tipping erratically as it reached back toward the sky but stayed in place, as if frozen there.

A long, dangling appendage was suddenly attached to the landing skin, preventing ascension.

Jean-Philippe rushed to the glass, shouting something in French Sara couldn't understand. Everyone stood paralyzed as they watched the helicopter gyrate over angry water, ever inching toward riled waves and then falling on top of them. The rotors snapped and broke apart, turning into projectiles that skipped through the night, one of them slicing through the yacht like a cannonball.

Jean-Philippe rushed for the ladder through the chaos, reached it and glided down. He sprinted across the bow and fired a flare just over the spot where the helicopter had gone down.

A twisted mass of metal floated there, ebbing against the hull as storm waves tried to swallow it.

"God," Carly cried, her words on the cusp of breaking.

Sara didn't see it at first. The helicopter's fuselage was dented and damaged, but as the flare light shifted and fizzled, she noticed part of its undercarriage was shredded.

Then she saw why. Eager teeth rising from below, chopping the metal away, cleaving through the wreckage to reach the flailing pilot trapped inside the sinking coffin. His hands slamming against cracked glass just before the flare light died out entirely.

The pilot's scream was louder than the lashing rain and whipping wind. And then the helicopter was gone, en route to a soggy grave.

THIRTY-ONE

Kaahin flailed beneath the water as the *Frozen Cocktail* went to its final resting place. He swam until he couldn't hold his breath any longer, his chest beginning to ache.

He surfaced slowly and did a 360, confirming he'd lost the American in the chaos. Had lost everything in the chaos. The darkness was impenetrable. The shoreline, nowhere. He knew in his heart whichever way he ventured would be wrong. The fates had decided he was a dead man, his spirit just another in a long line that would give power to the Death's Head.

Each time Kaahin's legs knifed through the water, he imagined the demon gliding up to take a bite of him. He was embarrassed by the panic that pushed him to paddle blind, as fast as his spent body would allow.

He splashed around like a child in a bathtub, squinting through the dwindling storm to find his bearings. Just a light on the horizon, a hint of the shoreline somewhere distant would be enough.

"I could kill you, pal." That voice was behind him. He turned to see a lifeboat bobbing behind him, far enough away but gaining fast. "But I have a feeling I'm going to need you."

Kaahin hated to admit it, but he was never happier to see anyone, least of all an American. He tried to keep his composure but the charade was short-lived. He laughed at the sight.

The American helped him climb aboard and motioned for Kaahin to sit opposite him. He did as he was told, so grateful to have been temporarily rescued that he very nearly said "Thank you."

Very nearly.

THIRTY-TWO

A tale of two Guillaumes.

There was the man by the pool, intense and passionate eyes that sliced through the game, saying what he wanted without having to speak it aloud. Guillaume claimed to prefer the company of men, though the way he'd looked at Sara, his needs were maybe a bit more fluid. She got that. Variety was the spice of life or however the hell the saying went.

Something about him had excited Sara. She always thought her own sexuality might've been somewhere on a sliding scale, and wondered if more people weren't really born with similar proclivities. She hadn't given it a ton of thought, though she was surprised sometimes where her mind wandered when she indulged her most private instincts.

That was the Guillaume she'd gone to dinner with. Had relaxed her at a time when she needed to relax. He'd provided an emotional Band Aid at the precise moment she needed one.

But it'd been a ruse.

Because there was also the man who'd knocked on her door later that night. The man whose eyes were equally intense and much colder. A smile devoid of what she had assumed was natural charm. A smile that was instead a sneer. He was sinister. And terrifying.

That Guillaume stood on the helm, pointing an automatic rifle at her.

"Two men." It was the third time she'd answered the question. "Two pirates. We killed them."

"Why are you on this ship?" he demanded. "Where is your husband?"

Sara answered and he had no reaction.

Guillaume must've realized his presence was confusing and intimidating. Clearly, he was used to dealing with rougher clientele. He lowered the gun and it went back to dangling from the strap around his shoulder. He lifted his hands to signal a truce. "Please, Sara," he said, a bit softer. "May we speak somewhere?"

Behind them, Jean-Philippe stood at the helm window, looking down where the helicopter had vanished. "Daan," he said softly. To no one in particular.

"It is a tragedy," Guillaume said without taking his eyes off Sara.

Jean-Philippe swiveled his head and glared. "That you have barely acknowledged."

Guillaume sighed. "Grieve later. Tonight, there is work to do."

Jean-Philippe grumbled something beneath his breath and returned his attention to the ocean.

Carly seemed afraid to speak. She hadn't taken her eyes off Sara either. "Who are these guys?"

"I don't really know," Sara said.

"Please." Guillaume extended his hand toward the door that lead down into the kitchen. "Sara, let us speak in private."

"No way," Carly snapped. "I'm not staying here alone with him."

"She comes with me," Sara said.

"We are not the bad guys," Guillaume said, tiredly. "We can help you."

Jean-Philippe was looking at Carly now, eyes widening as he recognized her. "I cannot believe this."

Carly crossed her arms, uncomfortable with the spotlight.

"*Three Nights in Malibu*?" Jean-Philippe asked.

"Oh Christ," Carly said.

"I knew it." Jean-Philippe pointed at her. "I know who you are."

"A fan," Guillaume groaned. "Leave it to Jean-Philippe to find one of his favorite actresses on a derelict boat in the middle of the ocean."

"Look," Jean-Philippe said, stepping toward Carly. "I can get this boat turned around. You can help me. You want to hold a gun, a knife, or whatever else you need to set your mind at ease, do it." He pulled his sidearm from its holster and handed it to her.

"You will be fine," Guillaume assured her. "We only need to speak in private for a moment, and then we will return. This isn't about either of you."

Sara didn't believe there was any danger here. Not immediately. These guys might've been cold-blooded criminals, but she didn't believe they would murder the innocent. "Anything happens to her," Sara said, "you won't make it off this boat."

"A necessary threat and a fair deal," Guillaume said. "Sara, please, this way."

Carly held the gun on Jean-Philippe as he moved in front of the boat's controls. "It's fine, Sara, just hurry back."

"Much better company up here," Jean-Philippe said without looking at his husband.

The walk to the living quarters seemed to take forever and Guillaume didn't bother with small talk along the way.

Once they reached the bar in the entertainment space, he tapped his hands on the counter and said, "No reason for this to be contentious, let me pour you something."

Sara thought she might've had more alcohol in her system than water at this point. Whatever kept the edge off. When Guillaume slid a glass in front of her, she didn't even look. Just took it and sipped.

"You know what we're after," Guillaume said.

"Pretty badass for a couple of antique store dealers."

"Field expeditions are a different thing."

"Makes sense." She chinned toward his tactical gear: The bungee cord dangling off his belt, the holstered handgun, the night vision. All of it. "You're pretty well connected."

"My employer does what she can to ensure success."

"Where does she stand on losing a helicopter?"

Guillaume took a sip from his own glass. Refused even the faintest smile. Sara was ashamed of how much she wanted it.

"Go ahead," Guillaume said. "Ask."

"You knew who I was. At the resort..."

He nodded matter-of-factly. "An instance where business and pleasure were able to mix."

"But how did you know me?"

"When your husband responded to that 911 call, it was one of my associates he found shot to death on the floor there."

"Holy shit."

"Small world, right? Our guy had gone there to meet the old man, to get the map. Legally, of course. Rent paid until the end of his life. What he found instead was a halfway senile old man who wasn't all that trusting."

"How did you find him in the first place?"

"After he burned through his entire savings trying to find Roche's secrets, he tried soliciting help from others. His condition was always twenty percent. Nothing anyone seriously wanted to consider. But his request crossed our desk. My employer... she was well aware of the stories."

"Your employer sent someone who couldn't close an elderly man. That's why I'm in this shit?"

Guillaume laughed. "Never heard it so eloquently put, but yes. Regrettably."

"Yeah," Sara said. "Regrettably."

"Here's the thing," Guillaume said. "My employer is not unreasonable. She has more money than she knows what to do with. She can buy and sell ships like this without a second thought. She will compensate you. You and your friend above deck. We only wish to be the ones who retrieve Roche's treasure. And we must do it quickly."

"Before that fish eats us all?"

"Take your pick," Guillaume said. It was the closest he got to smiling. "The fish, the Coast Guard, the pirates..."

"That fish is more than just a problem." Sara gave him the rundown. "You saw it wrestle a helicopter into the water. You think that thing's just going to take off somewhere else just because it's got a bellyful of blood and metal?"

Guillaume nodded but did not reveal his thoughts. He simply waited for her to finish speaking and apologized for the loss of her husband. "Perhaps it is all the more reason for you to help us find Roche's secret. So that people stop ruining their lives on such a stupid errand."

"You need me," Sara said. "And I don't trust you as far as I can throw you."

"What would you have me do?" Guillaume's laugh was inward, almost nervous.

"I lost the pages when the pirate threw us overboard. You want to find the treasure you're going to have to find the *Frozen Cocktail*."

"Yours is the only ship out in this mess."

"You're sure?"

He only nodded.

That meant Holloway was gone. The hopelessness of that news filled her with despair. She asked Guillaume to pour another drink. "So you lost the notes," he said. "But you've got them in there." He stroked the side of her cheek. His glove was thick with tactical padding.

She brushed him away.

"I meant what I said." Guillaume tapped the countertop. "My employer's generous when she wants to be. But there is another side of her. A ruthless side."

"You're going to play me like that?"

"Not if I can help it. Help me, Sara, and you are rewarded. You cheat me..." he shrugged. "I'm tired of this job. Tired of hearing my employer speak about Roche's treasure as though it's the last secret on this shitty planet. Let us find it together."

Sara weighed this. It wasn't outside the realm that Guillaume might be telling the truth about paying her a finder's fee and sending her on her way.

She shrugged. Her way of saying maybe she could live with this arrangement. What other choice did she have?

"I will radio for another chopper as soon as this weather passes," Guillaume said. "For now, we'll use this ship as our hub. We'll unpack the gear and get our bearings."

They went back to the helm where Jean-Philippe and Carly were hitting it off. She was in the middle of a story, regaling him with an anecdote about the time she vomited on a horse she was supposed to ride into a scene. The animal was so mad about it he took off running and didn't stop until he'd bucked her into nearby marshland.

Guillaume picked up the astrolabe sitting on the counter and turned the golden disc over in his hands. "This is probably worth close to a million," he said, eyeing Carly as if she owed an explanation.

"Belongs to Jesh," Carly said, then turned and looked out at the water as her shoulders slumped, remembering everything that happened. "Never mind."

"Think your employer will be happy enough with that?" Sara asked.

"She's got ten of them."

"Well, I need that one."

He handed it to Sara.

"Let's step outside," she said.

The four of them went onto the deck where the rain had stopped, though the wind continued to gust.

"Give me your hand," Sara told Guillaume. "Don't move."

He stood still as Sara lifted his arm so that it was level with his shoulder. She pulled his elbow straight and slid the astrolabe ring around his index finger.

The golden disc dangled from Guillaume's hand and danced in the wind.

"Hold it still, Carly," Sara said.

The actress held the bottom of the discs between two fingers. Sara twisted it around so that she could approximate their location. She wasn't an astrologist, but knew the night sky was very different now than it had been three hundred years ago.

But Isabella, or Roche, more accurately, probably hadn't planned for that.

Jesus, Sara thought. The clue's faulty.

She looked up as the storm clouds thinned, revealing the sprawling star scape beyond. This was some "Where's Waldo" shit. A thousand shining stars up there, none of them clustered noticeably closer together.

"Isabella I can understand," Sara said. "But how does Roche not know stars rotate?"

"He knew," Guillaume said.

"Then, what?" Sara asked. "He never wanted anyone to win?" Given what she knew of Roche, that did make the most sense. Though it was just as easy to believe someone like him would want the challenge. This game was tough, sure, but she believed it was built to be played.

Sara paced the deck while Guillaume continued to impersonate a statue. The astrolabe dangled off his finger, locked into place by Carly's clamped hand.

"Think, dammit," Sara growled. She was back in Mrs. Zimmer's class, taunted by riddles she couldn't solve.

When using the astrolabe at night, stars are observed by aligning the pinholes on the revolving ruler in order to see the star through both ends of it. That gives altitude on the degree scale, and the angle is then compared to star charts and tables in order to find latitude.

"We're not in the Northern Hemisphere, are we?" Sara said. "So Roche wasn't using Polaris to gauge his location. So what's he talking about?"

"Are we sure he's speaking of the stars?" Jean-Philippe asked.

"I'm not sure of anything," Sara said. "Follow the path of the plate to the glaring twins, who watch the sky to see the sign."

Carly looked like she was desperate to say something, but stayed appropriately shy, considering their guests.

"The plate," Guillaume said. "What if he's not talking about this damn thing?" He jiggled the astrolabe and then put his arm down. "But instead the plating of a ship's hull..."

"Telling us we gotta sail," Sara said. "Okay, but where to? And we still need to watch the sky? For what? Stars? If it ain't that then what is it? Clouds?"

"His island," Carly said and everyone looked. "Jesh, uh, my boyfriend, was looking for an island. He and his friends were searching all the local clusters."

"It wouldn't be a local cluster, would it?" Sara said, to which Carly flapped her palms against her hips, wondering why she should bother contributing at all. Sara picked up on her frustration and said, "I just mean... Isabella spoke of total isolation, feeling as if the rest of the world had been a dream and that the only reality was the small strip of land Roche kept her prisoner on."

"Some small patch of land, then," Carly said. "How many can there be?"

"Hundreds," Guillaume said.

Jean Philippe was smiling. A shit-eating grin that couldn't be contained. You had to work hard at wearing a face that smug. "The twins," he said. "I know what Roche speaks of."

"Enlighten us then," Guillaume said.

"Better just to show you." Jean Philippe headed back to the helm.

"The sky," Sara said. "What if it's clouds that mark the spot?"

"There are more clouds than islands," Carly said.

"Yeah, but that makes a certain kind of sense to me now that we're in the eye of this riddle."

"You are earning your pay, Sara," Guillaume said.

"One of my first times on the ocean, the fishing vessel I was aboard picked up a distress signal. To this day, it's the creepiest thing I ever heard... a garbled voice saying 'help, help, it's eating the sky' over and over. Thing was, we were in this desolate part of the Atlantic our captain called the 'Vacant Corridor' on account of there being nothing around for hundreds of miles."

"What was on the radio?" Guillaume asked.

"Young guy's sailboat sprung a leak in a storm, and he managed to get to this small patch of land in the middle of nowhere. Should've seen this place, barely the size of a house. But he had his radio, and he just kept begging for help."

"Wait, what was 'eating the sky' then?" Carly asked.

"Gonna get to that if ya'll let me finish," Sara said. "This was a summer day and the sky was clear. Our captain said that was good for our missing person. Had everyone take turns on the telescopes, watching the skies. An island can be spotted from a far off distance because clouds tend to form right over them. Land heats up quicker than the sea, right? So the air begins to swirl up above it, making a localized low-pressure area that sucks up moisture from the sea. You spot cumulus clouds in the distance there's a safe bet you've got a landmass beneath it."

"You didn't answer my question, though," Carly said.

"We found the guy and he was so dehydrated he thought the cloud looked like Pac Man."

Carly laughed out loud and kept laughing. It was contagious and spread to Guillaume.

"You get a prize," he said.

Sara allowed herself a prideful smile. "Holy shit, Isabella," she said, never closer to her.

"Welcome to the team," Guillaume said.

"Still need to know where to look," Sara said. "Think your man in there really knows what's up?"

"He is so arrogant because he is so often right," Guillaume said. "This is the first time in my life I have been happy to admit that."

"So he definitely knows how to drive this boat?" Sara looked to Carly for that answer and Carly nodded. "Good," she said. "We're going to go pass out for a minute."

Guillaume smiled. "Have a good night." He followed them back inside.

They went through the helm and toward the bunks. Carly leaned in on Sara once they were safely out of earshot. "Are we really going after it? Instead of going back to Madagascar?"

"Don't you want to?"

Carly shook her head and then rolled her neck around. Her shoulders were wider than most women. It gave her a sense of power she didn't seem to comprehend. Like she could land a punch with all the force of a sledgehammer. "Not really," she said. "I'd like to go home."

"We're close," Sara said. "Don't you think we're entitled to a little taste of what put us in this mess?"

"Did you forget about the fucking dinosaur that's chasing us?"

It was Sara's turn to shake her head. "I just think if we find this treasure, we're set for life. Money, yes, but also respect and recognition. Can you even put a price on that?"

"You know just what to say to me," Carly said, reaching out and touching two fingers to Sara's collarbone. "Okay."

Sara thought it was time to hone this girl into the killer she'd proven herself to be. There was an alliance with Guillaume and Jean-Philippe now, but tomorrow was another story.

"I don't think I can do it without you, Carly."

"That's funny," Carly agreed. "Because neither can I."

THIRTY-THREE

Mr. Reeves sat at a folding table at the back of the empty airport hangar. He pressed a can of Brisk to his forehead where the cold first stung, then refreshed. He dragged it around his sweat-laden face as the door across the way opened and Mr. Davis entered.

"You had to set up all the way back there?" Mr. Davis's voice was all echoes. Acoustics in here were like standing in the belly of a cave and screaming "Fuck."

"Need to get my daily steps in," Mr. Reeves said. "This way I gotta walk half a mile each time I need to take a piss."

"Steps is for soccer moms," Mr. Davis told him. "And I wouldn't get too comfortable."

"Who's comfortable?"

"Not me," Mr. Davis said as he neared. "And we're moving out." He dropped a folder on the table and Mr. Reeves twisted it around in order to read it.

"Distress call?"

"Not exactly a mayday, but close enough. Chopper went down near those coordinates last night."

"Not surprised," Mr. Reeves said. "Storm was bad."

"Storm didn't do it."

"Our man couldn't have done it either."

"Sure about that?"

Mr. Reeves didn't know. He just didn't want to leave this hangar on another bullshit errand. Their hot tips had been colder than a brass bra. But could he say for certain their man hadn't blasted that bird out of the sky? Maxamed Abir Kaahin was a career professional. Resourceful. Would he waste the equipment? Yes, if it was some private military corporation on his ass then he certainly would.

"I'll take your silence as a no," Mr. Davis said. "Which means we're going out there."

"Shit," Mr. Reeves said.

"I know," Mr. Davis agreed. "But our man's been too quiet. He's not on this island. And those fireworks are the only lead we got."

Mr. Reeves popped the Brisk and swallowed the iced tea in three gulps. "Those assholes in Algeria had him dead to rights."

"We're not going to make the same mistake."

"We're not," Mr. Reeves said and crushed the can, hurling it into the wide-open hangar. "Know why? We're killing his ass on sight."

"Langley wants him."

"Langley can suck my dick," Mr. Reeves said. "I was in Marshall's wedding. Had to tell his wife what happened. And Langley thinks the plan's the plan?"

"They're sweeping it under the rug because we've got interests here."

"Langley's got interests. I don't."

"Another thing that worries me," Mr. Davis said. "A few of those online assholes are starting to piece it together. A few of them know exactly what happened in Algeria."

"Hooray for citizen fucking journalism," Mr. Reeves said. "Call our boys in Silicon Valley and have them shut it all down. Ban every last account if they need to."

"Hard to keep things buttoned up anymore."

"Things would be easier if we brought back the gulag and filled it with those assholes."

"Just so I'm clear," Mr. Davis said. "You think we shoot him dead? 'Sorry, boss, guy was a cornered animal.' Like that?"

"That's what I'm saying," Mr. Reeves said. "Blow his brains out, get out of his country. Be home in time for bacon."

Mr. Reeves watched Mr. Davis carefully, saw reluctant agreement turning over in his eyes. Only rub was that they'd have to do most of the wetwork themselves. Couldn't afford to use hired help because hired help talked. And this was better. A little trip down memory lane. A time before cubicle life. A chance to remember where they came from. He savored those memories, thinking they'd travel light just as they had. Easier to control the narrative that way.

Mr. Reeves stood. Thought about crossing the hangar space now in order to get the day's steps in one shot.

"I think we can be ready to leave before lunch," Mr. Davis said.

Mr. Reeves only nodded, choosing to leave his Brisk off the day's calorie count. "Let's hurry up and find him."

THIRTY-FOUR

"You trust them?"

Carly and Sara were two girls at a sleepover. Carly sat Indian-style wearing an overgrown UC Santa Cruz Banana Slugs shirt.

"I don't trust them at all," Sara said, her back against the wall, fingers rubbing the carpet. Each time she closed her eyes she saw that terrible fish launching out of the water like a missile, catching the helicopter between its mouth and wrestling it down to hell.

"That thing," Carly said, watching Sara turn the golden plate over in her hands.

"This thing," Sara repeated before flinging it to her feet, "is a waste of time. I really thought it was the answer." She imagined Mrs. Zimmer somewhere making that *tsking* sound as yet another riddle slipped past Sara.

"You did have it," Carly said. "That cloud shit was one hell of a pull."

Carly's sincerity made Sara smile. "Thanks."

"Jesh talked about treasure," Carly said. "Not this treasure, specifically, not to me at least. But he used to imagine all these little caches scattered around the world. I figured it was just some fantasy he had. Never thought more about it because, like, who really believes in buried treasure in this day and age?"

"Men," Sara said and turned away. She listened to the sound of crinkling paper as Carly pulled a few loose sheets from a small backpack and handed them over.

The map was marked up, slashes through the island clusters they'd already checked. It was hard to know how off-base they'd been, given Sara didn't know where Jean-Philippe was bringing them, but most of the places Jesh had searched looked closer to Madagascar.

The other sheet of paper was a hand-written note, this one in English. She scanned the signature and the author's name was familiar.

Martine Vernier.

Isabella, the pirate's whore, told me how to find the island. Information I keep in my head. We leave in four days.

Tell your men to be ready the morning of the seventh. I will not wait one moment more than necessary.

As for Isabella, your men they may have their way with her, should they require the incentive. My gift to them... in addition to their cut of loot, of course. She is soiled from where I sit. Once I return, I shall buy myself an actual princess.

Your former partner,
Martine Vernier

"He didn't care," Sara said.

Sara told Carly the whole of Isabella's story and it bothered the actress just as much. All too relatable, no matter your walk of life.

"I need to say something, okay?" Carly said. "I haven't known you more than a few hours, but the second you showed up, my luck changed."

"We've made a good team so far."

"Back home, people are as nice as your last project. Rather than suffer death by one thousand cuts or, death by thirteen straight VOD releases, I high-tailed it out of town because foreign investors were still eager to work with me. And my name makes foreign markets pay attention. For now. It's a career adjustment, but nothing stays the same, right? I was beginning to think my best life was over, and then here you come with promises of treasure on the tip of your tongue and all I can think is it's not over yet."

"My gig back home ain't all that sympathetic to my needs, either," Sara said. "And it's super discouraging to hear that this shit can happen to Carly Grayson."

"You think we should trust them?"

"You just asked that."

"Did I? Shit, I don't know, Sara. I'm trying to keep it together."

"We're not trusting anyone else," Sara said. She pointed to her temple. "But they want what's in here so we're safer than Roche's treasure at the moment. They won't try anything until we're Land Ho."

"You mean that's when they'll kill us."

"I don't think they'll make that much trouble for themselves, though I'm not sure they'll be cutting us checks."

"I'll write you one," Carly said. "We get out of this, I'll give you a grant for whatever research you're doing."

"We'd better survive, then."

"Will we?"

"You were doing just fine without me. Two months in their capture? I was ready to lose my brain after two minutes. And the way you took that pirate down? You're a badass bitch, Carly Grayson."

Carly reflected on those props. Her features brightened.

Sara got up with a loud pop of her knees. She shuffled over to the bed and sat down. The bed creaked. She dropped onto it. "I think we should try to sleep for a few hours."

"You go ahead," Carly said. "I can't."

"Carly—"

"I can't. When I close my eyes, I see things I'd rather not think about."

"You want to talk?"

"Oh, where to start? My daughter probably thinks I'm dead. Jean-Philippe wouldn't let me use any of their equipment to communicate because he said it would compromise the operation."

"How's that?"

She mimicked his French accent. "If a movie star turns up on the radio screaming mayday, your president will have the entire Navy out here. You think we want to explain what we're looking for?"

"Everything serves the hunt," Sara said.

"Yeah," Carly sighed. "He told me he'd give me the phone the second we open Roche's vault. 'When we're rich beyond our wildest dreams.'"

"God," Sara said. "We're in this up to our necks so why doesn't it feel real?"

"I just want her to know I'm alive. That I'm okay."

"Not much longer now."

"These guys aren't any better than producers. Men like Jesh promise the world and then under deliver by half. For you, they'll cut a check. For me, they'll fly me home first class. Whatever they need to say in order to get us on their side."

"I buy it," Sara said. "It ain't charity, but cutting us loose with a little money is still the easiest way to make people shut up."

"I didn't swim through a cesspool of producers in my line of work to take men at their word now."

"He did give you your gun back."

Carly took it and slid the magazine out into the palm of her hand. She started for the door when Sara sat up in the bed.

"Hey," she said. "Don't."

"You're taking their side?"

"No sides, Carly. Just come get some sleep. You're more exhausted than I am."

"Too tired to sleep." Carly slid one foot toward the bed but then looked back at the door. "And I wasn't going to do anything crazy. Just, you know, check things out."

"Nothing's going to happen tonight."

"If that fish comes back—"

"It's a big ocean."

"And it's all over us."

"Come here, Carly. Please."

Something in the blonde's face changed. She was looking at Sara like there was a piece of meat on the bed. Comfort Carly was suddenly desperate to feel.

"Look," Sara said. "Nothing sexual. But I'll relax more with you beside me. Throw that chair in front of the door if you really want to make sure nobody else comes in."

Carly sighed, too bad, but took Sara's suggestion. She wedged the chair back right beneath the doorknob and then lowered the plastic blinds so there could be no peeping.

She pulled her shirt away and threw it on the floor, crawling across the bed like a cat, smirking as she tried to make Sara reconsider.

Sara's heart raced, fleeting urges and curiosities that she tamped down.

Carly curled up atop the covers, trembling. Sara's body was perfectly straight, her palms pressed into her thighs.

"I've never felt so alone," Carly said at last. "My career is basically over. My kid... doesn't need me. Off to college. Truth is she probably doesn't even know I'm missing. Nobody does."

"What about your boyfriend? His family?"

"Jesh? Shit, I was so stupid about him. Oil baron who wanted to break into the movie business just so he could show his dick to actresses."

"How can you stand it, then?"

"Can't. You take meds to forget. Why do you think there's so many overdoses? Breakdowns? Because it's a perfectly nice town to work in?"

"Never gave it much thought." Sara threw a gentle elbow against Carly's arm. "Shit sucks, but today's the first day of the rest of your life. We make it to that island and help them find what they want, they're gonna let us walk."

Carly closed her eyes. Sara listened to her breathe.

It was enough in that moment. Sleep managed to follow. For both of them.

THIRTY-FIVE

Two men. One lifeboat. A single paddle.

They shared the labor.

Kaahin clutched it in his fists and considered swinging for the American. One crack across that skull and he would be looking at a red waterfall streaming down a lacerated scalp. All he'd need to do then was lean to one side and tip him overboard.

Tempting.

But Kaahin was in no rush to do this, for it would mean condemning himself to death too. Given the vast sprawl of ocean around them, they would need to conserve every bit of strength and save it for the labor at hand if they had even a small chance of reaching land.

Overhead, an expanse of bright blue sat high above turquoise waves. Hours passed looking at the same view. The American said very little. He hid behind a steely gaze that was busy calculating its own odds. At last, he asked, "This all part of the plan?"

Kaahin had to swallow a good amount of pride before he could look the bastard in the eye. His overworked fingers felt like jelly, otherwise he'd crack that insufferable smirk off his stubbly mouth. "What would you have done?"

"Hauled my ass back to port."

"I find that hard to believe," Kaahin said. "You don't think I know you. Your reputation."

"That a fact?" the American said.

"Some cowboy comes south, lives on a boat, and spends his days chasing after women he has no right to."

"Yeah." The American grinned, his reputation preceding. "Broke a few of your boys' noses, you know. Ones who call me *colonizer* like it's supposed to keep me up at night."

Kaahin didn't have the energy for this. The constant paddling reduced his muscles to mush.

The American lounged across the bow as if he were a passenger, visibly amused by Kaahin's struggle. "Gotta say I'm disappointed in you, chief," he goaded. "Steal my ship... for what? Lose the ride you came in on, and the one you lost all your guys trying to take."

"The fish—"

"I saw the fish. A hundred other ways to roil that sucker."

"Please," Kaahin forced a laugh that was both sarcastic and inviting. "Teach me something."

"Depth charges, for one."

"I see," Kaahin said. "Just raid a naval yard, then? Or perhaps swim down to the ocean floor and find a submarine that will hand over its munitions?"

The American brushed him off. "Redneck firecrackers, pal. Made 'em back home all the time. Flash powder. Seven parts potassium perchlorate to three parts powdered aluminum. Can't get that stuff in the states without bringing the ATF around, but what you can do is make friends with any sort of fireworks wholesaler. And we've got about as many of those per capita down south as we do mosquitos."

"What's done is done," Kaahin said.

"That so?"

"What use is there in dwelling?"

"Alexein Rabetsitonta," the American said. "That's one reason."

Kaahin did not acknowledge that. The only sound was the gentle lapping of ocean green against the wooden hull, heavy paddle drips each time Kaahin lifted the blade.

The American continued, "Ykem Andrianantoandro... Ikem Rajaonarivelo..."

He spoke each surname in almost perfect Malagasy. The esteem this man held for his crew had taken Kaahin by surprise. He felt more than a twinge of embarrassment, even now, because Kaahin hadn't bothered to learn the names of those who'd died for him.

"We have both lost much," Kaahin reminded him.

"Whose fault is that?"

"If we wish to survive—"

"Right," the American said. "Conserve our energies. Speak only when necessary. Pretty convenient for you, huh, pal?"

Speaking hadn't been necessary. Not at all and not for hours. It wasn't until a stitch of land appeared on the horizon, far off in the distance, like seeing a spec of dirt on a television screen, that it became necessary.

Kaahin said nothing, flexing his muscles and pushing harder to reach it.

The American took notice. He sat up and craned his neck. Laughter as soon as he saw what Kaahin paddled toward.

"Can't believe it," he said. "I really can't believe it. Hitting this straight on is like throwing a fuckin' dart at forty feet and landing a bullseye. Vingt Cinq... has to be."

Kaahin smirked.

Vingt Cinq was one half of the Agaléga Islands. Two small islands governed by the Republic of Mauritius, an island nation some eleven hundred kilometers to the south of Madagascar. While Mauritius was mainly a tourist trap, annexed from one hundred and fifty years of British rule in 1968, nobody could understand precisely why the dominant language there continued to be French Creole.

And the American was not entirely correct in his assertion. Vingt Cinq referred to the capital city on the northern island, where most of the three hundred people on Agaléga called home.

Kaahin had never been. He suspected it would be incredibly difficult to navigate without arousing suspicion. Still, he paddled on thinking about the demon fish that was almost certainly following them.

"What are the chances?" the American snorted.

It shouldn't have been possible, Kaahin agreed. He smiled inwardly, certain the elders were smiling down on him, bringing good fortune because his quest was too important and they had finally realized this.

The American whooped like an excited mutt, sticking his forearm into the water as if that might get them there any faster. Then he crossed himself, thanking his own god.

Kaahin paddled faster. Given the sun's position in the sky, and the island spec still on the horizon line, the risk now was reaching safety before nightfall. If they lost the light while paddling, it would be too easy to accidentally go wide and float right past that island in the dark.

He smashed the paddle through water so hard his already tired arms went numb. But once the distant land at last unhooked itself from the horizon and grew just a tiny bit bigger, he knew they were going to make it.

Kaahin continued to hold the paddle until he couldn't. Until there was no choice but to relinquish it. His arms dropped and dangled like hooks of beef as the American began beating on the water like it was a defiant animal.

Kaahin lounged back and wondered who would try and kill the other first. He also knew the American sense of justice—*lex talionis*. One of the few things he admired about their hamburger culture. One of the things he agreed with.

Kaahin could not afford to sleep. Because he did not trust this man. So he sat with loose eyes on the distant island, really watching the American. Wondering when their reluctant cease-fire might end.

***

They reached land well after dark.

By the time the wooden hull came upon the shallows, Kaahin had never felt more relief. He was tired. He rolled out of the boat and dropped into knee-high water, resting on his forearms that sunk beneath cool and moist ocean sand.

The American moored the boat by dragging it to the beach and leaving it slumped against a palm tree that dangled so low it was nearly horizontal.

To Kaahin's surprise, the American propped himself up against that tree. A burly silhouette that watched with folded arms. For some reason, he was waiting for him.

Kaahin took just another moment and began to wade toward the shore, noticing the elongated structure off to the right, an old ship dashed upon shallow rocks.

"Ever hear the story?" the American asked.

"Of that?"

"Sure, you're nautical."

"I have not."

The American seemed to like Kaahin's wanting answer. "Story goes she was a coastal trading vessel under the British flag. Ran aground right here a couple of hundred years ago. Kinda adds to the atmosphere of this place if I do say so myself."

Kaahin stared at the decaying ship. The mast was snapped clear, sails long stripped away. The wood on the exposed hull looked battered and recessed. Other patches were punctured straight through. Holes too large to be from cannon fire.

They walked the length of the island in an hour's time. The one village on this southern landmass, Sainte Rita, was close to the northeastern shore. A row of rural homes accessed by coral and sand tracks served as the sole road through it. Houses had uniformity in the same clay-colored and slatted roofs designed to catch rainwater for all purposes: drinking, cooking, and bathing.

The one market sported hand drawn advertisements for Sprite and Coca-Cola.

Three sides of the coast showed endless sprawls of water that stretched and stretched. And the north led to another, slightly larger island that was connected, not by a bridge or road, but by a reef of sand and coral.

"The one time I was here," the American said, "I could walk across at low tide, where the reef is awkward and sharp enough to pierce most footwear. Either that or we had to wait for transportation."

Transportation was a carriage pulled along by an ancient-looking tractor that had long turned the color of rust.

"We should walk," Kaahin said.

"Sooner or later we're going to have to explain why we're here."

"What have you come up with?"

"Tell me, boss, just how famous are you?"

"They will not know me on sight," Kaahin said. "Our story should be mundane enough to satisfy them."

"We're not exactly storytellers."

"Why were you here?" Kaahin asked.

"Worked in Mauritius for a few years after getting discharged. Bounced around a few of the resorts. Got a job for a telecommunications company there and they sent me out this way to make sure the satellite connection was good enough right before the World Cup."

Kaahin laughed as he started across the thin island connector. "Of course."

The American followed, but Kaahin did not like keeping his back to him. He turned and waited until they were side-by-side. The American could've finished him off on the beach had he wanted to, but reluctance did not make them allies.

They reached the northern island's hub just before sun up. Unlike the peaceful village they had moved through on the southern island, the settlement of Vingt Cinq was as modern as a forgotten little village could afford to be.

Generator hums said they were getting close. They marched beneath a canopy of palm trees, stumbling over the occasional fallen coconut.

Kaahin decided the American would take point, and that they were to pose as the only two survivors of the *Frozen Cocktail*: The captain and his deck supervisor.

They moved in knee high brush toward the administrative building—La Grande Case. A row of guest bungalows lined the path that moved up toward the central structure. In narrow slats of moonlight, all the curtains on those accommodations were drawn wide.

"Can't imagine they're full up," the American said.

They were about to emerge from the brush and move the rest of the way on the proper road when Kaahin snatched the American by the elbow and tore him back as headlights bounced toward them.

They went prone as the area around them glowed yellow, pushing the darkness further into the forest. Severe shadows grew and twisted on the buildings across the way as the jeep steered along the curved road.

Both men held their breaths.

There were three or four police on this island. Very little need to employ more than that. Most of the time their presence was symbolic, a reminder to residents they still belonged to society. It was otherwise the sort of beat men would kill for because there was hardly anything to do.

The jeep slowed as it passed the front steps of the administrative building. A quick rumble and it was past their hiding space. The yellow light receded, taking the deepest shadows with it, leaving red brake lights to stain the night.

There was no guarantee that reaching this building would solve their problems. Though if they could plant their excuse first, really sell it to the bureaucrats, the law here would fall in line.

Kaahin rose to his knees and watched the brake lights as they continued skipping south in between the trees. They froze abruptly, squeaking brakes that sounded like a yelping animal. Excited voices followed as Kaahin and the American looked at each other.

The police were looking for them.

The American mumbled, "Shit."

A shadow jogged back up the road and a click followed—the unmistakable sound of a weapon being drawn.

"Out." The voice spoke in Creole.

"Jig's up, aye?" the American whispered.

Kaahin did not know. They were capable men and could pacify a single officer, if necessary. These were not the department's best, but rather the laziest. Dulled edges. Blunted skills. There was no place to hide on an island this small. And if Mauritius had an opportunity to bring reinforcements from the mainland...

"Our story stands," Kaahin said through a clenched jaw. He stuffed the jewel into the dirt at the base of the tree and covered it with a few leaves. Then he stood and stepped to the road with his hands to the stars. His Creole was bad, but it would be enough. He fed lines to the nervous officer whose face remained hidden behind the blinding flashlight.

The American followed his lead and began to blabber a similar story. Behind them, the jeep wound back up the trail in reverse. This was time they could not afford to lose.

If they couldn't sell this, they'd sit in jail and wait for the arrival of a magistrate. Magistrates visited the island once or twice a year in order to preside over all matters of law. It had the potential to be a very long wait.

They got on their knees and the officer waited until the jeep got all the way back. The officers then traded Creole at furious speeds that Kaahin couldn't follow.

The officers didn't have much to say to their prisoners. They simply bound their wrists together with zip ties and loaded them into the back of the jeep. They headed away from the administrative building, taking with it any hope of making it through this arm of their journey without suspicion.

The American looked to Kaahin for a lead. His reluctance stood. He hated to admit it, hated feeling constricted by these binds, but it was the only choice they had.

For now.

THIRTY-SIX

The weight of the handgun in Sara's fist brought relief. That was a strange feeling to reconcile as she stood amidships with Carly, trying to understand who she was anymore. Her memories and experiences felt alien now, part of someone else's life.

The sky was crayon blue, a scribble of clouds dotted across it. Sara stared up at it and a scoff passed her throat as she realized she was still technically on her honeymoon.

"Here," Carly said, taking Sara's arm. "Let me show you the trick to aiming that Keanu Reeves once showed me."

Sara pulled away. "Told you I've shot a gun before."

Carly lifted her hands and widened her eyes, gesturing "excuse me all to hell."

It brought a smirk to Sara's face. "Sorry," she said. "Guess I should be willing to hear what John Wick has to say."

"That's right," Carly agreed. "When most people aim, they tend to look beyond the iron sight. Don't. Look right at it. Your target will be a bit blurry and that's normal. Your sight will hover around some because we're not robots and no one, not even Keanu, can hold a handgun totally still."

"Ladies, I do not want to die of old age," Guillaume called out. He had fastened some empty liquor bottles to the port bow's rail.

"Want me to show you?" Carly asked.

"Go right ahead," Sara said.

Carly lifted her Desert Eagle. The gun was far bigger than Sara's and was absurdly oversized in Carly's fist. But the actress knew exactly how to use it. With all the movies she'd done, firing a gun was like a reflex.

Sara braced for the shot. It was still startlingly loud. An explosive burst that prompted angry squawks from circling seagulls. The old scotch bottle exploded while Carly slid her aim just a few inches to the right and fired again. Sara bucked at that noise, too, as more glass shards joined the pile.

"One more," Guillaume said, unable to hide the condescending bemusement in his voice. "Convince me you're the real deal."

The Jack Daniels bottle blew apart like a gunfighter had shot it. Carly did everything but blow on the smoking barrel, eyeing the Desert Eagle with a satisfied smirk. "I think I'm in love."

"Then it's yours." Guillaume went to the pile and used his boot heel to brush the glass overboard.

Carly slid the vertical weapons holster around her shoulders, clicked the safety switch on the slide before sheathing it. She looked like some 70s detective show character as she leaned against the cabin, eyebrow cocked and eager to see if Sara could match her. "Need me to show you again?" Carly asked.

"Nah," Sara said, suddenly and stupidly competitive. She lifted the SIG Sauer P226, which is what Guillaume had told her it was, as if that was supposed to impress a marine biologist. Did it fire? Would it kill? Then great. She looked down the gray slide as the distant bottles blurred. Carly took a few exaggerated steps away and Sara turned to her. "Gee, thanks."

Carly chuckled.

Sara raised her other hand to cradle the SIG Sauer's grip. The gun barked and the glass broke.

"Beginner's luck." Guillaume's words and accent were smugly French.

"Bullshit," Sara said and blasted the next bottle into oblivion. And then the last. "Keanu fucking Reeves," she said, and then to Guillaume, "You can clean that shit up now."

Guillaume did while Carly bumped shoulders like the actress was hip to her secret. "Look at us, all armed and dangerous. We find that island and—"

"We still don't know what could be there," Sara said.

Guillaume returned to the conversation and handed Sara a tactical thigh holster for her weapon. She attached it and tucked the gun away.

"She is right, you know." Guillaume popped a stick of chewing gum into his mouth. "Never know what you'll find out here. Ever hear of the Sentinelese?"

Neither woman had.

"Cannibal tribe off the coast of Sri Lanka," he said. "Last people on this planet to go entirely untouched by modern advancement. Primitive hunter-gatherers, incredibly hostile to the outside world."

"Poor people," Carly said.

An unfortunate display of clichéd Hollywood ignorance. Sara thought she saw visions of a charity dinner pass through Carly's eyes. "Save the Cannibals" or whatever. The actress hadn't meant anything by it, but Sara appreciated that parts of this world still lived in the past. It wouldn't always be that way.

And Guillaume challenged Carly. "Who says poor them? It's the life they know."

"It's all geography," Carly said. "I mean, they don't know how much easier their lives could be..."

"Again, who says?"

"The world could at least try and make contact."

"The world has tried," he said. "Indian government, Christian missionaries... They're not having it. So perhaps it's best to live and let live."

"Yes," Carly said. "Of course."

Jean-Philippe appeared two decks up. He waved for them to join him.

"Shooting bottles is one thing," Sara said as they walked. "But shooting people—"

"—is much easier," Guillaume said. "When someone's trying to kill you, you'd be surprised what you're capable of."

Sara remembered all the confusion and desperation aboard the *Frozen Cocktail* as the pirates took it and figured the mercenary was right. She wished she could've killed any one of them. Blake might still be alive then. The ship might still be afloat.

She went to the rail and stared out on the ocean, eager to glimpse the monster that followed. The water was so calm it chilled her, knowing what could be just beneath the surface of serenity, keeping its distance until the time was right.

This ship took ocean waves with more smoothness than the *Frozen Cocktail*. The *Star Time's* hull displaced water by brushing it aside as opposed to tipping upward and riding atop it as Holloway's vessel had done.

Sara was the last to reach the helm and Jean-Philippe was already in mid-speech.

"This boat was never intended to be out here this long," he was saying.

"Pirates were most likely going to do an open water auction," Guillaume said. "This thing's valuable enough to fund them for years."

"So you're saying we're out of fuel?" Carly said.

"Almost," Jean-Philippe admitted. "This thing holds five thousand liters and we're losing it fast."

"Is there a place to refuel?" Guillaume asked.

Jean-Philippe grinned. He had retrieved a GPS device from one of their drop packs. "Everything is working out," he said.

That seemed good enough for Guillaume. "Carly will stay on the helm with you while Sara and I discuss that other thing. Does that work for everyone?"

Carly seemed hesitant to leave Sara, but the women exchanged trusting nods.

"I have more questions about your films," Jean-Philippe said.

"Shoot," Carly said, trying to hide her delight behind modesty as she dropped into the helm chair.

"Tell her instead how you converse online entirely in reaction gifs from her movies and refer to her exclusively as 'the queen,'" Guillaume laughed. "Because I think she will actually love that."

As Sara followed him from the helm, she heard Jean-Philippe concede, "I apologize for nothing."

"They seem to get along well," Sara said once they were removed from earshot.

"I have never seen him so star struck," Guillaume said. "He blames me for what happened to our pilot. Hasn't said much since, because it was my decision to take this ship in the storm."

Sara was glad they were here, even if the relief wouldn't last. Had no comfort to offer him, though.

"No matter," Guillaume said. "I am glad she is here for him."

They went down to his cabin. The only sign of occupancy was a bulky Toughbook laptop sitting on the writing desk.

"I know that I have not yet earned your trust," he said. "I do not blame you. But I am serious about this partnership and would like the opportunity to discuss it further."

He opened the laptop and connected to the hotspot "football" the mercenaries had attached to the top of the ship's helm.

The screen blinked and beamed them into a high-class bedroom of hard right angles and minimal design. Bodies rested atop a king-size bed in a slumped tangle.

Guillaume cleared his throat, which prompted the mound beneath the bed sheets to stir. A slim figure lifted from the center, a petite female frame. Groans and exhausted shuffles as two larger bodies rolled to their respective sides, forming a valley down the center of the bed as the woman emerged in full beneath the sheets and descended, her feet touching the floor as she stretched for the sky.

She stood and crossed the room in the nude, too important a person to give a damn about modesty. She adjusted the laptop screen and smiled at the prying eyes.

"It's early," she said in a raspy pack-a-day British accent.

"Apologies, Baroness."

"Oh, please." She was older, but had staved off the aging process in a way Sara found impressive. Her body was baked golden and there wasn't a trace of fat to be found. If there was a fountain of youth, then only the wealthiest players in the world knew where it was.

The Baroness mumbled some kind of smarthome command as the window blinds in the background began rising, filling the bedroom with early morning sun. The floor-to-ceiling windows glowed hot enough for Sara to feel it. Outside was a gracious view of the London skyline.

Behind the Baroness, two naked men stirred and groaned and shambled their way out of bed. Washboard abs, strong muscles. Boy toys who slumped out of frame like trained pets.

"Is this our partner?" Baroness asked.

"It is more complicated than that, sadly," Guillaume told her. "But this is her. Sara—"

Sara cleared her throat. "Just Sara."

The Baroness smirked and stared at her for a long moment. Sara read every inch of her confident smile. It said,

"I'll know everything about who you are by the time I end this call." And Sara didn't doubt that.

"Okay," the Baroness said. "Just Sara, I would like you to know that I pride myself on reputation. For all matters similar, I am fair and honest. The treasure we search for, that of Alejandro Roche, will be mine. That is non-negotiable."

Guillaume's hand moved like lightning, raising his weapon. Cold steel bit Sara's temple.

"Say that you understand and we will move at once beyond this unpleasantness."

"That shit you're after cost me everything," Sara said. "I don't want it."

The Baroness continued to scrutinize Sara with a slow, almost imperceptible nod. "Here's what I'm prepared to do as a gesture of gratitude, Just Sara. I am prepared to fund your field research to the tune of one hundred thousand dollars a year over the next decade. On top of which you earn a living wage through one of my companies. Forty years with pension. Retirement. And you never have to show up."

"My parachute out of this rat race?"

The Baroness smirked. She was impossibly gorgeous, and better suited for a James Bond movie. Sara couldn't believe people like this existed. "Exactly," the Baroness said. "I take care of those who are loyal to me."

Guillaume took the pistol away and exhaled silent relief. He stood there looking mildly apologetic.

Sara shrugged. "Just tell me where to sign."

The Baroness flushed her smile away the moment business was concluded. "I will meet you once this is over," she said. And that was it. The screen flicked and was dark.

"Pretty shit way to earn my trust," Sara said.

"Sorry about the gun." For the first time, Guillaume couldn't look at her. "When the boss speaks—"

"Yeah."

"Why do you look like sour milk then?"

"Because I don't trust her any more than I do you."

"Her offer is a peasant's wage where she is concerned. It is much, much easier for her to grease your wheels that way than do anything disreputable."

"If you say so."

Guillaume stuck his hand out. "You're on our team now. Welcome."

After some reluctance, they shook.

He took Sara above deck, to where one of the rooms beneath the helm had been retrofitted into a makeshift supply depot. All the cases the helicopter had dropped off, apparently.

"The first time I briefed the Baroness on the situation," Guillaume said, "she wanted me to bring you into the fold." He pointed to a spread of equipment in the far corner. "So that's roughly your size. Figure out what you like and suit up. I'll go make sure Jean-Philippe isn't making Carly sign his poster collection."

"So you two really are..."

"Married?" Guillaume said. "No, but... we are involved. That much is true."

He left for the flying bridge and Sara changed into a thick pair of sandy shorts. They were a little on the short side, but the humidity out here was as monstrous as the creature in that ocean. She stripped her top off and slid a white belly tee over her body and then covered that with a sleeveless olive top. She looped the holster through her belt strips and gave that SIG Sauer P226 a comfortable home.

Boots were halfway to her knees and the half gloves would prevent the weapon from slipping from her hands if the world got really wet again. She was ready for whatever Isabella and her psychotic boyfriend might throw at them from beyond the grave.

There was news when she got back to the bridge. Carly stood there like a little kid at her birthday party, eyes beaming.

"What is it?" Sara said.

They had intercepted a communication from some place called Agaléga. It was a request for the immediate presence of a magistrate. They were also asking the coast guard to investigate a man there who claimed to be the captain of a sunken vessel called the *Frozen Cocktail.*

"Holloway's alive," Carly said as if Sara hadn't been able to piece that much together on her own.

The others seemed less enthused by this development. On their end, this complicated things.

"We need to beat that magistrate to land," Guillaume said.

"We will have to refuel there," Jean-Philippe said. "It does not look like they have a port, so that's easier said than done."

"And there's more," Guillaume said, looking right at Sara.

"That's right," Jean-Philippe added. "Follow the path of the plate to the glaring twins. The clue is exactly what I suspected. Has to be."

"Which is?" Sara asked.

"The island itself," Jean-Philippe told her. "It's really two islands joined together by sand and coral."

"The glaring twins," Carly said and hugged Sara, warmth she hadn't felt in days. Sara allowed herself to relax inside the actress' soft grip for just a second.

"Holy shit," Sara said, wiping a single tear on Carly's shoulder.

"If you look at those islands on a map," Jean-Philippe added, "they are almost on top of one another."

Sara pushed away from Carly as she looked at the digital GPS map. The actress kept a supportive hand on the small of Sara's back, might've even been massaging her with small, calming rubs, but Sara couldn't focus on that. The puzzle was clicking into place and filling her with adrenaline. "Right," she said. "So it cannot be north or south. The 'twins' cannot glare together in either of those directions."

"East or west then?" Guillaume said.

All eyes were on Sara.

"We need Holloway," she said. "He might have the jewel."

"What is the jewel for?" Carly asked.

"I don't know," Sara said. "But I think we need it. For the game."

"Then we will not leave Agaléga without it," Guillaume said.

Jean-Philippe tapped the GPS and confirmed to the group they'd been heading toward Agaléga since yesterday.

And they were closer than they realized.

THIRTY-SEVEN

The northern Agaléga island prison was two holding cells on the building's far end.

A wire fan tucked into the furthest corner oscillated and was only a meek disruption to the punishing humidity.

Every few minutes, Kaahin looked to the American for a plan and saw only his downturned eyes.

For Kaahin, this was bad. All the American needed to do was keep his mouth shut. The truth would come out.

The Agaléga police claimed their little island was receptive to visitors. Especially those who arrived carrying this kind of trauma. Thing was, though, word traveled. Word reached these small islands, for even out here at the end of everything, pirates were news. Mauritius had sent word that the waters around Madagascar had seen a sharp increase in pirate activity.

The police claimed to believe their story, their truth through omission, but they also had orders. Orders that required both men to be tossed into prison cells until the magistrate could arrive and sort through the details.

Kaahin had no intention of waiting. "We are close to the treasure," he whispered. Then, taking his voice down even lower, added, "If we separate, we may not succeed."

They were in separate cells, but the men sat close. Their backs each faced the stonewall that formed the building's rear, and that area was divided by iron bars that split the space into cells.

Kaahin kept the conversation confined to whispers. The officers came and went so often it was like they were searching for excuses to avoid actual police work.

"I said we have a serious decision to make, American."

The American didn't look. "We don't."

"The only people closer to the treasure are your acquaintances. If those women find it—"

The American looked up. That thought apparently too much to bear.

"Pretend you are ill," Kaahin told him.

"You want to get out of here, or do you want to get us cuffed to these bars?"

His way of saying he had a better idea. They waited for the officers to return. When they did, it was not the men who had taken them into custody last night, but two nondescript uniforms who stared from across the way. They weren't used to guests.

"Hey, pal," the American said. He crossed the cell and closed his fists around the bars. "I'm going to need you to let me use the radio."

The officers exchanged mutual shrugs.

It wasn't enough to prevent the slick-mouthed American from continuing. "My ship went down. You know that much, right? Well, I lost some good men. One of those boys had a wife... a kid on the way any day now. I need to get word to her. Can't wait for the magistrate."

The police traded a few whispers before realizing the airy hum of the wire fan was all that prevented their words from being overheard. They stepped outside.

The American smiled and watched them disappear. "They're going to let me do it."

One officer returned before there was a chance to take the conversation further. He unlocked the American's cell and ushered him out. "I take you to port." The officer stopped and glanced back at Kaahin. "They are cooking your lunch now. Meals are prepared at the administration building. My partner goes to get yours."

His meal was delivered fifteen minutes later. The officer balanced a tray containing a plantain sandwich and piping hot coffee.

Kaahin waited for him to begin fumbling with the key ring and sprung. He struck with the reflex of a tightly wound cobra, catching the iron door the second it unlocked, and shoving it back into the officer's face with a thick and brass-filled clang.

Steaming coffee scalded the officer and his skin began sizzling. Screams filled the room and escaped through the opened windows like liberated prisoners.

Kaahin was not finished. He seized a fistful of the uniform and tugged it. The officer tumbled into captivity, his scorched and blistering face smashing the ground.

Kaahin slammed the door as soon as he was beyond it, leaving the officer begging for mercy. Kaahin snatched the handgun off the desk and considered ending the man's suffering. Only the entire island would hear the gunshot and then they'd never escape.

So he headed outside, down the winding path. No matter how far away from the police station he got, he heard the officer's desperate cries hanging in the sky.

***

He got off the road and moved toward the western shoreline.

First thing he did was retrace his steps from last night. He reached the spot where he'd stashed the gem. It sat against the base of the palm tree, obscured only by a few discarded fronds and broken branches.

Once it was tight in his fist, he raced toward the water.

Last night's officers were presumably off duty and so there was only one man they needed to worry about. Maybe the American would take care of him.

He suspected the American would be his obedient whore right to the end as long as treasure was involved. They'd never be able to resolve their differences. Too much spilt blood for men of their type to simply forget.

Through the fronds he spotted a fishing party standing in the shallows off the beach. Three women in cotton sundresses waded out alongside two shirtless men. They spread outward into a circle and cast a wide net across the space. They closed in, drifting toward one another, making the net smaller and smaller, hoping to catch a day's bounty.

Kaahin stuffed the gun into his waist where it was obscured by his shirt. He waded out to join them, arms outstretched and wearing his best smile.

"My friends," he said in their tongue. "Help me with my bearings, please. The last time I was on your island, I visited by ship. We had to dock at a port five hundred meters from your jetty."

One of the women pointed up beach. "Follow and you will find," she said.

"There is not much use for ship travel these days," one of the men added.

"What does that mean?" Kaahin asked.

The fishermen fell quiet. Nervous chatter skittered around the circle, but nobody wanted to confide in the stranger.

"Please," Kaahin said.

"Tell him," demanded the woman.

The other man strode inland. "Most of the supplies are delivered by plane these days. That is all."

Kaahin smiled warmly. He looked at the woman, who seemed disappointed by the group's consensus to remain silent. She stared helplessly for a second and then returned to her task of bundling the net.

"Plane would be good for you, too, friend," the man said and tapped Kaahin on the shoulder. He hurried back to the task, dragging the overflowing net from the ocean. There was enough catch in there to feed half the island.

Kaahin laughed. The catch he sought wouldn't be captured by plane. He started down shore, toward Point St. James, turning back once to catch the group staring.

They were bunched together while behind them, the entire ocean seemed to be creeping up on them.

He knew what they feared because he feared it too.

THIRTY-EIGHT

Land was a half-mile out. The ship was anchored and rocking on calm water. Carly took Sara by the elbow, nails drawing shallow blood as she pushed her against the wall and whispered into her ear.

"Are we sure we don't want to get out of this?"

"Carly," Sara said, so startled by the actress' urgency that she returned the whisper. "We can't." She didn't have a good excuse as to why. Not one that she'd admit. She hadn't told Carly about the Baroness' offer.

"Why?" the actress snarled. "It's right there, goddammit. We could swim and—"

"We don't know what's over there," Sara said. She pushed the blonde off and gave a threatening look as she wiped trickles of blood from her forearms.

Carly acknowledged her mistake with a measly nod.

From this distance, the island looked to be all trees. Whatever civilization supposedly lived there looked like Guillaume's Sentinelese—a world trying to hide from progress.

"You go there," Sara said, "and there's no telling what happens. I know these guys are shady but—"

"I'm famous," Carly said. "They'll help." The first truly stupid thing she'd said in Sara's presence.

"They look like they've seen too many movies?"

That shut Carly up. "I hear you," she said. "It's just, seeing land right there... hard not to think about making a break for it." She walked off toward the bow, chewing her fingernails.

"What the hell are we whispering for anyway?" Sara asked, and both women laughed at their stupidity.

Guillaume and Jean-Philippe had taken the Zodiac boat inland. There was no refueling mechanism here, meaning they were going to have to bring the gasoline back in cans. Their plan was to enlist the help of however many boats were willing.

They'd been gone a little over an hour now, and Sara was beginning to swear them off until she spotted a growing speck zipping toward them. One Zodiac boat flanked by a fleet of dinghies.

They reached the *Star Time* and loaded jerry cans at the stern, passing them boat-to-boat until the entire set was offloaded. Jean-Philippe and Guillaume climbed aboard, and Jean-Philippe negotiated to bring a few hired hands on deck to help get the cargo below and begin the refuel process.

Carly made her way over and grabbed two sloshing cans. She followed the men below, a sudden selflessness that Sara found uncharacteristic.

By the time the last of the cargo had been lugged below, the islanders were set to return. The men looked absolutely eager, scrutinizing the water and discussing things in their nervous native tongue. With the empty jerry cans spread throughout five dinghies, the skeleton crew of the *Star Time* watched the islanders disembark.

Carly stood at the top of the ladder with knees bent. She took one last glance at Sara, desperate blue eyes brighter than the sky with hope her new friend might reconsider.

Sara went for Carly and took her by the arm, pulling her away from the ladder.

"What are you—" the actress began to say.

It was Sara's turn to shove her against the wall, and Carly seemed about as furious as Sara had been.

"Not going to let you make this mistake," Sara said.

"Take me!" Carly screamed at the islanders whose motorized dinghies began pulling away from the *Star Time*.

Guillaume headed for the commotion but Sara's glare warned him off.

"Carly, I know you're desperate to get home but this is the smart play. If you leave us now—"

"I don't need your protection," Carly said, watching the boats shrink into the distance with defeated eyes. "You're fucking with my life now."

"I'm protecting you," Sara said. "Please, we've both been through the ringer. I can't... I won't lose anyone else. You're the only person I trust."

"Then admit to me that it's your selfishness that's keeping me here."

"It's not." Sara couldn't muster an argument. She began to wonder if that was the truth.

"We're two days out," Guillaume told them. "Hold it together."

Sara was too shaken by Carly's accusation. The actress was right. There was something about being the only woman aboard she didn't wish to experience. When she was on the water for work, she remembered the way men looked at her. Quick and perverted glances. Wandering minds. Nothing ever come close to happening, but she couldn't stand to feel that sort of vulnerability on top of everything else.

Guillaume and Jean-Philippe didn't have eyes for the opposite sex, though she remembered the way they'd eyed her at the resort pool and decided that distrust had served her well so far.

Except, she trusted Carly.

There was excitement on the ocean. Booming voices that drowned out the half dozen motorized boats. Sara and Carly looked at each other and took a few synchronized steps to the rail.

The men in the boats screamed. Some waved their hands overhead. It was unclear if they were trying to signal the *Star Time* or those on the island. It was the same word over and over. A foreign tongue Sara couldn't understand.

Guillaume appeared beside them.

"What are they saying?" Carly asked.

"Hurry," he said.

"They're never going to make it."

Carly had Sara's arm again, squeezing it. The actress' body pressed against hers, desperate for what little comfort contact might afford. "Oh my God." Her breath was lower than a whisper.

Two hundred feet separated the *Star Time* and the boats, but the expressions on those dinghies were clearer than crystal.

The *Star Time* rocked hard. Beneath them, the hull gave a nails-on-the-chalkboard screech. Sara and Carly wobbled and fell against Guillaume, whose hands flexed and became fists that wrenched the rail, holding all three of them in place.

The blurry shadow glided out from beneath the hull. The sparkling aquamarine water made the fish shimmer. It sliced toward the small boats as if guided by magnets.

Sara couldn't help it. She screamed. It might've been "watch out" or "hang on" or something just as futile.

Carly buried her eyes in the round of Sara's shoulder, hands squeezing Sara even tighter than before, only this time Sara said nothing.

The men were helpless. The fish broke the surface and continued to glide right for them. Its stone-shaped head barreling down on the sputtering boats like a missile.

Its head rose further so those aboard the *Star Time* heard the grinding of its self-sharpening teeth. Even at this distance, that sickening sound of scraping bone put goose bumps on Sara's arms.

The fish chomped away the first stern with a potato chip crunch. Its bites came fast, breaking through rubber like a blown tire.

A few graceless bodies tumbled right into that mouth, and Sara saw blood explode into the air like paint splotches. Screams were loud and severe as diligent teeth shredded the bodies into silence.

Those in surrounding boats began leaping overboard as if they could out-paddle the fish. The creature went next for a wooden boat, chomping its hull into mulch. The people onboard wobbled and fell, repeating the ghastly process over again.

One of the men fumbled against the fish, his upper torso bending right over the creature's eager head. For a second it looked as if he might scale the thing and escape down the length of its body. He looked up at the deck of the *Star Time* and his eyes locked with Sara's.

He never screamed. Wide eyes began to fade as the body slumped to one side of the fish's head and then slipped into the water beside it. There were no legs beneath the torso, and what little remained of him quickly slipped beneath a stain of red water.

The fish took each of the boats down without effort, zipping back and forth through the commotion, snapping up the survivors like an old arcade game.

For a while, Sara watched. She felt obligated to witness it. She stared at the carnage until she grew numb to it. And after a while she turned her head and nestled it against Carly's. The actress still burrowed into Sara's arm as if eagerly trying to escape this grim reality.

"We need to go," Guillaume said. "Away from here."

From the helm, Jean-Philippe was already beginning to pull away.

"What about Holloway?" Sara said.

"He wasn't in the jail," Guillaume said. "Pirate must've killed him."

"What do we do now?" she said.

"We find that island."

Sara started to follow but Carly held Sara by the shoulder. She turned back around and the actress let her go. Cleared her throat and passed Sara an unspoken "thank you."

"Don't thank me," Sara said. "I think you might've been right about me."

And then she hurried off to rejoin Guillaume.

PART THREE

ANGATRA

THIRTY-NINE

Kaahin found the second policeman unconscious on the floor of the procurement office. Blood darker than motor oil pooled around his head.

"Had to crack him a few times," the American said, hunched over the receiver. "Could've just taken a dive, but that Frenchman had some real *gilets jaunes* fight in him."

The waterfront was visible through the windows. A few small boats had delivered gasoline to the *Star Time*, which sat just a few kilometers at sea. Reunion was close, but entirely out of reach.

"Maybe they will spend a day or two in port," Kaahin said. A display of optimism even he did not believe.

"As soon as word gets out the island's got unwelcome visitors, they'll skip the magistrate and throw us in the ocean."

The scalded officer in the station had probably fallen unconscious by now, but someone must've heard his screams.

"Still got the jewel, pal?" the American asked.

Kaahin opened the palm of his hand.

"That's our leverage," the American told him. He lifted his chin and gestured toward the ship. "They need that and they know it. Gonna have to find us."

The commotion out there was suddenly familiar, panic rising in the throats of every islander nearby. The two men swapped looks, realizing what that meant.

Frenzied screams. Frantic splashing. Kaahin succumbed to curiosity while the American refused to look.

Less than a mile out to sea, right before the ocean floor crept up and became shallows, Kaahin's worst fears were confirmed. Death's Head was there, chomping boats into oblivion like what it really wanted was to eat its way ashore.

Islanders swam for safety but the creature swept through the water and made pieces of them all.

"The airstrip," the American said. "Use that fucking thing to our advantage while we can."

They went. Bounding down wobbly stairs away from the water, sprinting like the thieves they were.

"The hell is that thing?" the American said once they were out of sight.

This was not a conversation that Kaahin wished to have with a westerner. But something else bothered him more.

Here was the first time the American sounded terrified for his safety.

***

The airfield was a brisk jog away.

They passed several locals hurrying toward the shore as word of casualties spread.

"It ails them just as it does Madagascar," Kaahin said. "Only its presence is much harder to ignore on an island of three hundred."

The American didn't respond. He stared at the single plane sitting outside the runway hangar, fear draining from his eyes, swapped out for a hopeful shimmer.

"Can you fly that?" Kaahin asked.

"Does a yeast infection smell?"

"I am thankful I cannot say."

"That's a Dornier Do 228. Twin-turboprop STOL. Once you learn, it's like riding a bike. Can I fly it? The hell do you think?"

The American gave him a forceful shove and trotted off. The terminal building was the size of a small roadside garage and couldn't house a large pick-up truck, let alone a plane.

Every light inside was off. The plane departed in the afternoon and certainly not every day if the handwritten schedule was any indication. The comms room was to the back and the plane key dangled off a single nail on the wall there.

"Let's flap her wings, hoss." The American took off for the runway.

A few curious people had taken up position on the side of the airfield, staring gape-mouthed at the unusual break in ritual.

The twin engines were spinning up before Kaahin hopped aboard through opened cargo doors. He closed them as the American buckled into his seat.

"Might want to come up here," he said. "Plane ain't pressurized or air conditioned. Cold's gonna bite your ass deeper than a polar bear no matter what, but it'll be much worse back there."

Kaahin buckled in, sitting shoulder-to-shoulder with the American who started to accelerate down the small runway.

"Hope they refueled or this will be a short trip," Kaahin said.

"We're right as rain," the American told him, easing up on the yoke.

The small plane achieved lift and zoomed off over palm trees where it glided as a distorted shadow over treetops. That same shadow chased them over emerald seas, shrinking as the American took them higher.

"That's what I'm talking about!" the American screamed, punching the ceiling like he was trying to tear through it. "We live to fight another day. Again. Goddamn it, I thought we were dead to rites down there."

Kaahin tried to suppress his grin. Failed. In another life, under different circumstances, he could've liked this man.

"What've you got for me, hoss? This ain't exactly my neighborhood."

"There is one airstrip on Madagascar that might take us," he said. Without greasing the appropriate gears, however, there was no guarantee the government wouldn't have real problems with a rogue plane touching down out of thin air.

"I'd like to know for sure," the American said.

"We've got time," Kaahin told him. "A three-hour flight, I believe." He dropped a headset over his ears. "Let me try and raise my people."

"Do what you gotta," the American said. "Unless you think we can land there?" He pointed to the luxury yacht pulling away from the island, already in open water.

"So close," Kaahin growled.

"And we can't even follow them. We'll be empty before they get to where they're going."

"Let the fish chase them for a while." Seeing it out there, even from the safety of land, its calm automation while dooming a dozen men to death, had chilled him like nothing else. Kaahin carried many superstitions, but there was nothing worse than that fish's destructive indifference.

The Malagasy believed their ancestors transformed into protective spirits once they passed, forces of guiding light. But that belief went the other way, too. Malevolent men could go to their graves and transform into something else. Become vengeance personified. That's what scared him.

This fish was more than a fish. It had to be.

Kaahin caught his reflection in the side window and was too disgusted to keep looking. The monster there glared back. He saw a lifetime career of misdeeds that had aided in the creation of that demon.

"What is it?" the American said.

Kaahin took a deep breath as his body trembled. The truth was, he was beginning to feel grateful for the American's presence. The last thing he wanted was to face that demon alone.

"Come on," the American said. "Level with me. What is that fish?"

"Angatra," Kaahin said.

"Never heard of it."

"You can live somewhere all your life without ever belonging."

"Story of my life."

"In Malagasy culture, the angatra are the fallen ones. It is said they are forever on the prowl against those who have offended them."

"That's why you're so shook," the American said. "You think it's all about you."

"I have much to atone for. I can only believe my ancestors have decided to punish me."

"You think your grandfather was a fish? C'mon, pal."

"That response could not be more American."

"Damn straight."

"What does it matter to you?" Kaahin said. "It is something uncommon. How many times have you seen a fish like that?"

"Don't watch the Discovery Channel, so I don't know."

"There is karma in your culture, yes?" Kaahin said.

"Of course."

"Close enough, then."

"That thing's killing us 'cause we deserve it? Nature is indifferent, pal. Doesn't care whether we go to church on Sundays or screw our step moms."

This was not nature, though Kaahin dropped it. "Once we reach the treasure island," he said, "it will be a race. And people will die."

"Appreciate your confidence, but a lot of things need to go right before we get there."

"I do not intend to fail."

"Let's say we find it. What happens next? They've got a boat. And equipment from the looks of things."

"That is my boat," said Kaahin. "I took it once. I will take it again."

"I'm not going to hurt the girl."

Kaahin nearly laughed at the misguided chivalry. "I would not have you do that," Kaahin said, thinking, because I will kill the western girl myself. He said, "I believe it is the men we must remove."

"More for us, right?" The American threw a side-eye. It might've been threatening if Kaahin hadn't watched the angatra devour several men today.

"They need us," Kaahin said. "But they will be suspicious." It felt like a month had passed since throwing the women overboard.

"I think I got a way around that," the American said.

FORTY

Carly and Sara retreated back to Carly's bunk.

The decision was made to head east of Agaléga, because the ocean was a lot smaller if you sailed west. All shipping lanes and tourists venturing far, but not too far, away from Madagascar. Roche wouldn't have hidden that close to anything.

Agaléga was the gateway to a deep blue nothing, and Isabella's island must've been beyond it.

Carly threw her arms around Sara once they reached the room.

"I told you, Carly, it's fine."

"It's not," the actress said. "I was three seconds away from making a fatal mistake."

They sat on the end of the bed facing each other. Carly's eyes were glassy, little tear streaks beginning to fall. It was the face of someone who hadn't really believed in her own mortality before now. She'd been traumatized out here, by disappearing boyfriends, attacking pirates, and of course that awful monster, but today was the first time her instinct might've brought death.

That had to shake you.

"I was so stupid," she said.

"You weren't," Sara assured her. "Civilization was dangling in front of you like a Christmas ornament. Of course you were thinking about it."

"I can never thank you enough."

Sara's motivations were worse, keeping Carly around for her own self-centered needs. "We get out of this and you might have to sign an autograph for my brother," she said.

"We get out of this, I'll suck your brother's dick."

"Jesus, Carly," Sara laughed. "Don't you dare think about wrecking his shit. He's married with three kids." Despite her mother's insistence that James be the sole heir to the Mosby name, Sara was happy for her brother and his political aspirations. But the reality was that she'd been looking forward to becoming Sara Jovish. All anyone thought about when they heard the name Mosby was James, the good-looking future politician whose star burned bright. Every time Sara introduced herself the first question was, "oh are you related to James? I'm going to vote for him. I think he might be president someday."

It was frightening how quickly your identity could be snuffed out.

"I'm joking," Carly said. She lay back on the bed and stretched. Her bones cracked softly and the relief she sighed was a sound Sara had never before heard. A hand reached for Sara's shirt, took a fistful of fabric, and tugged her down beside her.

There was calm in each other's eyes. Steady acceptance. Mutual strength. It didn't matter who'd been motivated by what, they knew, only that they were still alive.

And together.

Sara thought of Blake and, oh God, it felt like he'd been gone for years. The wedding. Nervous vows. Dancing in the open-air like shooting stars. A best man speech about unwritten futures. All of it less than one week ago.

It's true that Carly's presence comforted her. But to think about Blake made her tremble. Sara's body was suddenly hot, and once the tears came, she was happy to let them fall.

Carly reached out and touched Sara's cheek. Just the soft press of fingertips. It was enough.

They stayed like that, eye-to-eye, until the day was gone and the ocean shined beneath bone white moon glow.

"Air's a little stale," Carly said at last. "Take a walk?"

They did. Seeing the ocean was enough to drum up panic. Carly gave Sara the last prescription pill in her bottle and promised it would take the edge off. It didn't, or maybe it did, and Sara was beginning to panic about so much that it just wasn't any help.

They found Jean-Philippe on the stern, admiring the vastness around them. He smiled when he saw Carly standing there. "I am truly thankful that you were not on those boats," he said.

Carly gave him a gentle nudge. "How are you doing?"

"Trying my best to forget about Daan," he said. "Focus on the rest of the job."

"Without you we might not be anywhere near completing the rest of this job," Sara said.

Jean-Philippe flashed a polite smile. "Almost wish I'd said nothing."

"Really? You don't want to be the one who—"

"Baroness will be the one," he said. "If history remembers us at all, it'll be as her foot soldiers. On to the next job, and so on until we end up like Daan."

"You don't have to keep going," Carly said. "You can quit."

"I can," Jean-Philippe said.

"Any more sightings of that fish?" Sara asked.

Jean-Philippe shook his head.

"How does it keep showing up wherever we go?" Carly asked.

"I would just like to know what it is," Jean-Philippe said.

"I might know," Sara told them.

The mercenary's face tightened. "Please," he said. "I am interested in your professional opinion."

"It's going to sound crazy," Sara said.

"Let us judge."

"Come on, Sara," Carly said. "It's a long way to the island."

"Yeah," Sara agreed. "Okay. First time I saw it, I was too terrified to think straight. You see something that unnatural up close and your brain rejects the sight. You gotta reboot, but can only do that once you've got some distance. Weirdest feeling ever."

"It is always that way when you see something out of the ordinary," Jean-Philippe said.

"I wouldn't know, thankfully."

"You will be old pros by the time this is over," he said. "Both of you."

"Maybe I'll change careers," Sara said. "Take your gig once you quit." She winked and was reminded of the holster strapped to her shorts, of the weapon stuffed inside it.

Jean-Philippe laughed. "Last time we excavated on Madagascar, we set sail for one of the uncharted islands on the western side. Hired help swore that a demon lived there. They refused to row with us to the beach. Guillaume was able to buy some of their loyalty. We disembarked on rowboats, five men came with us. None returned."

"So it always goes well for you guys?" Carly said.

Jean-Philippe didn't think that was funny. His face was suddenly sunken. "The job is the job. We were there looking for the remains of an Arab trader buried with his fortune. Madagascar was a serious trading post back then, you had the whole world in those ports, so there was good reason to believe his treasure was substantial. We rowed ashore and found we were not alone..."

"Your demon?" Sara said.

"Something hunted us," Jean-Philippe said. "Demon to some, certainly. A feral man, snarling, growling, completely crazed. His eyes were red, like somebody had poured vials of blood into them. His fingernails were sharper than knives. Tore the throats right out of our men."

"Shit," Carly said.

"I believed the superstition at first." Jean-Philippe looked ashamed to admit it. "We are programmed to believe the unexplainable. It is hardcoded into us because it is in our nature."

"But sometimes a fish is just a fish, right?" Sara said.

"Correct," he said. "The men swore this vengeful spirit was resurrected to prevent anyone from disturbing his grave. In reality, he was a poor leper who left his family behind in order to die in isolation. I shot him through the eye and put him out of his misery. For a while, though, I really thought—"

"Well, the thing that's after us is most definitely a fish," Sara said. "I'm drawing on some pretty old college lectures at this point, but I'm also pretty damn sure."

"I want that university expertise," Jean-Philippe said.

"No such thing," Sara told him. "Everything I learned came after I walked."

"You learned this."

"Yeah, by accident. Which is the only way you learn shit inside those walls. Anyway, it's a fish from... well, a long time ago."

Jean-Philippe's poker face was not field-tested like Guillaume's. He couldn't suppress the grin creeping north from the corners of his mouth.

"You already know that," Sara tsked her tongue.

"I know that whatever hunts us is something the world has not seen for a long time. If ever."

"You'd be right," Sara said.

"If you're right."

"Yeah, okay, if I'm right. But I'm telling you... my gut's talkin' loud. I took a course on prehistoric fish. A stupid elective to satisfy my major. And if I'm remembering correctly, this fish is a straight up descendant from the Devonian Period."

Carly and Jean-Philippe didn't seem to know what to make of that information.

"That's old," Sara said. "420 million years ago, to be exact. So I know how this sounds."

"That's an old ass fish," Carly added.

"Most people can't grasp how old," Sara said. "You tell people that the Jurassic Period was 65 million years ago and their eyes glaze over. Devonian? The vases and shit you run around finding for your Baroness are from last weekend, comparatively."

"I know the Devonian Period," Jean-Philippe said. "When all the landmasses were one and the same. Before dinosaurs roamed the earth. An age of fish."

"Right," Sara said. "Pretty sure that thing's called a dunkleosteus." She laughed as soon as she said it. "It's stupid, but you can thank Dunkin' Donuts for my sterling memory. America Runs on Dunks, and that shit's tenfold if you're from New England. I didn't walk into that class one single time without an iced coffee in my hand..."

"A mnemonic device," Carly said and nudged Sara's arm excitedly. "I use them all the time to remember lines."

"Yeah," Sara said. "I had that cup on my desk. Dunks. And when we got to the page about the dunkleosteus..."

"What are the chances?" Jean-Philippe said.

"So much of the ocean remains unexplored," Sara said. "I would argue with my professors about the certainty of extinction."

"I might agree with you, Sara. For what it's worth." Jean-Philippe had no intention of sharing anything further. He wished them goodnight and started back toward the helm.

Sara and Carly edged closer to the rail and watched the ocean fizz as the *Star Time* passed through it. Sara pictured the old fish tailing them, following the bubbly water, knowing exactly where they were.

Part of Sara couldn't get past the idea of catching that fish. There was, of course, no way to easily do that, but hadn't Jean-Philippe been thinking the same thing?

She smiled like the Grinch as she considered it, imagining being invited back to her alma mater to speak about it. She bit the inside of her cheek. All those times her damn professor laughed at her "naiveté."

Watching the water, Sara realized that everything was easily explained. Whether it was crazed lepers or ancient fish, everything had a scientific explanation. That should've pleased her. Instead it made the world feel smaller.

"You might've been right, Blake."

It was the first time she'd spoken his name aloud since his passing. She repeated it with a broken inflection. "Blake." The horror that struck her was severe. The word no longer had any familiarity.

"What'd you say?" Carly asked.

"Just thinking aloud."

That was enough to open the floodgates again. Sara threw her head into her hands and started to cry, mourning not only Blake, but all those who'd lost their lives along the way.

Her thoughts were a mess. Her identity, gone. She didn't know who she was. She'd been eager to get out into the world and find herself. Sara Mosby was long gone and Sara Jovish had never really existed.

She thought about this while watching cracks of lightning shatter the horizon sky. The wind picked up quickly.

"Jesus," Carly said. "Let's go back down and get beneath the covers."

"Yeah," Sara said, once again happy that she didn't have to spend the night alone. "Let's go."

The ship sailed on as the rain started to fall.

FORTY-ONE

The American had done his part to bring them in.

He landed the plane on the makeshift airstrip tucked into the base of the Maromotokro Mountain.

The men swapped a sliver of repressed appreciation. They sat in the cockpit listening to the double engines cracking and cooling as the propellers wound down.

"How long until they come for us?" the American asked.

The airfield was actually the remnants of a depleted rice field that had been ruined by activists from Antananarivo. An anti-GMO lot who got their intel wrong, hiking up here to raze the earth when the target they really sought was a hundred kilometers west.

The island had slashed about twenty percent of its remaining forests over the last few years in order to maintain a competitive export economy. Residents seemed not to care, and certainly had zero political clout to stop it. They were instead too intoxicated by western promises of iPhones and streaming services.

Kaahin thought this field should be brought back to life because the people could stand to use it. But its current use made his life easier in certain situations, like hiding from the authorities.

The arrangement was simple. From the ocean, Imani was available at specific frequencies at certain times of day. A critical piece of their partnership. One word from Kaahin about a rogue airplane coming in hot from Mauritius territory and Imani put his people to work, dispersing runners who knew the language.

Legs that found the right officials. Palms were greased in order to ensure important eyes remained averted. And those who tracked errant flights were fed stories they couldn't refute. Emergency landings from local money. Vacationing royalty that didn't wish to pass through customs if you know what I mean...

It was a system. Imperfect but beneficial. It was enough.

The American had repositioned the plane so that they could take off again in a hurry if it became necessary.

"There is a safe house over there," Kaahin said, getting ready to point it out when the American lifted a sawed-off shotgun from out of the space on the far side of his seat.

The barrel crashed into Kaahin's ribs so hard it was guaranteed to bruise. "Sitting right here beside me the whole time. Believe that?"

"My friend—"

"Don't."

"What, then?"

"Tell me what you're really planning, pal."

"You do not have to do this," Kaahin said. "As you can see, there is nobody here."

"You keep saying that." The American studied the surrounding tree lines like Kaahin's men might've been chameleons. "They tell stories about you to this day. You're a living legend."

"Recall then that I had a small army with me when we took your ship. Those ranks are not easily replenished."

"Hard times."

They watched each other like bitter enemies. Kaahin knew this was not a person to be underestimated. He'd never lost more bodies than during the assault on the *Frozen Cocktail*.

He also suspected that the dark-skinned girl would listen to the American. Him and no one else.

It was easier this way. Their alliance necessary.

"Know what kills me," the American said. He did not wait for Kaahin to answer. "I had good people working for me. People who only wanted the opportunity to support their families. Working class."

"There is no working class here," Kaahin said. "Only the working poor."

"Sounds a lot like the way politicians have made my country."

"Hardly," Kaahin said. "People are born into this life and some will never earn so much as the plane fare out."

"You got the means, pal. Fly them out."

"Like Robin Hood?" Kaahin mocked.

"People I employ only wanted to earn a wage. You pay people to be murderers. Your economy is blood. They work for you because they think it's viable to pick up an AK-47. Your world tells them there's no other way to do it. So they don't come work for guys like me."

"This is not a land of opportunity, American. And you may pay a few men more than others, but you are not doing anything to change the way of life here."

"Maybe you need to think about it differently."

"What should I do? Spend the rest of my life taking westerners, Saudis, Japanese on ocean tours? Cruise these waters with a smile plastered on my face because the hypocrites who come here pretend to respect us? Maybe employ ten other people at most? Is that what I am supposed to do?"

"Better than being a murdering thief."

"Is it?"

"Your life expectancy's so short they wouldn't print it on the side of a cigarette pack, pal. People who follow you get dead before their kids are out of diapers."

"You think they would follow me if there was a better life on the other side of that mountain? I'm not exploiting anyone. I'm giving them a chance to change things."

"By terrorizing your own people," the American said. "We had weapons on our ship in the event of guys like you. And you know what? There wasn't a person in my employ who hesitated to kill you. You're a parasite. Exploiting a weakness in your homeland for profit."

"So your half of the treasure goes to charity?"

The American laughed hard and long. "I'm my own charity case. We find that island, I'm going to disappear off the grid forever."

"What a legacy."

"Not everyone's concerned with one of those."

Two men appeared out of the tree line, pulling a bull that had gasoline cans hooked all the way around it. The American pressed the shotgun barrel deeper into Kaahin's ribs as if they could see that gesture from their position.

"There is no easy way up here," Kaahin said, ignoring the pain in his side. "That is the best way to bring the fuel. They will fill us up and be on their way. I mentioned the safe house..."

The men shuffled past the plane window without acknowledging them. They fumbled with the gas latch and went to work on refueling.

"You do not care about my land," Kaahin said. "I do not blame you."

"Whatever you say," the American sighed. "Want to know what I'll do with my share? Pay the widows of the men you murdered. Make sure they never have to worry."

"Noble."

"Someone's got to, don't you think?"

"Know what I will do?"

The American's nod was sardonic.

"Once that fish dies," Kaahin said, "and we have raided Roche's vault, and I have more money than I will ever need... I will sponsor an uprising that will change my land once and for all."

"How realistic."

"You know what's realistic?" Kaahin said. "Our health and education systems are crumbling. And our leaders—"

"The ones you bribe to look the other way?"

"A necessary evil for now," Kaahin said. "For they are in charge."

"Can't win if you don't play the game?"

"Exactly. And they will never see me coming. Something needs to change. We are one of the world's poorest countries. Negative GDP, an external debt of five billion to your country, the United States... everyone's friend. More than half of my people live on less than two dollars a day. Should I begin telling you about our infant mortality rate? So, yes, something must change. I will bring it."

"Let me tell you about a guy I used to work with," the American said. "Guy called Zarif. Story ain't exactly about him, though. His wife, Kya, waitressed at a resort. Her beat was the pleasure cruises. One of those got boarded by pirates. See, you guys have changed everything up. More often than not these days, you leave the Americans and the Europeans alone. You don't want the attention of those governments. But you'll disappear your own people without a second thought, won't you, motherfucker? Yeah, that's what I thought. People who ain't got a pot to piss in get to beg their corrupt government for help with ransom. My guy, Zarif, got pictures of his girl, naked and hog tied, in his fuckin' Facebook DMs... you believe that? Fucking Zuckerberg says there's no way to stop it. 'Reconnect with old friends and allow terrorists to reach you wherever you are.' What a fuckin' world we've made."

"Your point has been made."

The American continued like he didn't hear it. "They kept Kya for one whole week. Pictures coming nonstop. Gun in her mouth. Gun to her head. Gun between her legs. Pay up or we'll make her wish she was dead. Government wasn't going to do that. You fuckers knew that. And Zarif... well, he got real desperate. This working class guy that you care so much about got himself shot to death trying to rob a resort casino. Only way he could pay your goddamn ransom."

"That was not me," Kaahin said, his throat feeble. "There are others who—"

"I give a shit who it was," the American growled. "You done people just as raw. So when you tell me this is all in service of Making Madagascar Great Again or whatever the fuck, I think you need to remember the people you destroyed to get there."

"Every war has casualties."

The American looked him over for one long, unending moment. A difficult man to read, especially now. Something bothered him. It was either Kaahin's greyed out moral compass, or the fact that he understood where that compass was coming from.

"I will recover the *Star Time* and sell it to the Saudis. Use that and my share of the treasure to directly finance a movement. No more piracy. That is the past."

"Glad to see you've got a new lease on life."

"Some things are more important."

"I don't think you're going to stop at your share."

The gun dug so hard against Kaahin's chest that his ribs were beginning to bruise. "You seem to be looking for reasons to shoot me."

"Save myself a headache later on."

The men outside finished refueling and disappeared into the trees without acknowledging completion of their task.

"Okay," Kaahin said. "Are you going to trust me enough to have dinner at the safe house?"

"No."

"Wherever the *Star Time* is headed, we can close the distance in a few hours. If we take off now, without aim, and have to come back, I may not be able to prevent suspicion."

The American didn't like it. He performed an exaggerated groan so that Kaahin knew it. But then he followed him down a thin trail to a tiny hut roofed with cornhusks.

The place was unlocked. The interior sparsely populated. A few pieces of equipment on the far table, a machete, a few handguns, and a rifle. Beside it, a rickety desk that possessed a few different radio types.

The place was useful. Well-hidden. Nearly impossible to access because of the surrounding terrain. It was outfitted with enough amenities to pass a few hours as the rain followed them off the Indian Ocean, beginning to soak the island in a furious tantrum.

Tonight there would be food and drink and an attempt to find common ground. He needed this man's loyalty for at least a few more days. This was the first westerner to ever set foot inside one of his safe houses. Every so often, Kaahin caught a death glare and thought the end was coming. That this rabid dog cowboy would try killing him on the spot because Americans loved to think justice mattered above all else.

Couldn't Kaahin drum up a few more loyalists to take back the *Star Time* in one final push? He didn't know. He'd left the island a few days ago with a handful of men who would never be seen again. This immediately following a failed CIA sting that had murdered his longtime friend. Following the Pirate King was a deadly business these days.

The only leverage Kaahin had over the American was possession of the jewel. It was the one thing that prevented him from losing everything.

Kaahin steamed some rice and boiled a pot of water to heat up some legumes. "I think probably your employees appreciated working for you," he said.

"Tryin' to romance me before dinner?"

"We are a beautiful country here. There is no ethnic nationalism, which is my way of saying there is plenty of room for you. And for what it's worth... you were well liked among your men."

The American wasn't interested in compliments. Or in this heart-to-heart. He fell quiet and turned toward the corner.

"I've got to get a hold of Sara," he said. "Find out where they're going. And where we can meet them."

"In due time." Kaahin sat with a satellite phone in his hand while he waited for the water to boil. He dialed the number and closed his eyes.

It only had to ring once.

"Yes."

"Lissa," he said and tried to keep the American from hearing his throat wobble, repeating the name into the receiver. "Lissa."

The reception wasn't good. It popped and crackled and Lissa's voice was static. "I'm here."

"How are you?"

"Certain you were dead."

"I couldn't contact you sooner—"

"You still shouldn't."

"Tell me quickly, how are the kids?"

"Trying to pretend their lives are normal."

"What does that mean?"

"They are not hiding anymore. Black vans at the end of the driveway. Following the kids everywhere they go, thinking they'll find you there. How long until they get desperate and take us? Take us to lure you out? Would you even come?"

"Of course," he said without a trace of conviction.

"Yes," Lissa gave a spiteful laugh. "Of course."

"Are they close by?" he asked. "The kids."

"They are at my sister's... I think... I think I am going there, too."

His heart dropped through his chest and cratered at the bottom of his stomach. Across the room, the American fiddled with the maritime radio, flipping through frequencies.

"I am sorry," Kaahin said. There was more to say, though he couldn't now.

"Me too," Lissa said. "I regret everything."

The phone clicked and she was gone. Kaahin felt as though he was standing outside his body, staring at himself slumped in the seat. Watching the tears begin to nest in the corners of his eyes. Lissa was right. It was his fault. He didn't get to regret it now.

"Take it your wife wasn't in a talking mood?" the American said.

"She is going to her sister's."

"Ouch. Nice to see some things don't change no matter where you are in the world."

"She doesn't have a sister," Kaahin said. It was her way of telling him to stay away. Far away. Kaahin had made her promise never to use it unless there was no way back.

He dropped the phone to the floor. A piece of it broke off and went skittering beneath a cabinet. His life was in tatters and there was nothing left to lose.

FORTY-TWO

Wherever Sara went on the boat, she felt stir crazy.

No more sleeping. Even Carly had taken to pacing the bow, doing her best to spot the clouds that could signal Roche's island.

The sky had cleared at some point during the night, and by the time early evening had rolled back around, the world was back to being baby blue.

Sara changed into sweat shorts and snuck into the onboard gym to jog the treadmill. After six miles her legs were jelly and she wobbled above deck to do some cool-downs.

No matter how hard she pushed, she felt no better. No more relaxed. Just a heap of discomfort and nothing that could be traced back to a single point of trauma.

She went to the main deck with her gun, drawing on the sea and screaming as she imagined the dunkleosteus knifing straight for them. Fifteen shots broke the surface and she pictured every one of them bouncing helplessly off the creature's plated face.

The way the gun rocked in her wrist was power. It gave some catharsis. And she reloaded with a satisfying click.

By the time she put her elbows on the railing and watched the shifting waves, she realized what had been eating her.

Isabella.

The girl was near.

This wasn't something Sara wanted to do, but it was closure. She was determined to bring it for the both of them.

Neither Guillaume nor Jean-Philippe had bothered to come out and check the gunshots. She didn't see either of them until nightfall and only then because she spotted Guillaume watching in shadows from the next platform up. He puffed a cigar that smelled like the ones her father used to smoke. The only time she could see him was when he took a drag and the embers lit the edges of his face.

There were four people aboard this ship, and it didn't even feel like that many.

Something had happened to the couple. Something had turned them into strangers. The pilot's death, yes, but it had been there even before. Sara thought back to that night in the Emerald Tides bar, the way Jean-Philippe had griped about his job, and Sara realized the discontent had always been there.

Jean-Philippe spoke to Carly more than anyone. He remained friendly with Sara, though there was iciness there. Probably because she had gravitated toward Guillaume since the beginning.

Nearly two days later and it was Carly who called "Land Ho" while leaning over the rail off the portside. She passed the telescope to Sara. "Look straight on."

The island was a tiny scratch in the distance. A sole puff of midnight-colored clouds hovered over it, lightning cracks sparking from inside. The most ominous sight Sara had ever seen.

"Do you want to turn around as much as I do?" Carly said.

"Kind of," Sara agreed. That wasn't true, but she had no desire to go out there, either.

"I just want to get back to my daughter," Carly said. "Please let me get back."

"You will," Sara told her. "Look, there's something I want to tell you before we make land—"

Jean-Philippe cleared his throat as he appeared at their backs. "You've already seen it, I see."

"Tell me you've got a plan," Sara said.

"Not one we can agree on."

"Carly and I should get ready then."

"We wait for daylight," he said.

So they told Jean-Philippe goodnight and walked down to the supply room. Sara slipped back into her tactical gear, stuffing her holster with spare magazines and attaching climbing equipment she couldn't imagine needing. Better to be overprepared than not at all.

Someone had to survive this ordeal.

She found Guillaume in his bunk, doing push-ups in the nude. He made no effort to cover his modesty when Sara and Carly appeared in the doorway. His body was oily from sweat and he stood glistening like a centerfold model. His uncircumcised business swung between his legs.

Carly was suddenly diffident. Hanging back against the far wall, eyes anywhere but on the naked man.

"What's the matter with you two?" Sara said. "Shit's been weird ever since leaving port."

"A difference of opinion."

"Anything we need to know about?"

Guillaume shrugged this off with the wave of his hand. No desire to discuss his relationship with the expendables. The silence between the three of them grew.

"Good talk," Sara said and left him standing there.

Carly followed but couldn't keep up. Sara went to the bar and perched atop one of the stools. Carly slid behind the counter and poured two glasses of Stoli.

"Jean-Philippe doesn't think we can retrieve the treasure," Carly said. "He thinks our troubles are only beginning as soon as we land."

He might be right. But Guillaume hadn't come all this way to be talked out of it. And neither had Sara.

"It's more than that," Sara whispered. "Jean-Philippe wants out, and he thinks catching that fish is his ticket to freedom."

"He hasn't said—"

"He doesn't have to say it," Sara said. "You see the way he stares out at that ocean, like he's trying to wrap his head around crazy."

"Shit," Carly said. "I think you're probably right."

"Need you on my side more than ever, Carly."

Carly put a hand on Sara's forearm and smiled. "Wouldn't have it any other way."

The women clanked their glasses and drank in silence.

***

"Sara would you come up here?" Jean-Philippe asked over the ship's intercom. It was morning and he was still at the helm.

Sara sat up and rubbed her palm against her temple. Beside her, a naked Carly rolled over onto her side and grumbled something beneath her breath.

Sara took a cold shower and dressed in yesterday's fatigues.

Jean-Philippe waved to her as she came up through the kitchenette. "Someone's on the radio asking to speak to you."

"Tell me you're there, darlin'?" Holloway's voice was all static and crackles.

She was glad to hear him. "Yes."

"Lost my boat but I'm still in this."

"Glad you're alive, really."

"Still hunting it?"

"Yeah, I have to know."

"Makes two of us. Look, I got the jewel..." And there was nothing else to say about that.

Sara wanted to ask how, because the pirate had taken it off her. A million things could've happened onboard the *Frozen Cocktail* once they tossed her over, though.

"I've got it," Holloway repeated.

"And I'm glad you're okay," she said again.

"Where are you?"

The bluntness of the question gave her pause. Jean-Philippe shook his head, do not answer. A moment later, Guillaume appeared on the kitchenette stairs, the same protest in his eyes. Sara pressed a finger to her lips.

"Heading to the island," she said.

"Where? I'll meet you." The silence that barbed his simple words felt sinister.

"Where are you, Holloway?"

"Believe it or not I was close by. On Agaléga. Saw you there, refueling."

"Then you saw—"

"The shark? Yeah."

"You still on that island?"

"Close by."

"Get another boat?"

"Let's catch up in person. Seriously, where you at, darlin'?"

That was it. Any familiarity that might've once existed between them, however briefly, was gone. They were strangers now, two people feeling each other out, concealing their truths.

Guillaume and Jean-Philippe gathered close around the radio.

"He's got the jewel," Sara mouthed.

Guillaume nodded grimly. He scribbled the coordinates and handed them over.

Sara read them out loud and felt Holloway's smile from here. "Perfect." It was more of a snarl. "See you soon, darlin'." Then he was gone.

"Your friend is dead," Guillaume said.

"That was his voice."

"He gave them what they wanted, and they killed him for it."

"No," Sara said. "He's not that stupid."

"Everyone's story ends."

It was suddenly hot on the helm. Sara rushed for the door, for the clear air.

"There will be men coming to kill us," Guillaume called after her from the doorway.

"I know," she snapped, climbing down to the main deck. What difference did it make? Everyone would be dead out here before all was said and done. Christ, she was beginning to believe that.

Guillaume followed her. "How hard are you willing to fight?"

"Jean-Philippe told me what happened with the leper."

"What did he tell you?"

"That he shot him through the eye."

"Still in therapy for it, too. Now, after Daan and after seeing those islanders turn to fish food before his eyes..."

"Why does he do this, then?"

"For me." Guillaume shrugged. "Every relationship, regardless of gender, has an alpha and a beta. Beta always makes more sacrifices. Just how it goes. And... I, uh, think he hates me for it."

"You're going to lose him," Sara said.

"Already have." Guillaume's face nearly cracked. He came in close and dropped his voice to a whisper. "And I think he's sabotaged us."

"You can't mean th—"

Guillaume pointed to a black dinghy that drifted far behind the stern. Someone who didn't think they'd need a ride off this thing. "Empty," he said. "But it wasn't always."

Sara felt weightless. Someone had boarded the *Star Time* without anyone noticing.

"Holy shit," she said and slid her pistol free.

"Come," Guillaume said.

The helm erupted in gunfire. Broken glass exploded out the starboard windows as Sara and Guillaume dashed for cover, rushing through the living space and working their way up from inside, taking every corner with caution.

They spotted Jean-Philippe on the ground when they got there, his back against the helm's controls. He faced Sara and Guillaume who stood in the kitchenette, crouched behind the countertop. A man in paramilitary gear towered over Jean-Philippe, an automatic weapon hovering in his face. "Call him," he ordered with swagger that was unmistakably American.

"I am telling you," Jean-Philippe wheezed, "there is no reason to do that. He is already on his way."

"Then I don't need you."

Sara couldn't get a confident shot off at this angle. This was a lot different than shooting glass. If her aim strayed and hit Jean-Philippe—

Guillaume fired off a burst round. Three shots sunk into the attacker's neck and back. He spun to face them, eyes wide, almost bursting. Guillaume squeezed the trigger again and the next three bursts gave him a facelift. Red-caked brain matter painted the helm windows behind him and then he dropped beside Jean-Philippe, who was wiping his blood-smeared mouth with the back of his hand.

They cleared the helm and Guillaume knelt beside his lover, surveying his wounds while Sara kept her weapon drawn on the kitchenette, should anyone else have come aboard. "Shoulder's out of commission," Guillaume told him, "but you'll live."

"I'm sorry," Jean-Philippe coughed. "He came out of nowhere and—"

"Did you call this guy?" Guillaume demanded.

"Of course not." In that moment, Jean-Philippe appeared mortally wounded. He started to say something defensive, and then paused. Reshuffled his thoughts and took a deep breath before continuing with sadness etched across his face. "He wants the pirate. Did not believe me when I told him that he was on his way."

"CIA," Guillaume growled. "They never travel alone. So we need to search this ship and be fast about it. Because the clock's ticking."

***

Except, CIA wasn't there.

Sara stayed back to guard Jean-Philippe while Guillaume fished Carly from her bunk to assist with the search. For one hour, they checked every nook and cranny, and once it was clear that nobody else was aboard, it was time to hit the water.

Guillaume was certain they would find the CIA on the shore of Roche's island, waiting for them.

The Zodiac boat ebbed against the stern. Sara leashed it to the nearest trellis, then helped Guillaume stock all the necessary equipment. Her biggest concern was whether or not she had enough ammunition.

Sara didn't wish to leave Carly on board. Carly was standing on the deck with her wetsuit folded over her forearm, ready to go with. Sara argued that someone needed to care for Jean-Philippe, thinking that it was also probably the safest place for her.

Sara was cautious as she loaded the C4 on the boat, careful to keep the detonators in a satchel hooked to Guillaume's belt. They carried a jackhammer across the deck and found it couldn't sit onboard without pushing the whole boat beneath the water.

"Going to have to let that go," Guillaume said.

"C4 will do the trick, right?"

Carly placed her wetsuit on a rack beside a diving tank and her Desert Eagle, rushing up to Sara and throwing her arms around her. Carly gave a casual peck on the lips before hovering over her ear. "Please be careful."

The whisper was pleasant enough to drive Sara's eyes into the back of her head. "I'll be right back," she said.

She and Guillaume climbed down to the small boat, swapping nervous nods as they settled among the overstocked equipment.

Guillaume started the motor buzzing and swiveled the rudder to guide them alongside the ship. Carly gave a good luck wave from above, but Guillaume watched the deck for his lover, who hadn't bothered to come out and bid them farewell. Once they cleared the yacht's length, he steered them straight on toward the island where the tide immediately fought their approach.

The boat rushed against the constant thrust of eager waves. It was constantly shoved back by the flexing undertow. One hell of an aquatic gatekeeper. They weren't far from land, three hundred feet, if that, though it seemed they could get no closer.

Guillaume steered across the ocean in erratic zigzags. The waves tossed them back and he gunned the motor when the swell was weakest, strong-arming the current and gliding past the barrier.

Sara divided her attention between the endless crash of fizzing waves and the open water behind them.

A surge of undertow with suction like a vacuum reached up and swallowed the boat beneath the waves. Sara went headfirst. The current jerked her around and raked her against a coral bed.

She heard Roche somewhere in the beyond, laughing. Delighted that people were still being lured here to die.
She flailed her arms, desperate to grab hold of something. Anything. But her body rushed along without control, twisting and spinning as water invaded her lungs.

She pushed through it all like a baby bird that didn't yet know how to fly, flapping and kicking on instinct. She wouldn't hand this ocean such an obvious victory.

At last her arm breached the surface, followed by the rest of her. She broke through, sucking air. Unable to find her bearings. In the distance, Guillaume's cries were encouraging.

He'd made it to land.

"Swim," he cried. "Just swim."

It wasn't the undertow that had taken them under.

The dunkleosteus' dorsal fin patrolled the water between her and the *Star Time*. She prayed for a moment that it would head toward Jean-Philippe and Carly. They'd have a better chance to defend the ship. The fish wasn't stupid, though. It knew an easy meal. The fin came straight for her.

Sara paddled, throwing hard kicks behind her like her boots might somehow repel the creature if it got close enough to bite.

Rising waves lifted her and she splashed through like her life depended on it. She glided back down to what she hoped would be calmer shallows and another wave rushed to greet her. She dove through that green wall, knifing through the flexing current and punching out the back, emerging into the calm. Guillaume was submerged up to his knees, cheering her with hoarse screams.

He tossed something over Sara's head and the water behind her exploded. Sara reached the shallows and the mud cooled her hands and knees. The two of them sucked air like it was their business.

Sara lay on the beach, too spent to move, realizing this wasn't an island, but an atoll. Millions of years ago, its foundation would've been laid with the eruption of a seamount far beneath the ocean. The spilt lava would've hardened as it touched water, like crusted hot sauce outside the bottle. Eventually hard lava rose above water and created a new landmass while lava beneath the water became an ecosystem for all sorts of marine life.

Sara could think of a million things she'd love to study out here. Her hands curled through a fistful of sand, or dusted corals more accurately.

She tried to stand but could only reach her knees.

Guillaume was already up, but his attention was split between the task at hand and the sight of the *Star Time*, rocking on unpredictable waters.

"He's going to die there," he said. His voice genuinely panicked.

"Carly—"

Guillaume kissed the tips of two fingers and held them to the wind. Without saying another word, he reached down and dragged his equipment inland.

FORTY-THREE

The American took them down to an altitude of seven thousand feet and circled the small island, sighing because there were no serious options here.

"I can do it," he growled, challenging himself to make it work.

Kaahin tightened his belt straps and closed his hands around the door handle. It was the only thing in here to easily brace against.

The plane glided down to six thousand feet. Five thousand. Four thousand. Their teeth chattered in the frosty cab air. Kaahin gave his pilot the side-eye. The American's lips were the color of frostbite.

"Found the party," the American said.

Kaahin spotted the *Star Time* anchored off the island's shore. He hoped they had been dumb enough to leave it unguarded, rushing headlong to find their pot of gold at the end of the rainbow. The yacht was still his, after all. Law of the sea. And he would take it back.

The American eased the yoke against the dash, gliding the plane down further as something that looked like a single chemtrail launched off the deck of the *Star Time*. He realized too late what he was seeing. He only had time to brace as the rocket stream from a fired missile launcher rushed up to greet them.

The explosion outside the cabin took the plane's wing clean off. It shattered the windows, cracked the fuselage, and sent them into tailspin, spiraling through the sky as the pilot's door tore away and the air suddenly began sucking everything out of the cab.

Kaahin batted debris away from his head and tried to speak, though his words were little more than sputters, lost beneath the groaning sounds of a hemorrhaging hull.

He pressed his palm to the gun tucked against the band of his pants when an elbow collided with his jaw.

At last the American made his move, determined to ensure they died together. Kaahin had been expecting it. He realized his error in thinking it would happen on the ground. Down there, the game would be even. Up here, the advantage was not his.

Kaahin closed a fist and swung back, fighting every instinct to draw his gun and blast the American in his guts—if he still had the weapon. The world was spinning, parts of the fuselage breaking off. The wind speed tore at the plane like claws through butter, flinging parts of it through the sky.

Kaahin reached for his gun. In the chaos, he couldn't tell if he even still had it. The American saw this happening and lunged for Kaahin's wrists. Except the American wasn't going for the gun at all. His reach extended beyond it. Fingers clasped the door handle behind Kaahin.

The cabin was all tremors, the fuselage bending and cracking beneath the crush of hurried wind speed.

The American's body was pressed flat against Kaahin's. His arm was pinned in place against the door. The space here was too tight to maneuver. The American knew this, or perhaps it was the anarchy of the moment that made his weight so oppressive.

The door popped wide and then tore from its hinges and went flapping into the trees below.

Kaahin didn't wait. He rolled through the opened frame and fell sideways into the chop.

This while the plane shot inward toward the tree line like a bullet. Kaahin fought against sweeping undertow, watching the remaining wing break off. It dropped onto the beach like bricks and a nest of birds went flapping toward the skies with angry squawks.

A midnight plume of smoke followed the thunderous crash. Kaahin watched but felt no satisfaction for the American's death. He only slipped beneath the waves and began to paddle.

FORTY-FOUR

"Company," Guillaume said.

The island wasn't large enough for the explosion to go unnoticed. They drew their guns and Sara's heart drummed as they hurried toward the action. It would be best to neutralize any threat before the company could regroup.

The plane's twisted wreckage was barely inland, stopped at the base of some large trees that served as an entrance to the forest proper.

The wings and doors were torn free. The fuselage had more crinkles than an accordion. And the windshield was completely busted. A familiar body was sprawled across the plane's nose, so much blood running down to the tip.

"Holloway," Sara said and rushed toward him.

They eased his lower torso through the cockpit windshield and glided him toward the sand.

"Do we have first aid?"

"On the ship," Guillaume's words were cold. He was more interested in the area around them, suspicious that this man had friends nearby.

It was a shame they had nothing, because the old ship's captain needed a lot of something. His left leg was gone beneath the knee, cleaved off in the crash.

Holloway groaned with every motion, thick red globs pouring down his chin.

They made Holloway a makeshift hospital bed out of their heaviest clothes. Guillaume used his shirt as a tourniquet around the injured leg and then got a fire going in order to keep the impending shock at bay.

Sara's blade glowed red hot as she lifted it off the fire. Holloway was in and out of it, though he seemed to anticipate what was coming, tightening his arm around Guillaume as Sara brought the hissing blade to his bloody stump and pressed against it. The knife sizzled, the smell turned immediately to charred meat, and Holloway's screams uprooted every nested bird.

The captain had an onset of Tourette's, screaming a hundred profanities in between short breaths. He rolled back and forth as the pain rolled through him. After what felt like an hour, his eyelids drooped and he began to lose consciousness.

"There is nothing more we can do," Guillaume whispered.

"I know," Sara agreed. Her first instinct was to get him back to the *Star Time*. It wouldn't be as difficult to fight the waves on the way out, but that fish was going to be a problem.

"Where's the jewel?" Guillaume asked.

Holloway answered with a few soft grumbles.

Sara bent and performed a passionless search. It wasn't on his clothes. Guillaume was already checking the fuselage.

"Holloway," she said, but the captain's eyes were rolled all the way to the back of his head.

"We should search the island," Guillaume said.

"For a rock?"

"What else is there to do?"

"I don't know," Sara said. "Be smart about things?"

"This hunt has cost me everything," Guillaume snapped. "We see it to the end. No other choice. That is why we stand here now."

"You have balls saying that to me, as if I'm just along for the ride."

Guillaume wasn't willing to discuss it. He stalked off along the shore, promising to leave tracks that would be easy to follow.

Sara started her search by fanning out around the smoking wreck. She completed the next lap of ever-expanding circles and found Holloway sitting up on his elbow when she returned. He looked oddly conscious for the moment, sharp features and blazing eyes.

"He's going to kill you," he said, lapsing into a coughing spasm that painted the sand around him red.

Sara skidded through the bloodstains on her knees and brought her ear straight to his lips.

"They're paid to kill," he said. "Bitch they work for is ruthless."

"How do you know them?"

"Work where I do, you learn the players," he sputtered. "Don't tell me you think that guy's your friend."

"Where's the jewel?"

Another cough. His limp wrist gestured to the waves.

"The ocean?"

"Pirate's got it... jumped out just before the crash."

Guillaume had been right about Holloway's broadcast being compromised, but at least he'd tried to ditch the pirate before landing. The crash was a gamble that hadn't paid off.

Holloway was the color of moon glow and might probably be dead before sunset. He smiled red and the blood streamed down the sides of his cheeks, finding new areas of flesh to stain.

"I'm sorry, Holloway."

He shook his head. Didn't care to hear it. "Catch up to him." His hand brushed the grip of her pistol. "Kill him."

It was the last thing she wanted to do. Didn't want to believe Guillaume would kill her. She considered telling Holloway about the deal the Baroness had given her. But wasn't that more naiveté?

Before she could even consider that, she caught a glimpse of the *Star Time* in the corner of her eye. The ship was moving, coming around, and headed straight for shore.

What now?

She drifted toward the open beach and drew her weapon. Just behind the boat, the fin cut the water.

And then somewhere out of sight, Guillaume began to scream.

FORTY-FIVE

Kaahin could've gone for the island, but the vicious undertow would have cost him time and maybe more.

The yacht, on the other hand, was further out. The fish, here. He accepted his helplessness and swam for it, thinking the boat would grant him tremendous leverage, should he make it.

A hundred kilometers. Maybe less. The longest swim of his life. He pushed through water that was perpetually red. Blood pouring from unknown wounds.

A tired hand reached for the yacht's swim platform. He climbed onto it and scaled the stern ladder. He moved across the deck mumbling a quick offering of thanks to his god.

The living space was luxurious past the point of mockery. This boat would net him one large sum. He could take it right now, cast off for home and leave these foolish treasure-seekers to die. Only there was no chance he'd get far. The angatra wouldn't let him. Besides, the treasure was within reach...

"One hell of a swim." The thick French accent was almost too difficult for Kaahin to understand. He froze on the stairwell landing. A man in a flak jacket was on the next landing up, leaning over the railing, an automatic weapon pointed down. His face was smeared in blood and his eyelids seemed heavy.

"What are you doing on my ship?"

"You shot me out of the sky," Kaahin said.

"Didn't do shit. What are you doing on my ship?"

"Didn't want to drown."

"I'd have preferred it if you had," the Frenchman said. "I know who you are."

"Then you have the advantage."

"I'll keep it. Upstairs. Now."

Kaahin walked with his hands in the air. He wouldn't give this man one excuse to shoot him. They went single file into a supply room where the far wall was lined with weapons. Diving equipment and field-ready computers were sprawled across the table.

The Frenchman ordered him into a seat and then joined him, eye-to-gun barrel. Another soldier of fortune. No shortage of these parasites.

"You're going to go fishing with me," the Frenchman told him.

Kaahin laughed. The first time he felt like laughing in forever. Not only was the request absurd, but this man was nearly dead. Kaahin saw oversized gauze stuffed beneath his vest where someone had shot him. "Oh, fishing," he said. "Is that all?"

"We're going to kill that thing."

"And do what with it?"

"Worry about the killing."

"Why not ask your people?"

"The fish is hammering us now. I can't wait for my people to come back. I think it punctured the hull."

"Ah," Kaahin said. "Then you are running out of time."

"This isn't a partnership. You refuse, I shoot you in the face and use your corpse as chum."

"Tried that," Kaahin said. "It does not work."

"I will try again."

"It will not be easy."

"Let's cut through it, then, Pirate King. What do you want?"

"This ship."

The Frenchman's turn to laugh. "It's yours. For as long as it floats."

"It's a smart fish," Kaahin said. "Bait it and it will not come."

"She went after my people as they went ashore."

"I would guess your people were anything but ready for it."

The Frenchman considered this and lit a cigarette. He took deep breaths that sounded like someone blowing into a kazoo. "It haunts this ship. I wonder why it let you make it aboard."

"It is not through torturing me," Kaahin said.

"We'll turn those tables."

Kaahin felt bold. He reached two fingers out. The Frenchman stared back and at last slid a cigarette in between Kaahin's fingers. "I know how to catch it," he said.

"Start talking," the Frenchman said.

Kaahin did. The easiest way was to go inland. The fish would go for a living thing inside a Zodiac boat.

"We rig a second boat," the Frenchman said. "Send it straight for shore. It'll sputter against the undertow, make the fish think we're trying to follow our friends."

"And while that's happening we lift anchor and move this boat closer," Kaahin said. "Use everything we've got to take it out. Which begs the question, what have you got that kills?"

The Frenchman went to the back of the room and lifted a soviet RPG off the floor. "Funny," he said. "Used to be three rockets here. Now there's one."

Kaahin ashed his cigarette on the table and tossed.

"There is someone else aboard this ship," the Frenchman growled. "We thought they went to shore but—"

Kaahin nodded sadly. "It is me they want."

"And we need to find him fast," the Frenchman said.

***

Mr. Reeves grabbed the blonde by the hair and yanked her head.

Her eyes were soaked, but steely. Impotent hatred that bored him. "If I take the sock out of your mouth," he said, "do you promise to remain silent?"

A muffled uh-huh, so he pulled the dirty sock free and tossed it. She pressed her mouth to the bed sheet and gagged in silence.

Mr. Reeves thought she was a lovely sight. Very fit and with an exquisite body. Nice curves beneath the white and yellow lemon wrap dress she wore. The way it rode up around her thighs. He enjoyed the way one of her ass cheeks poked out from beneath the thin fabric, for he felt like he was seeing something he was not supposed to.

Very fit, he thought. In another life, he would enjoy sitting with her and inquiring about her workout regimen. He felt depressingly out of shape beneath his gear. It had been years since he'd worn this much and it was so heavy. Made him... tired.

The good news was that Mr. Reeves still had his fastball. He and Davis had taken this ship with ease. But Davis, young as he was, had suffered a tragic dimming of instinct. The boy had gotten himself killed for no damn reason other than thinking he could control the situation.

"Why don't you get up now?" Mr. Reeves suggested. "And stand in front of the door. Make a sound I do not like, and I will execute you."

The blonde did it and Mr. Reeves couldn't suppress his grin seeing how much fear he'd instilled in her.

Fastball indeed.

Mr. Reeves knew you did not underestimate your enemy, no matter who he was. Once Davis got his ticket punched for the Heaven Express, he knew they'd search the ship. Mr. Reeves found the one place to hide they wouldn't think to look. The small storage panel beneath the engine room floor, intended for tools and spare machine parts, but deep enough to take a body. You wouldn't even know it was there, hidden beneath floor matting, unless you'd read the owner's manual. This wasn't Mr. Reeves' first time at the dance, recalling circumstances that led to him being stranded on the Atlantic in a boat that wasn't at all dissimilar to this one. Him, alongside with a cadre of Washington types that included two former presidents. An amusing story that would have to die with him.

The problem now was that he couldn't use that spot again. Because pirates learned every crevice of their ships by trade, and this bastard would certainly know to look there.

"I almost hit him, you know," Mr. Reeves told her. "I mean, I hit the fucking plane. That could've been it. Why couldn't that have been it? I've got to clip him here and now."

"You don't have to kill Jean-Philippe, you know," the blonde said, her voice all trembles.

"Oh, I won't." Mr. Reeves popped the magazine from his submachine gun, dispassionately checking to ensure it remained loaded—a nervous tick he'd never been able to shake. He tuned her out. Thing was, it was less of a mess if he waxed them all.

The blonde eyed him with caution. She knew what he was.

"It's time we take the fight to them," Mr. Reeves said.

She winced as he crossed the room and put a gloved hand on her shoulder. She didn't see, but the barrel of the gun was an inch from her back. "You're on point," he told her. "Open the door."

She did as she was told.

There was no motion, save for the creaking boat that made more groaning noises now than when he'd boarded. Mr. Reeves knew the others aboard hunted him the way he hunted them. And he would've clipped the blonde already if he didn't think he'd need a human shield.

"Where might they be?" he said, almost inaudibly.

"Last time we searched from the top down," she whispered.

Yes, they had. Mr. Reeves recalled lying in the dark, listening to the humming engine while waiting to hear footfalls crossing over him. And it had taken a long time.

"We go up," he whispered. "Move too fast, and I will execute you. Got it?"

An affirmative whimper.

They reached the stairwell and Mr. Reeves made the blonde ascend to the next landing and hold there. He kept his gun trained on her just in case the others were on their way down. He wanted them to spot her first. And alone.

They did this until they got topside, passing through the entertainment space on their way out.

Mr. Reeves caught motion in the window beside him, a figure moving along the outside of the deck. He spun toward it and, through the glass, saw the other figure mimicking him.

Gunfire shredded both sides of the yacht wall at once. Electronics detonated into shrieking sparks as the deck exploded into a full-fledged firefight.

The blonde shrieked and ran for the open air. Mr. Reeves continued firing through the wall as he dashed behind the tattered bar for what little cover he could get.

Elsewhere on the deck, two male voices exchanged screams.

I got one of them, Mr. Reeves knew. He gave his own body a once-over to ensure he hadn't been hit and nearly laughed once he realized he was going to get through this.

He was on the move then, approaching the busted glass and peering through. He spotted a blood trail that went amidships.

Mr. Reeves rushed for the open deck. As soon as he crossed into fresh air, a fist smashed the side of his face, hard and unexpected enough to knock into him a stagger.

He spun, expecting to find the pirate there. The blonde's twisted and angry face inside a full body wetsuit. She had a diver's tank in her hand and hoisted it as he began lifting his gun. The tank cracked across his face, sending Mr. Reeves into a helicopter twirl. He fired his weapon toward the sky as he danced.

The blonde wasn't done. She cracked him a second time, harder. His vision crumpled. The tank struck him again. The crack inside his skull was like branches snapping on a winter's day.

He no longer had the gun in his hand and didn't know how he'd lost it. He reached for the blonde, found one of her wrists and tugged her.

They stumbled across the deck together. Mr. Reeves felt as though his skull was collapsing. He clung to the blonde, reaching for her face and thinking he could claw her eyes out before this was all said and done.

She shrieked and attempted to pull free, but it was no use. Mr. Reeves continued yanking her along, thinking she'd lose her balance and fall into his arms where he could snap her fucking neck.

And then the ground beneath him disappeared. And as Mr. Reeves realized he'd fallen off the ladder landing on his way overboard, the only comfort he took was knowing he was taking the blonde with him.

***

Kaahin retrieved the Zodiac boat from storage, then made a second trip for its motor, dragging it topside in order to attach it.

This while the Frenchman sat slumped against the ship's railing, bleeding out beneath the sun. They both knew he was a dead man, only the Frenchman did not wish to admit it.

"A fish is pure cartilage," Kaahin said. "As soon as we destroy it, it will begin to decompose."

"Its body will," the Frenchman wheezed. "That awful head will not."

"That will be enough?"

"That will be everything."

Kaahin sprinted back to the helm and lifted the anchor. He spotted a curved trimming blade resting in the pot of one of the ship's decorative plants and picked it up, deciding he could never be too careful.

He returned to the deck to find the Frenchman looking out on the water and said, "You know that you are going to be the one to go, correct?"

The Frenchman had a pistol in his hand, and he thought about lifting it but instead threw it across the deck and sat wheezing for another moment. "Yes, I can avenge Daan," he said. "I can do that much. I can't believe he killed me. They came for you. And killed me."

"I will help you down," Kaahin said. "You will still help take this thing out of the ocean. You will become a hero."

The Frenchman's eyes rolled, blood spilling from his mouth as he stirred. "You did not even try and help Carly."

"The woman is not my concern."

"After everything you did to her—"

"She is at peace now," he said. "Think of it like that. Let's go."

The Frenchman oozed blood as he descended the ladder, Kaahin expected him to bleed to death on the swimming platform. But he struggled into the boat and dropped against the wall of the tubing, where Kaahin thought he might've died on the spot.

Then he stirred, enough strength to give the motor cord one good tear. It sputtered and hummed and Kaahin motioned to the shore. "Godspeed," he said flatly and started back for the helm.

Take him, Kaahin thought, watching the small boat zip off. He wanted it so badly he could almost visualize the dying Frenchman being swallowed whole.

A coarse grinding somewhere beneath the hull disrupted his thoughts as the lower decks whined. Noise that became an almost permanent groan.

"Death's Head," he whispered and raced for the yacht's controls. He started the ship inland while around him the navigation equipment continued to spark and sizzle from a previous gunfight.

The ship continued to screech like nails crawling a chalkboard. He imagined the fish dragging the tip of its head along the hull's length just to keep him irritated.

The Zodiac boat veered off and Kaahin watched the dorsal fin break the surface directly behind it. The Frenchman rose on a fast-flying wave. At that speed, he was able to punch straight through the water wall and disappear into the thin channel beyond.

Kaahin gave chase in the yacht, accelerating toward the same spot. The grumbling hull grew louder as it scraped coral bottoms, slanting as the portside shallows lifted the ship on an increasingly severe angle.

The Frenchman's boat was long out of sight. In a moment, his screams echoed somewhere beyond the twisting river.

At last, the fish had done something stupid. They had seen from the sky that the river did not slice its way through the entirety of the island. There was no exit. Now that the yacht was wedged between beaches, Death's Head was trapped.

The *Star Time* was taking on water, slipping beneath the waves and going lopsided. Kaahin knew his dream of selling this to the Saudis was finished, and here was the next best use of it.

He was careful to traverse the ladder, climbing down with his back almost directly over the ocean. Much of the equipment had slid across the deck and clustered against the rails. He tossed it into the sand over the starboard side.

The jackhammer plopped into the mud and Kaahin had to abandon ship in much the same way, falling straight into the shallows, then wading up on the shore, dragging the jackhammer onto dry sand.

He stood over the spill of salvaged weapons and tools, realizing how desperate the situation had become. They were trapped here with a sinking ship and a crashed plane. No other means of escape.

Kaahin stroked the curved blade that dangled from his belt loop. He turned to watch the ship tilt further, all the way onto its side. He mourned its passing like a dying relative. The only solace he had left was in his pocket. He reached deep and freed the ruby red jewel.

All of his misfortunes for this.

Something lifted out of the water and rose against the yacht's stern. A figure in a diving mask. The blonde bitch. She clung to the overturned swimming platform, using it for leverage as she unholstered a pistol that looked like a cannon in her fist and wasted no time drawing down on him.

Kaahin was wide open. No cover for a hundred kilometers. He thought about diving for the sand when a whip crack rang out and the bullet sunk through his shoulder. It dropped him to his ass as the bitch fired again, this time going too wide overhead.

"Please," he screamed.

The blonde's eyes blazed with the kind of madness you couldn't talk down.

There was one chance, and Kaahin took it. He scampered for the water on his hands and legs, leaping into the deep as two more gunshots plunked into the mud around him.

Kaahin swam inland, wondering how he could survive this.

FORTY-SIX

The scream from the shoreline was Guillaume's.

Sara found his comms gear smashed and scattered across the beach, just before the trees. Blood was already hardening in the coral sand, and small dots of it formed a trail into the forest.

She called his name and nobody answered. She didn't know how to use a submachine gun but took it anyway and just as she did, another scream tore through the distant sky, this one more familiar.

Holloway.

Sara broke into a sprint against the trees in order to shave off some distance. She was drenched in sweat by the time she reached the now vacant site of the plane crash.

Another scream. This one somewhere inside the forest. Someone had taken Holloway. Sara rushed after the noise, using trees for cover.

Jagged mountain stabs rose over the treetops. Sharpened points confined to the northern most side of the island. Looking at them was enough to make Sara tired. Her fingers brushed against the spool of dynamic nylon climbing rope hitched to her belt.

Right, she thought. You knew you were going to have to use that.

At her back, distant gunfire was a muted echo. Jean-Philippe would have to defend the *Star Time*.

She picked up her pace and rushed through the trees on a steady jog. Sweat soaked through the fabric beneath her neckline. The submachine gun in her hand brought minimal confidence.

Her chest tightened, wondering if she wasn't feeling a few native gazes all of a sudden. Muscular fingers gripping bowstrings, eager arrowheads pointed at her chest. This place was obviously home to someone. Difficult to find, near impossible to land.

The more island she saw, the more she began to wonder if they were in the right place. Isabella had claimed that she and Roche lived here, in a manor that had taken years to complete. Even if that was long gone, there had to be some trace of it.

"Sara, they're killers..." Holloway's voice broke across the sky. The next sound out of his mouth was full-throated, guttural, and could only mean one thing...

"No." Her voice was so soft it was nearly silent. She leaned against a tree, light-headedness taking hold. She was nearly abandoned out here and had no strength to continue. "I'm sorry, Holloway," she said. He had been as good as dead, Guillaume was right about that, but no one deserved to go out this way.

Maybe it was best to get back to the *Star Time*.

She turned on her heels and a tomahawk was raised above her head. The blade was firm inside a gnarled fist of tri-pronged and misshapen fingers. Nails like train spikes. The forearm was wisps of grey, ghostly hair. Bulbous white eyes glared out from behind the anonymity of a human skull that masked this thing's true face.

Sara stepped back and screamed at the sight.

It wore a loincloth of animal pelts. Its torso was a display of open sores and broken scabs. A banded headdress stretched in a ring around its malformed head, various bird feathers jutting out atop it like jewels on a crown.

It opened its mouth and hissed, flashing a scramble of chiseled teeth that would flay her in a single bite.

Sara squeezed the submachine gun trigger, mostly in panic, burying rounds straight through its heart and chest, halting its charge before it could begin. The thing stuttered back and collapsed, flailing through the dirt with a horrible death rattle vibrating in its throat.

Sara kept her weapon fixed until its wheezing breath wound down into silence.

Its weapon was a sharpened fish bone, fashioned to a stone hilt with leather strips. She kicked it into the brush just to be safe.

This thing was humanoid. Three toes on one foot and six on the other. The missing digits weren't removed, the flesh was too clean and rounded where they should've been. Curved animal talons were in the spot where a human had toenails. The feet were callused. Were these the red feet that Roche's clues intended her to sit among?

Eruptions of gunfire on the beach, more frequent. Sara tensed and got low as if the bullets might be coming for her.

"Sara." Another far-flung scream, this one belonging to Guillaume. "Sara, help!"

She held her breath as if the simple act would betray her position.

Sara stepped toward the mountains with reluctance, fanning out in order to go around its base.

The jungle kept humidity the way her father's walk-in humidor had. Her palms itched. Beads of sweat tickled her skin beneath her bangs. Her utility belt consisted of rope, a climbing axe, a holster, and a canteen, but she felt as though she were lugging bricks.

The square footage of this island atoll was somehow deceiving. The day stretched and became afternoon. Her steps turned to shuffles. She fantasized about taking another sip of water, but hadn't she just done that? Couldn't afford to spend another drop so soon. There was, after all, no telling how long she would be stranded here.

No telling how many of those monstrous skull things were watching.

Sara feared living out the rest of her days here—just as Isabella had. Surrounded by treasure that might as well have been rotted food for as useful as it was. The cruelest irony. One final way for Blake, her husband in sickness and in health, to hurt her.

Her boot tip dropped onto the forest floor and something snapped. Reflexively, she threw herself down, face-first and bracing for death. A dozen blades carved through her back at once, drawing thin rushes of blood. She screeched into the earth, as the blades lurched back from the other direction, slicing her again.

Sara dragged herself out from beneath the obstruction and rolled to her side, feeling the blood pour off her back. She jammed her fingers into her mouth to keep the cries from getting any louder.

To keep those awful skull faces at bay.

A log, cut to precision so it would fit between the trees that lined either side of the path, was suspended three feet from the ground, swaying in the breeze. It wore a slew of carved and fastened spikes, many of them blood-stained.

Roche's trap? Or had the locals done this?

Close to her boots, an old bird's nest had fallen as the trap dislodged. Two homeless birds circled it, firing off mournful squawks. One landed to survey the damage and Sara only now realized there were a few eggs spilled out around her. None had cracked and she was surprised by how much relief this brought.

In the distance, Guillaume's voice came roaring back, begging for help. He was closer now.

Sara retrieved her weapon off the forest floor. Those things must've been hunting him.

A second bird landed and began chirping. Sara stepped away, ready to continue when her eyes fell upon the creature's feet. Its talons were a dark shade of red. And it wasn't blood.

"You clever bastard, Roche." Sara was surprised by her willingness to smile as her hand slid down to the metal spool that housed her climbing rope.

Guillaume's voice came back another time and she thought the best thing she could do was take to the skies, suddenly eager to sit among red feet.

***

The birds must've been indigenous to the island. Sara wondered at first if she had to climb the very tree that had spilled the nest, but thought better of it.

She knew where she was supposed to go. To the largest stone structure the island had.

She was climbing before she knew it. Her hands fell into the natural crevasses. Padded and half-fingered gloves protected her while granting flexibility. She stretched against the old rock and pulled herself up. From beneath her arm she caught a whiff of her own perspiration and laughed that she could be so vain in such a desperate moment.

"Sara!" That voice again. This time, practically nipping at her heels.

She was going to signal him when his voice came calling again, stopping her cold.

"Where the fuck are you, Sara?" She wanted to know what made Guillaume so certain she was alive, but then remembered the thing she killed. He might've found it, or at least heard the shots.

She kept scaling. Once she was about equal with the treetops, she unspooled some of the climbing rope and hammered a stake through the rock face, never quite sure of how she knew what to do. The end of the rope hooked through the grip and at the very least she'd probably prevent herself from splattering on the forest floor. Now she'd just swing back and break her head open against the rock face.

"Sara!" Roaring gunfire somewhere below.

She climbed to escape that world, the sweeping chaos she feared would inevitably catch her. Things had happened too fast to comprehend. She wouldn't speculate. Only climb. The gunshots beneath her turned to sporadic pops. Guillaume was probably close to dead.

Climb.

Her hand got caught deep inside a crevice, tearing the skin off her knuckles as she yanked it free. Her muscles begged for a break, but Sara refused.

Climb.

A gunshot like cannon fire roared past her head, whizzing for the sky. Her body tightened and she pushed herself forward until she was flat against the rock face.

"Guillaume, what the hell are you—"

"Need to get your attention somehow if you refuse to answer me!"

"Dammit, I—" Sara glanced down and gasped at the sight.

"You're bleeding, Sara." Guillaume stood at the base of the mountain. "Quite badly." He barely looked like the man she knew. The flap of flesh hanging off his jaw was like a loose patch of chicken skin. Half his face had been peeled away, picked down to the bloody bone beneath. His eyeball was completely gone from that socket, and the ear on that side of his face had been cleaved away. Nothing but a wide dark hole where it had been.

"I'm fine," she insisted and kept climbing.

"You are going to get yourself killed." His speech was about as clear as oatmeal.

"Only if you keep shooting at me."

"Thought you were another of those things," he slurred. "Let me dress your wounds and we'll regroup... what are you going up there for?"

Sara left the question unanswered as she continued her ascent. Next time she looked, the treetops were like broccoli heads.

"Tell me what you are doing."

"Finding a vantage point." Trembling hands reached for the ledge where the stone receded. Her fingers curled around the landing as another jagged blade leapt for them. Sara yanked back her hand, but was too slow. The bone blade scraped stone. Her pinky finger came away and a small stream of blood painted the rock face.

Sara pulled her hand back and felt the blood rushing. She went for the submachine gun that dangled off her belt and swung it up toward the landing just as the skull appeared over the ledge.

Its face seemed equally crazed behind the human bone façade. The eyes behind the empty skull sockets were also white. These monstrosities were without eyesight.

Its hand was a creature's claw, slashing the gun barrel as Sara squeezed off a round that blew straight through its palm. The thing lost none of its strength. It yanked the weapon up toward it with enough force to tear the strap from her belt and send the gun sailing back to the forest floor below.

With the weapon gone, the thing closed its fingers around Sara's wrist and yanked her up too. Her knees scraped and bled and her body seemed to sail up and over.

The thing was hunched, readying the blade for its next attack. In motion, Sara saw the creature's curves, realized it was female. It had the same pattern of runny sores on its chest. Breasts were bare, though one appeared to have been eaten away, with only a flappy piece of ribbon flesh remaining, obvious teeth imprints.

Sara pulled her pistol free as the blade lunged. She scurried back while taking aim. It cleaved through the round of her toe just as she got her shot off. The bark was louder than an explosion and a quarter-sized hole broke through the skull mask.

The creature plopped face down. The back of its skull, a jagged exit wound.

Sara rolled onto her side, just about the only piece of her that wasn't bleeding. She sucked air until her heart slowed, vomiting just a little.

Far below, scraping and rustling began in earnest as Guillaume started his ascent.

"No," she said. Then, a little louder, "what are you doing?"

She peered over and caught his gaze. His body moved upward with strength he couldn't possibly have. His one remaining eye refused to move. Locked in a permanent, wicked glare. Underneath the charade, he was determined to be the one who took the treasure out of here.

"Think," Sara said to herself for no other reason than to refocus her thoughts.

On this ledge sat the remnants of several red-foot nests. Tiny twigs and leaves mottled together and reinforced whenever time demanded it. There were more eggs against the recessed wall space, but no sign of overprotective mothers looking to clamp down on trespassers.

An engraving was cut into the enclave stone, looking first to Sara's eyes like caveman markings. She used the fingers on her uninjured hand to scoop away as much muck as possible, running her fingertips through the rivulets until the gunk was clear.

The image beneath was a pair of stone eyes. Almond-shaped and mostly shallow, a small nose and parted lips. There was a deeper recession on what looked to be its tongue.

The jewel. It was necessary.

"Guillaume," Sara called. "Stop climbing. We're going to need to get the jackhammer. Or the explosives, if they survived the trip."

There was no response from the cliff face.

"Guillaume," she repeated. "We need that jackhammer if we're going to break through this."

A dark hand curled around the cliff. A second hand appeared gripping a curved and soaking blade. Sara gasped as the head appeared next. The face of the man who'd thrown her overboard.

"Please," he said in slow, measured English. "I do not wish any more bloodshed." His shirt was cut into ribbons. Pieces of it torn away and wrapped around the still bleeding shoulder wound. He used part of his shirt to clean the blade and then tucked the weapon into his waistband.

"What happened to Guillaume?"

The pirate did not answer. He reached into his pocket and took hold of something. Opened his fist to show the jewel that had come a long way and passed through many fingers to be here.

"What about Guillaume?" Sara repeated.

He lifted his hands in surrender and with his foot, gestured cliff side.

Sara limped to the edge and looked down. Guillaume was swinging like a pendulum on the safety rope, halfway to the ground. His shoulders stooped and his neck was torn so wide that the dark paramilitary uniform was stained crimson.

Sara lifted the gun and knew in that moment she should've shot him.

Because he lunged for her, sidestepping her arm.

Sara tried to pivot, but he had lowered his shoulder and plowed her like a battering ram. She went over the edge and dropped like a sack, rushing toward the earth below.

FORTY-SEVEN

Kaahin reached for his knife as the girl screamed below, caught by her safety rope.

As far as he could see there were two pegs. One was just a few feet beneath him. His reach extended that far and he hacked at the nylon rope there, the material fraying into thinner strands with each pass of the blade.

The western bitch screamed something desperate, but the pathetic tone of her voice only made him angrier. One final hack and the rope snapped, sending her sailing. The second peg caught her, but snapped her body and flung her around, bashing her against the rocks and knocking her silent.

He hoped she was dead, though there was no way of telling. It would have to be enough. His eyes went naturally to the work the girl had done, clearing away animal debris to find the spot where the jewel called out.

It was all so obvious.

He pushed the stone into the engraved space that resembled a human tongue. Tremors enveloped the wall and the stone slid away with a protracted groan. The stale air that lived beyond it came rushing out, setting him coughing.

Kaahin turned away, hungry for the fresh air his seafaring lungs craved.

He had no light, and cursed his haste for failing to take one off the soldier he'd left dangling below. He was going to have to do this in the dark.

With the blade in his fist, he headed inside.

FORTY-EIGHT

Sara's gnarled hands gripped Guillaume's belt strap for dear life. Overhead, the clip that kept them suspended in the air via the wall spike whined and groaned, dislodging with the addition of extra body weight.

Sara swayed back and forth atop the dangling corpse, stunned to discover just how far she'd climbed. Falling at this height meant splattering. She eased her weight and the body swung like a bell, away from the rock face while the wall spike continued to pull clear. Then she sailed back on momentum, trying to get close enough to grab.

The holding spike stuttered, dropping them a few inches as it fell free. Sara reached out, punching her fist inside the nearest crevice, burying it wrist-deep in order to anchor herself there. Her shredded knuckles were threads now, and the pain from her severed finger throbbed all the way up to her tonsils. The anchor overhead fell clear and sent Guillaume plummeting.

Sara resumed the climb. Her muscles blazed as she stretched and pulled herself up.

It took longer this time. The afternoon sun gave up beating on her back and disappeared behind a puff of clouds. The ocean breeze was cooler up here, and when she closed her eyes, she could fool herself for a second or two into thinking this really was still her vacation.

The day was nearly done by the time she reached the top again. Sara caught her breath alongside the skull-faced woman she'd killed.

And soon, the sky was black. It summoned jungle sounds she hadn't noticed until now. She imagined an entire tribe of these things prowling the darkness, hunting for intruders. She wished there was a way to get word to Carly and Jean-Philippe.

"I'm sorry, Carly," she whispered and turned toward the mountain entrance. "Please be safe." The way inside the mountain was even darker, a passage straight into nightmares. She gave a dispassionate laugh when she saw the jewel plugged into the stone tongue. The taste bud had in fact opened the way. She wrestled it free and held it tight before stuffing it inside her pocket, half convinced it was a good luck charm. It had carried her this far...

"Okay," Sara said, rallying. She reached into her supply pack and took a glow stick in hand. The snap of her thumb sent the darkness scurrying. Sara took the small pickaxe in her free hand and stared at the entrance, half with wonder, half terror.

The pirate was in there. With a knife. Fuck him, because she had an axe. Though, somehow, the advantage was his. He could sit in the shadows and wait. He'd see her coming because the light in her fist would betray her.

"Isabella," she whispered, carrying the light over the threshold and into the musty air. Despite everything, just being here was validating. Like Blake hadn't ruined their lives for nothing. She wished he could be here now and wiped her eyes with the back of her bloody hand.

There were steps. Lots of them. Descending deeper into what she had to assume was a man-made mountain.

The interior was confined, almost like winding stairs inside a lighthouse. She passed unlit wall sconces and tried to make her boots fall with stealth, but the echoes made gravelly clops.

The descending path led to a stone landing, though the stairs continued into unbroken darkness below. The wooden doors before her were ajar. She reached out and touched her palm against them. The wood flexed, soft to the touch. The pirate had gone this way. She should've gone somewhere else, but the descending staircase was anything but inviting.

Besides, Sara knew she had to kill that fucker.

She passed through and found a cold stone antechamber. A candle chandelier swayed on a rusted chain, delivering haunted house creaks. Two chairs sat on opposite sides of the entrance, withered by time and seemingly too brittle to hold any weight. The door beyond them was half open and flickering light danced inside that space.

She moved through, at last invading a sprawling living area. One center hallway stretched on, with doors lining both sides. Shorter hallways to her left and right led to other doors. A dirty carpet wore hints of long-faded royal red. It lined the floor in all directions, soaked by hundreds of years of humidity.

Stepping on it brought a squish of water. She goose-stepped and stuffed her glow stick inside her pocket. One path took her to an old kitchen complete with a rusted cauldron and sacks of old grain.

Sara headed back the other way. Mustiness tickled her nostrils and provoked a sneeze. She stuffed her arm into her elbow and held it there until the urge passed. Somewhere down the long corridor came the sound of rummaging.

They were the first people in centuries to be here. She imagined Isabella gliding through then-lavish surroundings, unimpressed with everything because Roche could not buy her love. And once he'd realized that, he decided this place would instead become her tomb.

Their tomb.

Knowing that, Sara could hardly be impressed by any of this.

So let's put that money to good use, Roche.

Opposite the kitchen sat the library, loaded with books as musty as the furniture. They had yellowed and twisted pages, bubbled covers. Roche's reading chair was positioned beside the fireplace, hobbled by a missing leg.

On the far wall, window indentations were blotted by small plates of stone. The pulley system under it implied there was a way to slide them aside and get actual fresh air and sunlight through.

Power windows. Gotta love it.

From down the hall, more rummaging interspersed with impatient grunts. It was impossible for Sara to search any further. The pirate was too dangerous, too rabid in his quest. And there was nothing in here with which to trap him, so she gripped the pickaxe. Only way to get on with it was to go through him. The more she thought on that, the better it sat inside her. This motherfucker had tried to throw her to her death twice in as many times as they'd met.

There would not be a third.

Sara slow-stepped toward the center hall, careful to keep her damaged back from scraping against raw stone. At the corner, she peered out at the empty space. It was suddenly as quiet as it had been the last three hundred years.

The pirate was going to have to pass this way on his way out. It was the only place where she could gain the upper hand. She waited with her fingers curled around the axe, trying not to think too vividly about the task at hand. The sound it would make when the blade broke his rib cage. The look in his eyes. The way his bowels would loosen.

Considerable time passed. The place stayed quiet. Maybe the pirate had fallen victim to the same kind of trap that had taken ribbons off her back, though she knew deep down she'd never be that lucky.

She shifted impatiently as the sudden onset of hysterical shrieking pinned her in place.

Coming from the darkness ahead.

Sara forced herself out of hiding. It might've been a trap, though not even Carly could give a performance that good.

The doorways she passed had all been opened. One of the spaces was a ballroom complete with a shiny floor that looked to be on fire because of the way the torchlight hit it. She crept past additional quarters, a dining space, other areas whose uses weren't as discernable.

The hall was longer than she thought, and it seemed far larger than the space the mountain concealed. The torch sconces along the wall made her shadow loom large in a stalker's pursuit.

The last room on the right neared, and the scream had diffused and become low-level grumbling.

Sara peeked in.

The pirate had discovered the bedroom. He stood at the foot of the bed, crumpled papers balled between his fists. He kept lifting one page to his face, reading it over and over, shaking his head and mumbling to himself. Then he tossed them across the floor with disgust and in the process found Sara watching from the jamb.

"I was right," he said, sounding like a completely different person.

The bed housed two bodies. They were little more than jagged shapes at this distance.

"We are destined to die here," the pirate said. He no longer seemed to care about much, steadying himself on the stone wall. He tossed his knife into a darkened corner of the room, signaling surrender.

Sara felt emboldened to step inside now that he was unarmed, because her blade wasn't going to go slipping out of her hand.

The paper had her curiosity. She scooped the pages, eager for whatever had upset him. She floated the glow-light over what she instantly recognized as Isabella's handwriting.

No translations. No way of knowing what was said. It was the first time since beginning this trip that Isabella felt like a total stranger. But then, maybe not. Because as soon as she glanced the bottom of the page, she thought maybe she could guess what the whole thing was about.

Down in the footer was a hand-scribbled drawing of a fish. Swimming beneath an old galleon that Sara guessed had been added for scale. The fish was double its size, and the front of its head had been colored in and drawn larger than the rest of its body, as if to emphasize the bone-like protection.

"My God," she said.

"It is retribution," the pirate told her. "The angatra will not let us leave. It will not let anyone leave."

"She was never getting off this island..."

"Neither are we," he said. "There are other letters here. In English. Journals from the night three galleons approached this island carrying ninety men. Except..."

"The fish. I mean, its great, great, great grandfather fish."

"Two galleons never got close. Attacked by the same kind of creature that plagues us. The last ship managed to anchor, rowboats ashore..."

She drifted to the bed as he orated. Two skeletons rested atop damp fabric, faceless cavities with jagged skull domes where the faces had been bashed free and removed.

"What are those things that attacked us?" Sara said.

The pirate held out another page. "It is here." He dropped the stack at his feet. Sara took them. The pages were English scribbles and glowed green as she hovered a light stick over them.

Vernier never had any intention of taking the whore home. She rushed the beach as our rowboats came ashore, bloodied and hysterical, begging us to kill Roche, to kill him now, and take her away.

But Vernier was unmoved by her plight. Enraged by the massive losses we had incurred to reach land, determined to find reimbursement inside the pirate's vaults. Vernier dragged the sobbing woman back to the keep where we suffered further defeat, for the mad pirate had dismantled his ship and lined the parapet with every last cannon, raining hellfire down upon us.

We managed to breach with six men remaining, imprisoning the pirate inside his own jail, leaving him to rot while we searched for a way inside his vault. Vernier wanted him alive so he could witness losing everything.

We rotated responsibilities. Three men searched the keep according to the whore's words. This while the rest of us took the whore to bed, releasing our loneliness inside of her. Maybe Vernier wanted nothing to do with her, but if you could overlook her madness, there was plenty of beauty still prevalent.

But she was never meant as anything more than a distraction. Until of course I awoke one morning to find my crewmen slain, swollen throats and vomit the color of black tar plastered to their faces. I knew she had poisoned them, but why not me?

I rushed to find Vernier as he continued excavation, and he was nowhere. The galleon, gone. I was certain I'd been abandoned. I was certain that Vernier had loaded the treasure in the middle of the night and fled, but Isabella appeared on that beach, laughing at me, and what she said there filled me with irreparable horror.

"If you will not take me away from here, then I must keep you with me. Forever." And her laughter was sinister enough to make me realize she knew exactly what she'd done. That she was not out of her mind. That she simply was not prepared to suffer alone.

It's been at least a year. The whore's belly is swollen and I do not know if the offspring growing inside her is mine, or the men whose names I can no longer remember. I ask her to tell me what happened to them, but she only laughs. And that laughter has invited my own madness. I hate her. And I hate this island.

The letter was unsigned. It was either unfinished, or the unnamed crewman had declined to identify himself. Maybe his admission was so vile that he'd chosen anonymity.

Isabella had seen her dreams dashed twice in one night. First, as fish chomped through two rescue galleons, and second, when the man she so desperately wished would rescue her, proved not to care at all. And it turned out, that was only the beginning of her problems.

The pirate stood beside Sara. He offered nothing in the way of comfort.

Sara stuffed the pages inside her pocket.

"There is no escape." The pirate spoke as if this was his realization.

This guy was on a ledge and Sara wasn't about to try talking him down. Better to let him jump. She went to the door.

"Anyone who comes here, dies," the pirate said. "Don't you understand?"

"What can we do?" Sara asked.

The pirate had nothing else to say. He waved her off and his shoulders slumped further. "Go," he said. "It does not matter. It will never stop."

"Unless we stop it."

"My people try. They sacrifice themselves to it and its hunger only grows."

Sara thought of the leper woman back at Emerald Tides who'd thrown herself willingly to this fish. They had probably been doing that for as long these things had grown accustomed to feeding on humans.

The pirate was vacant and Sara was glad to leave him there. Let him stew in whatever superstitions had slaughtered his ambition.

She was nearly to the damp entryway when he screamed.

She spun back around and saw the pirate stumble into the hallway, recoiling in the presence of another hulking skull face.

It hacked his chest with an oversized bone hatchet and his dancing blood was darker than shadows in torchlight.

The pirate slid up against the wall with his forearms raised as a desperate shield. The killer towered over him. Its weapon so high and so fast the blade sparked against the ceiling.

Its head whipped to the side, catching Sara in its side-eye. Rather than follow through with the killing blow, it growled at the sight of her. The bone white skull mask was smeared in gore and dirt as it began to charge forward beneath the flickering torchlight.

Sara stepped back through the stairwell, onto the landing, and pushed the door shut. Another primitive squeal overhead. A shadow performing eager leaps down the stairs, rushing to catch the action.

The only place left to go was down.

FORTY-NINE

Carly sat with her back to the water, right up against the shallows. She stared out at the man who'd nearly killed her. His body floated face down and the current dragged him along the *Star Time's* overturned stern.

One of his equipment straps must've gotten snagged on some part of the yacht, because he ebbed in place, despite the ocean's efforts to banish him.

Once she was certain the bastard was truly dead, and wouldn't be pressing his thumbs into her eye sockets again, Carly began to settle her attention on the overturned ship, trying to determine what she should retrieve from the inside of it.

The diving tank on her back was clunky and heavy and she didn't dare remove it. It had saved her life when she'd gone overboard. She'd been able to slip it around her back, pop the breathing apparatus inside her mouth and swim away from the maniac who pursued, chasing her into the deep with a gushing head wound that should've summoned every shark for miles.

Maybe the best thing to do was find Jean-Philippe and the others. The island wasn't that big. The pirate was out there, injured. But not dead. If she could've hit him just once more, she might've been able to end this. Got off a few shots, though the rest of the magazine was soggy from her swim, denying her the full load. She sounded like that babbling government lunatic and decided to dwell on her failures no longer.

Carly was caught between these two trains of thought. She stood and stretched, beginning to slide the tank off her back when she spotted someone walking beneath a canopy of sloped branches. Right off, she knew it wasn't one of theirs.

The shadows kept the figure hidden, but the way its hand raked through the leaves as it walked turned her into a statue. Because it grew more brazen then, stepping clear to reveal itself.

The thing was naked. Grotesque. It throbbed upright at the sight of her and made deranged chittering noises as Carly's fear went airborne. Its head twitched from side-to-side at the sound of her whimpers.

Carly kept the diving tank on her back and took a few loud steps into the water. The splashes set the creature hobble-running for the shore. It lifted its face to the air, and its nostrils puffed like a beating heart.

Carly dropped the facemask over her eyes and chomped the rubber breathing tube. She turned and flopped into the water, pushing into the deep while watching the surface.

Disgusting feet stalked after her, turning little springs of coral into dust as the thing waded into the Indian Ocean up to its torso.

Carly hovered there, watching as the creature then broke right, swimming out to the stern of the overturned ship. It reached the government spook's corpse and wrestled with it, tearing it free from whatever snag had caught it. Then it swam back, towing the body behind it.

Easily distracted, Carly thought. Thank God.

The creature returned to shore, dragging the corpse up the shallows through a haze of coral dust and then out of sight.

Carly spun and paddled into the gloom, reaching for the small light attached to one of her shoulder straps. She would have to kill some time hiding down here while waiting for the creature to hopefully forget all about her.

If it would forget.

She didn't know how much oxygen remained in the tank, but thought she'd have at least thirty to forty minutes left. It was better to go deeper in case that thing was just standing up there, expecting her to surface.

Past the shallows, the ocean floor dropped off like a cliff. She swam down along the vertical wall, glimpsing an overturned wooden hull nearly embedded in the floor on the next landing. Scattered across this seabed was a collection of broken and battered vessels, some of them relatively recent, others much older. Ancient.

Another ledge. Carly followed this declining mountain face downward. She reached the next landing and found a deep fissure there. An underwater canyon that ran beneath the mountain sediment and disappeared, as if years of shifting terrain had corked it.

Carly drew closer, the spirit of exploration inspiring her curiosity. No intention of going further, but she wanted to see, and pressed her facemask against the void, squinting.

The world beyond was ink black. One shifting shadow swirled and found shape as it rushed toward her, growing as it approached the fissure.

Jaws were wide and threatening. Lined with teeth so large they had their own teeth. Whatever this mouth belonged to spotted Carly at the hole, and charged to get her. The world's angriest zoo animal, imprisoned in natural captivity. The ground held intact as the thing struck sediment and then knifed away, returning to the sanctity of shadows, and leaving Carly to witness a shape so spindly and alien that she'd never be able to describe it.

She decided the best place to be was on the wreckage of the *Star Time*, and kicked back up toward it. There was nowhere else on earth, above or below, where she was safe.

FIFTY

The stairs brought Sara down to another landing. This one flooded with ankle-high water. The door was larger and Sara suspected it had to be this way in order to move furnishings and materials inside.

Which meant there was another way out somewhere beyond it.

It opened like an ancient meat locker. She flung it wide and tossed a glow stick into the darkness. A green trail skipped across the stone floor—just enough distance to bring some light to the narrow passageway below.

Sara lit another glow stick then, wound her arm back and pitched it even further. Then she broke another and kept it in her fist as she headed in. Overheard, footsteps echoed on the stairwell.

Sara rushed for the thin corridor. It was tighter than the hallways that ran beneath the decks of some of the commercial vessels she'd worked on. It didn't make any sense down here unless these walls somehow moved. Given the sliding window mechanisms she'd seen above, there was probably a good chance that was the case.

Roche wouldn't hand his treasure over so easily.

Sara's shoulders scraped stonewalls. Inhuman grunts huffed somewhere behind her. She wouldn't allow herself to look, instead taking careful steps toward the first glow light. The entrance door rumbled and slammed shut as she reached the first marker. Around her, the walls began to thrum.

She sprinted for the next glow light, throwing the stick in her fist further into the beyond, ensuring she knew where to run. In the same fluid swoop, she bent and picked the next stick off the ground without breaking stride, following the green light as she went.

The closing walls pressed on her shoulders, an undeterred squeeze that threatened to grind her skin right off the bone.

Once more, Sara hurled the glow stick into the beyond. The open space ahead appeared in the haze of a lime green filter. The room there was wide open if she could reach it.

On either side of her shoulders, two slabs of stone rushed to touch. She was nearly through, diving the rest of the way but failing to get clear. The walls caught her ankle. She tried to tug it clear, but the grip was unrelenting. The pressure began to feel like the prelude to a pop.

Sara reached for her scraped shoulders. The fresh injuries there were raw and tender, painful to touch. Her hand came back coated in fresh blood and she used that to lubricate her ankle.

It tore the skin off either side of the bulbous bone. She rolled back in an awkward summersault and whined, her body throbbing in a half dozen different places.

She wanted nothing more than to feel sorry for herself, but there'd be time enough for that if she survived. Right now, she rolled onto her stomach and crawled across the room, refreshed by the occasional cool air that gusted through this space like Isabella's ghost.

Sara hobbled though endless caverns and storage spaces, much of it flooded. There were old cages littered with skeletons, collapsed stone shelving, and rusted swords that rested on a busted weapon's rack.

As last she reached a spot where twirling stone steps disappeared straight down into open water. Squatting to look out across the low cave ceiling, she knew this would lead all the way to the ocean.

The stairs that spiraled up led to another set of rooms. These were directly above the chambers from where she'd come.

The floor there wore specific patterned tiles.

She hovered the light over them. This space seemed undisturbed because nobody had ever made it this far. But could that be true when Vernier had spent days down here?

There had to be a purpose to these designs. Some kind of method.

Roche had lived a pirate's life, so the puzzle's language was nautical. She stepped onto a square plate that seemed like an engraved ship's stern. The other choices were farm implements, a soldier in uniform, and a powdered wig.

Those wouldn't work.

The plate depressed as soon as her boots landed. From behind the walls on either side, bolt mechanisms clicked into place. She lifted her glow light to the nearest hole and found the sharpened point of a wooden spear ready to spring loose had she chosen poorly.

She hot-stepped next to the hull wheel, a diagonal jump that she barely made, and much harder given the injuries to her mangled foot. Her knees wobbled but she steadied herself against the wall. The path ahead remained easy to guess.

A masthead engraving was located directly above the wheel. Sara ignored symbols of government and order—Roche's dismissal of the world he'd fled. Next was an anchor. Her final choice was between a horse, a Renaissance-era dress, a gavel, and a cannon. She imagined the ones Roche had lugged off his ship and placed in the parapet and jumped right on top of it.

"Everyone's got a little pirate in them, huh, Roche?" Sara said, never more empowered. "I see you."

She was safely on the other side now. Her heart danced as the vertical door grumbled, then lifted.

Sara crossed the threshold and a plate beneath her feet depressed, rushing the door back into place.

"Didn't want to go back anyway," Sara mumbled, almost inaudibly.

One slab of natural light was filtered through two-dozen baseball-sized holes in the ceiling. As close as Sara could figure it, she was over the residential part of this place and the intrusive light here beamed in from the sky as the moon lifted over the mountain face.

If she paused just right, she could taste tiny instances of fresh air blowing through the holes—enough to keep the air from going squalid.

Sara walked the perimeter of the room in awe. In the center, she found what must've been the helm of Roche's old vessel—the ship that had earned him his riches. Of course he couldn't part with it.

She went to the wheel like a speaker approached a lectern, clearing her throat as she put her hands around the jutting handles.

"And what do you do?" she said from the side of her mouth, afraid that the mere presence of her voice was enough to ignite whatever trap lay in wait.

She turned the wheel slowly and the lights overhead shifted. The holes looked like spider eyes and they moved with the wheel. It took the light off of her and slid the beam forward, illuminating a pile of what she first assumed was broken glass. But the shards were too thick and clustered for that.

Diamonds. The light landed on them and threw kaleidoscopic fire onto the wall. A carved skeleton face with refracting eyes glared back from there.

"Okay," Sara said and tightened her hands around the helm, disturbed by the sight, giving the wheel another turn to see if the light would keep moving.

It did.

The holes moved on a circular arc and found another pile of diamonds across the way. The skull glowed once more, this time highlighting a single diamond's tooth inside its open and delighted mouth.

"What am I missing?" Sara asked.

She cranked the wheel and the lights moved even further away from their starting point. The holes clicked into place, illuminating the first pile of diamonds and making the skull's eyes burn hot once more.

Another crank and this time only half the holes in the ceiling turned. The second pile glowed along with the first and soon the skeleton's smile matched its beaming eyes.

It looked eager, delighted to see someone come this far.

Sara left the hull and circled the room, wondering how much the diamonds on the floor might be worth. Could she cut her losses?

The skeleton's grin widened as she approached. It wasn't a trick of the light. Its mouth had opened wider. The brick behind the fallen jaw came loose with a simple touch, revealing a cradle that held a blue jewel beside an empty cradle. The light touched it and a sliver of the wall across the way shook, then stopped.

"My words are ghosts," Sara said, thinking about Isabella's words, Roche's riddle. "They move across the moonlight, promises as purple fog."

She pulled the red stone from her pocket and held it in the palm of her hand, grinning as she realized what it meant.

She dropped the jewel onto the cradle alongside the blue one and let the moonlight have both. The merging light that came off the stones was a deep, throbbing purple.

"Eat it, Mrs. Zimmer," Sara shouted as a stuttering, disbelieving laugh fell past her mouth.

A small door swung open across the way and Sara pushed off the wall in order to sprint for it. The jamb rained stone shavings as she dove beneath. It slid shut almost immediately and Sara didn't want to think what it'd feel like to be stuck on the other side after all that. She kept moving up another slight incline.

She was directly beneath the living space now. She tossed the glow light into the dark and hobbled into Roche's vault.

At the sight before her, Sara began to cry.

The room was empty, save for two skeletons sitting across from one another, anything but at peace.

One single doubloon was wedged between two stone tiles. Sara stuffed it inside her pocket. In the center of the room, a single sheet of paper lay on the floor between the bodies. Only now did she understand that she was looking at Roche and Isabella.

The wall behind the larger skeleton was stained with faded blood. Bone was visible through shredded ribbons over his chest, that part of the rib cage blown inward.

The smaller skeleton was slumped against the other wall, a bayonet jammed into her ribs, wedged in between two bones. A flintlock pistol sat just outside its bony hands. And the ground around her was equally dark.

Sara looked at the page, recognizing Vernier's writing.

The bitch has birthed twins. They are my problem now, because she has lost her mind. One night, just to spite me, she confessed at last to watching Vernier take the treasures from Roche's vault and escape.

She wished so badly to hurt me, reminding me that I had given up everything to hunt for treasure and all I got was her.

Her. I caught the whore by the prison cells, on her knees for Roche, servicing him.

I should care. But there is too much else that matters. There is something wrong with the children. They grow violent, with each other and with wildlife. They do not kill to sustain themselves, but because they enjoy it.

I left the whore and her pirate inside their empty vault, curious to see if their love would remain intact after they were locked up. I have no intention of ever checking on them... may they die ever so slowly.

I fear the children will come for me soon, and there will be little I can do to defend myself from their madness.

I should never have come here.

Despite everything, Sara continued to sympathize with Isabella. You loved a man, she thought. A man who made bad choices.

Sara tapped the square stone plate that reached up from the floor, strangely confident in its function. The ceiling rumbled, raining down loose stones and pebbles. A small staircase grew from the wall. The pirate stood atop the steps, a wobbling blade in hand.

"Where are they?" Sara asked.

His voice was wheezy. A large red slice through his clothes. He gestured beside him. She came up to find one of those things on the floor, head separated from its shoulders.

"There's another," she said. "At least one."

"It waits for us," the pirate said. "Out there."

"Want to help?" Sara asked. "Let's kill it. Then kill the fish."

The pirate looked at her in disbelief. "You sound just like the American."

"I am one," she said and felt sadness for Holloway. "Now how do we get off this fucking island?"

"There is no way."

"Because of that fish? Nah, I'm going to cook that fucking thing for dinner."

"There is no way."

"If I told you we can kill it," Sara said, "would you help me try?"

FIFTY-ONE

"The Baroness," Sara said. It felt like such an inspired plan she even snapped her fingers at the thought. "Guillaume was in contact with a woman called The Baroness. His boss. She's the one who brought them here looking for Roche."

They moved through the jungle, both parties unable and unwilling to fully trust the other. The pirate led and Sara kept her distance. Eventually, it was the other way around. Nobody wanted to keep their back to the other for too long.

Every so often they forgot they were bitter enemies and walked side-by-side, attempting to find an escape plan.

They stood on the riverbank that cut straight through the heart of the atoll.

There was a slight incline there, a hill just off the river. A makeshift fire pit dug through the center, with a wooden spigot held in place by thick branch supports.

A corpse dangled from it. It was the color of char, cooked beyond its features. Hogtied with the same leather strips that fashioned the hunter's blades to their hilts. The body had one foot, the other leg amputated beneath the knee. Pieces had been sliced from its belly and arms, and a few finger bones were picked clean and discarded around the log stumps used for seats.

Sara dropped to her knees and vomited. The pirate stood solemnly and dipped his head in a motion of respect for one fleeting second. Then he went on the move, leaving Sara to follow.

The river wound through jungle terrain like a snake and they stopped again at its mouth when they came across the blood-spattered remains of a torn and deflated Zodiac boat.

"Let us keep moving," the pirate said. The yacht wasn't far. It lay in the shallows like an exhausted animal.

Waves broke over its deck, ocean fizz washing away debris.

Her heart drummed as she thought of Carly.

"Only one of us should go in there," the pirate said.

"We don't know what condition things are in."

"If we both die—"

"If we don't get that laptop, no one will ever find us," she said. "So we're as good as dead and you know that."

The pirate took a deep breath. He started for the wreckage and she followed. His footsteps left deep imprints in the sand, as if he was pressed down by greater weight.

They waded into the water and swam straight for the overturned helm. The windows there were either punched out or busted. Jagged glass edges promised to chew them up if they moved wrong. Undaunted, the pirate passed through, then reached back, offering to guide Sara. This as her light sputtered and blinked dark. One final sign to discourage them.

She ignored it and tossed it away.

Sara had spent several days aboard this boat, but the terrain was halfway inverted now, making navigation surprisingly disorienting. Floors were walls and the walls were floors.

Something as simple as the stairwell leading down into the kitchenette was mostly inaccessible. They took careful steps over broken glass floors that had once been windows, climbing up onto the small stairwell wall and then hopping down onto kitchen cabinets. It was like being back inside Roche's tomb, only that had been easier to traverse.

Sara thought something passed through one of the broken windowpanes, realizing the shadows here were exaggerated and expressionistic, wreaking havoc on her senses. Harsh angles that projected wide, crooked angles disorienting to look at.

Passage into the next hallway required a climb. The pirate boosted her in his hands so she could grip the ledge and hoist herself up. She turned back and begrudgingly offered the same courtesy.

The equipment room was located on the deck below. They fumbled across more stairwell walls and descended into ankle-high water.

The room they needed to reach was locked and submerged directly beneath them. If the *Star Time* had capsized the other way, they would've had to climb up into the room. A preferable option, because that awful fish couldn't fly.

"It's locked," the pirate said. Repeated stomps wouldn't budge it.

Sara hurried to the end of the hall and brought her boot heel through the safety glass now positioned on the floor. The glass broke away and she lifted the fire axe free.

The pirate tensed as he caught her stalking back toward him. She had a split second to think, good, but her eyes were plastered to the floor.

On where they needed to go.

She stood in a V with her legs on either side of the jamb, lifting the axe over her head. The blade slammed through the water and splintered the wood. Water bled out. Sara continued chopping until there was almost nothing left of the door but driftwood floating around their ankles.

The pirate didn't wait for an invitation. He dove through and went to work at locating the package.

Sara let him work. Bloodthirsty thoughts challenged her. She wondered if she shouldn't bury the axe in his skull as soon as he reappeared. He'd killed his way through everyone on this perverse treasure hunt. It was foolish to assume their allegiance was anything but limited. They were of mutual use to each other, but that lasted until the Baroness was called. Then she'd look him in his dimming eyes and tell him, "This is for my husband, you motherfucker."

The pirate reappeared in the submerged jamb, rising up over the water and gasping for air. No time to communicate. He slipped back under as her thoughts returned to murder. When? Now? But could she make the first move?

Next time the pirate returned, it was with an oxygen tank. He climbed free and slipped it around his back, pushing a breather into his mouth and sliding a mask over his face. He went back under and was gone for a long time.

So long that Sara began to think he'd left her for dead. That he'd found the laptop and took another way out. But she was careful to recall the parameters of the room beneath her and thought that was impossible.

When he returned again, it was with another diving mask and a tank.

"The laptop is nowhere to be found."

"Well he didn't take it with him," she said.

"Which room did he choose as his quarters?"

Sourness settled in her stomach. The diving gear meant they weren't finished exploring this ship. They needed to go deeper.

"Shit," she said with a tired sigh. "Let me show you."

FIFTY-TWO

Kaahin watched the girl suit up and slosh back to the stairwell.

The water in the hall was fast approaching their knees. Part of the yacht looked to be wedged on coral, but as the hull continued to take on water and weight, it was guaranteed to slip off that face soon enough.

The girl dropped into the cavernous hole like a bullet and he followed. Neither of them had any light, so they navigated the gloom with awkwardness. He followed the girl's basic shape around the sunken corners and into the next hall. Then another. The environment, once an idle display of unfettered luxury, was now a surreal and twisted hellscape that mocked their treasured pursuits.

They swam through the living quarters and the girl pushed into one of the larger bunks.

The bed was overturned. The twisted frame rested diagonally against one of the walls. Furniture was strewn everywhere and the lightest bits floated overhead, ebbing against the ceiling in the thin space of air there.

The girl waved to him in dark silhouette. He pushed through the murky to reach her. She pointed to a thick hard shell case that sat wedged beneath a bureau. They went to work on pushing it away from the wall space—just enough to wrestle it free.

Kaahin reached down and took the case by its handle, wound back and pulled it free. He turned toward the entrance and swam straight for it, unconcerned with whether or not his partner in crime was following.

He cleared the doorway and the world exploded. The surface that had once been the floor, but was now a wall, ruptured. Broken hull pieces rushed toward him. The ship's bottom punctured by a driving force moving like a bullet.

Kaahin had never screamed in his life. Not when his mother was gunned down on the beaches of Capetown. Murdered by police officers angry that she would not surrender her body. And not when his best friend and partner on the force was hacked to bits right before him with fire axes—retaliation for busting the wrong heroin den.

He'd always just internalized the pain. Let it attach itself to him like barnacles. Something he'd carry on his voyages as a reminder that life was pointless. Bad things happened to the people you cared for. And that he should simply adapt unless he wanted to be another forgotten victim.

Kaahin had never screamed before because that gesture belonged to the weak.

But he screamed now.

Because what came pushing through the darkness wasn't manmade evil, but fate. A rushing meat grinder, chomping and obliterating everything in its way. The hull, the floor, collateral furniture, and whatever else got caught in its insatiable path.

Kaahin pushed back and slammed into another body: The girl. Contact sent them both tumbling through the flooded space, spinning into the confines of the bunk. The hard shell laptop case tumbled from his fingers, slipping away into the gloom.

The wall before him cracked inward and broke apart with sledgehammer force. The armored fish head appeared in the mist like a battering ram. It moved in on him without the slightest resistance, filling so much space he could not see beyond it.

Kaahin pushed for less constricted waters, hoping the angatra's maneuverability down here was limited. But even as the fish fell from immediate view, that constant grinding continued to plague his ears.

The girl screamed. A swarm of oxygen bubbles rose through the space between them. The fish pushed in and its massive head craned to one side, its armored eye blazed, seeing him up close once more.

The broken blade that Kaahin had shoved inside the fish while on the American's ship remained embedded there, poking from the side of its face like stubble.

Does it remember me? There was a fleeting second of eye contact and Kaahin swore there was recognition there. That scared him even more. He kicked off the wall and paddled up through the debris, making a shameless dash for open water. Behind him, more soggy cries. Good, he thought. Have at her.

Except the fish didn't seem to care about her at all. Kaahin caught motion out of the corner of his eye and knew that it wanted him. He kicked and paddled and moved through the water, passing through the exploded hull like a torpedo.

Just get to the beach. To the weapons he'd tossed into the sand. The angatra wouldn't be expecting that arsenal.

The water fought him. Bad undertow. It dragged him back with every stroke forward. He bent his knees and pushed, managing only to inch further. He felt frozen in place.

The grinding grew louder, practically in his ear.

And now he realized it wasn't undertow. He was moving backwards, the water around him reversing direction, drawing back in a flash current. The angatra's rapidly upending jaws were responsible, moving so fast that it was sucking him in.

Kaahin slipped the oxygen tank off his shoulders and spun through the water so he faced the surface. Beneath him, the fish surged up. Kaahin dangled the tank in one hand while the continuing to paddle with the other.

The chomping mouth was close, flying up from the depths like a nightmare. Kaahin released the tank like a depth charge. It floated down to where the angatra's jaws cleaved it in two, dispersing compressed oxygen as both halves disappeared inside its mouth.

Then the fish charged up, undeterred. Kaahin bounced off its largest tooth again. He twirled along the fish's face, finding himself once more against its eye. He'd never known sea creatures to glare with anything but indifference. But this orb was loaded with fire, as if every one of his Malagasy ancestors sat nestled inside it, driving this creature to accomplish what it had been sent here to do—punish the wicked.

He kicked off the side of its face and knifed toward the surface, reaching the coral shore and wading up through the shallows.

The fish wouldn't relent. It tasted blood.

If anything, Kaahin had successfully driven it away from Madagascar. That might have to be victory enough.

He kicked until his paddling hands found soft, runny sand. Fingers disappeared into mud as he climbed up the embankment and into knee-high water. He rushed the beach, spinning and dropping onto his back as the dorsal fin sawed through aquamarine just beyond the shallows.

"Stay there!" Kaahin screamed. His breath was spent. His lungs burned.

Another figure broke the surface and stumbled ashore. Kaahin didn't look. He was too terrified to take his eyes off the angatra, as if his ancestors might somehow enable it aground to finish the job.

A shadow appeared over Kaahin, blotting the moonlight. He flipped his neck back and watched the thin figure tear a diving mask off her face. Icy blue eyes stared down, blonde hair in soaked, matted clumps.

"I should throw you to that fish," she snarled like a dog. "But I want to feel the last breath leave your lungs."

The blonde knelt so that her thighs boxed his ears. She planted the blade deep inside his chest. Two hands squeezing the hilt, driving the knife deeper until Kaahin felt his heart puncture, the sting of cold steel deep inside his body. She pulled the knife out and the splatter painted her movie star face with gobs of thick, rushing midnight.

Kaahin's vision turned to blood. His body jerked and the next thing he knew he was staring up at the stars. Thinking of his family. All the ways he had failed them. Taking relief in the idea that his disappearance might finally set them free.

His eyelids dropped like hammers.

FIFTY-THREE

Sara watched the pirate disappear into open water and the great fish followed.

She swam down to the floor and retrieved the hard case laptop, then headed for the *Star Time's* flooded hallways, where the water was now waist-deep. Maneuvering was harder by the moment.

The trip back to the helm was slow. A grumbling yacht quake shook the world around her, prompting Sara to place a hand against the floor-turned-wall and squeeze her eyes shut.

Somewhere below, another piece of the hull broke away as the fish cleaved through it, decimating what little integrity remained. The walls gave deep and guttural groans as if to say, we can't hold much longer.

Her hands coiled around the busted windowpane. She squinted into the murk for signs that the stone monstrosity was just beyond, waiting.

The *Star Time* shook again, and what little of the overturned hull was left, blew outward like an aluminum can, delivering the killing blow to the ship's structure.

The walls and floors creaked as cracks broke through them like opening fault lines.

The fish seemed to sense the *Star Time* was finished. Sara felt it punching through its length, a bullet through body armor, penetrating its structure like its walls and floors were soggy notebook paper.

The ship collapsed around her, and while the coast was anything but clear, it didn't matter. Sara kicked through to the ocean and kept pushing.

The terrible stone head burst through the space that had been the helm. Indiscriminate blades decimated everything in a rush to meet her. The hard case laptop slid from her hand. She couldn't alter her course to get it, just kept pushing because land was close.

She paddled for the shallows, twenty feet, maybe less. Breathing was hard. Panic making it harder. She reached the small incline and waded up out of the water, tossing her mask aside and letting the breather fall from her mouth.

"Holy shit, holy shit, holy shit," she said, dropping and crawling forward, unable to get far enough away from the water.

The corpse sprawled beside the weapons cache stopped her cold.

The pirate.

He was dead, the blade buried in his chest like Excalibur. The sight should've satisfied her, but there wasn't time for it. His death restored nothing.

Another figure sat upright in the sand a few feet away, rocking on folded legs. "Oh God," Sara said breathlessly, rushing for Carly and fearing the worst.

The woman was dazed, staring at the pirate's body. At the life she'd taken. It hadn't been the first, but Sara guessed this one had meant the most.

"Carly," she said and put an arm on her shoulder.

The blonde reached up and touched it. Said nothing.

"You did it," Sara said. She gave Carly's shoulder a gentle nudge and the actress looked up at her.

"That's a terrible noise," she said.

The constant *shink shinking* of grinding teeth. The terrible, unexpressive fossil head writhed on the surface, head above water and looking straight at them.

Cold eyes. An endlessly gnawing mouth. One of nature's most sadistic creations. Sara realized why it was no longer moving. The yacht's twisted and broken fuselage had pinned it against the coral beds.

Sara felt her blood go cold, even as she laughed at this bit of dumb luck—the *Star Time's* crumpled frame becoming its shackles, however temporary. Each time it reared its head to one side, the hull groaned and threatened to pull away.

Sara rushed the supply cache and snapped the rocket launcher from its rectangular case, nestling the cylindrical firing tube between her shoulder and neck. She pushed the trigger without hesitation and the rocket rushed off, bonking off the fish's boney head—a waterlogged dud that plunked into the ocean, and out of sight.

The fish managed to wrestle itself to one side, dragging the *Star Time's* frame with it. There were precious minutes left.

Maybe one. As soon as it got free, it would gain the upper hand once more and she'd be out of tricks.

"Let's see how you like this," Sara cried. She tore the Bosch-branded jackhammer from its sack and strode into the water, rushing headlong toward that killing mouth.

Its eye spotted her. She was close enough to see the damn thing actually widen. It craned its head to face her while the demolished ship frame whined and heaved in the same direction.

Sara's teeth scraped together with a similar *shink*, meeting the monster on its terms.

"Okay," she cried and with a flick of her thumb, set the jackhammer whirring. "Let's see you eat this!"

The chisel pumped forward with eager driving force, hungry for a target.

Sara's body disappeared as she sloped down off the shallows. The water at her ankles, her knees, her waist...

She lifted the hammer overhead as the Indian Ocean swallowed her up to her shoulders. Her injured hand throbbed, her remaining fingers working hard to tighten around the grip, a spill of blood trickling out like the last drops of a juiced orange. The flopping fish could only anticipate her approach with steady bite.

Sara's hands squeezed the jackhammer harder than she'd ever held anything. This was more than life or death. Flexing every muscle in her arms, she shoved it forward, straight against its killing teeth. The chisel cut bone like butter.

The dunkleosteus' largest tooth broke away. With nothing there, the jackhammer pushed further into its mouth, dragging Sara right up against it, standing on the tips of her toes in order to stay above water.

The chisel cracked through the dunkleosteus' face. Hammering through its rock veneer like it was highway pavement. A crack appeared just above its bite, where its nose might've been. Small sections of its protective armor began breaking away in an avalanche. The hungry hammer cleaved the scaly flesh beneath it, shredding it with ease.

Its eyes popped further wide, sensing imminent extinction. The jackhammer ate straight into the nearest socket, splitting away all the pieces of protection that had once protected it from natural enemies.

With a scream, Sara shoved the jackhammer inward until the chisel disappeared in full. It continued to burrow, tearing off its armor in even larger hunks. Blood began pumping through newly forged crevices until at last the chisel got gummed up on fish brains and cartilage, the assuring motor grind sputtered and then stalled. This as stone head slid away in hunks that sunk into the water around her.

At last, the body went limp.

Time to get the case, Sara thought, leaving the blade impaled inside the fish. What had once been the *Star Time*'s hull was unrecognizable—a hunk of twisted metal and broken plaster.

She went back to land to retrieve her gear.

It wasn't over until she could call for help.

FIFTY-FOUR

The Baroness was not happy to hear from Sara, or, more specifically, to learn that both her operatives were gone.

"They were bloody investments," she'd said with exasperation.

"Just come get us," Sara said and handed over the coordinates.

"Arrival in six hours," the Baroness told her.

Sara didn't mention that Roche's treasure no longer existed. She feared that would prompt the businesswoman to cut and run.

Sara and Carly passed the time dressing each other's wounds. Again.

Sara looked at the pirate lying on the far edge of the beach. Realized she was glad he was gone. "You did good," she said.

"Yeah," Carly said. "Maybe I did, but..." She pointed to the ocean where the round of the fish carcass was slumped against the shallows. "You had to show up, didn't you?"

"I saw it more as pulling my weight."

"You solved Roche's shitty riddles," Carly said. "People been trying to do that for a few hundred years. Victory lap's yours to take."

"Can I ask you something?" Sara said, eyes still with the pirate.

"Of course."

"What did it feel like? Killing the one who hurt you."

Carly wouldn't look at the body. She drew scribbles in the sand with a broken branch. "Same as when I shot that pirate on the boat. I wanted to kill them, knew that I had to." She looked at the corpse now and shook her head slightly. "But when I stuck that knife through him... and he pissed himself... shit himself... and I looked into his eyes and saw the horror that comes with everyone's final moments..."

"I'm sorry," Sara said. "I shouldn't have asked."

"No, hey, you didn't let me finish."

"Oh, uh, okay..."

"I'm glad I did it. Because someone like that, who can do what I just described like it's business as usual, all part of the job? That's pure evil. I don't know how many lives we saved by taking him out of this world, but I don't think I'll regret it for a second."

"If I had beer bottles, this is where we'd clink them," Sara said.

They tried to sleep, side by side, and in the softest bit of sand the beach afforded. Waterlogged guns beside them, both women keeping one eye each pointed toward the trees. With so much adrenaline driving them, chasing sleep was a completely useless gesture. They laid in silence, no pressure to fill it.

Sara stared at the stars and thought of Isabella. Gradually growing so used to the idea of captivity that in the end she'd favored companionship over escape, no matter how contentious. Given the way in which those bastards had treated her, Sara didn't blame her.

They sat up at the sound of every snapping branch or ruffling bird, positive that Isabella's distant, hideous offspring would come clawing. They surveyed the night and each time found only an empty beach.

It was only once the sky began to lighten that Sara dozed. Her breaths were deep enough to fool her body into thinking she was relaxed, and it was only when a tired snore got caught in her throat that she sputtered and surprised herself into springing awake.

She sat upright and saw a half-dozen bodies standing at the edge of the forest, each of them looking at the sky, sniffing the air.

Skull faces, heaving shoulders, eager bone hatchets.

"Oh shit," Sara said.

Carly sputtered beside her, coming to uneasy consciousness. But as soon as she was awake, she spotted them and went reaching for her gun.

The island residents started toward them as sunrise broke. Their horrible, scabbed bodies looked even worse, more diseased, in the morning's rays beneath the clearing.

Uncertain shuffles became more confident as the hunters converged on their prey. Their ranks had probably never suffered losses before, and so there was caution in their steps, stalking forward in solidarity.

Carly lifted the submachine gun, but held off until they were closer. Until her aim was sure.

The creatures crossed from jungle grass onto beach sand and now Sara heard eager growls in their throats. She also heard a motorized whirring at her back, but didn't dare take her eyes off the creatures, whose gaits were wholly confident now, stalking forward with weapons raised.

The helicopter swept in off the ocean and hovered directly over their heads. It startled the hunters into panicked retreat, but it was too late for them.

Gunfire erupted, and their skull faces exploded into hunks of jelly-red bone. All the bodies torn to pieces with exaggerated savagery. The helicopter floated inland as the hunters turned tail and retreated for the trees, the gunner reducing every last one of them to raw meat before laying off the trigger.

The chopper landed on the beach and armed men stormed out, clearing the area before the Baroness appeared. She stepped down and hurried away from the rushing blades.

"You two look much worse for the wear," the Baroness said. She smiled genuine. Given the bloodbath they'd just witnessed, her gesture was surreal and inappropriate.

"Tell you all about it," Sara said.

The British woman studied the beach. She looked at the pirate's body and nodded slowly as she processed the action. Her brown eyes settled on the *Star Time's* wreckage and then she looked at Carly with the same devilish grin. "I'm a big fan, you know."

"Jesus, who isn't?" Sara said, relief sinking in.

The Baroness held on Sara with amazement. "So you're my new hire?"

"I... uh, maybe?"

"Seems it was a good investment."

"I hope so," Sara sighed.

"Where is Roche's manor?" the Baroness asked.

Sara pointed to the mountains in the distance. "About that," she said. And then came clean.

The Baroness did not seem to care. "If this Vernier really did loot the island, we have ways of tracing his fortune." She ordered her men to fan out and search for any more creatures.

The Baroness gave the women an appreciative smile. "How about this?" She touched Sara's forearm. "Come back to London with me for a full debrief?"

"How about somewhere more neutral?" Sara asked. "And we bring my friend here."

"Oh sweetheart," the Baroness laughed. "You really must trust me. Do you think this is the first time one of my expeditions has ended in failure? That is the more common result in this business."

"Right," Sara said. "I thought it was pleasure for you."

"It can be both," the Baroness told her. She took a few steps toward the helicopter and glanced back. Threw two wiggling fingers at the women. "Of course you can bring Ms. Grayson, though I am sad she doesn't seem to recall meeting me." Another smile, this one aimed at Carly.

"Aspen?"

The Baroness pointed like, there it is.

"What about the ship's captain?" Sara asked. "If you follow the river you'll find—"

"I will arrange everything," the Baroness said. "Some of my men are staying behind to verify. Their work is just beginning."

"Can't you bring us to Los Angeles?" Sara asked. "Carly needs to get back to her daughter."

"Yes, of course," the Baroness agreed. "That is where we will go. But..."

"But?"

The Baroness helped Sara to board the helicopter. Then she pulled Carly in. "I am interested in offering you a job, Sara. I meant what I said to you."

Sara shook her head.

The Baroness raised her hands. "It's on the up and up, darling. I promise."

"What job?"

"Good help is hard to find," she said. "You're good help."

"I met your guys," Sara said. "I'm nothing like them."

"I do not want them," the Baroness said. "I want you. I'm sorry... I don't think you ever actually told me your full name, Just Sara."

Sara had to think on that—a surprisingly difficult question to answer. She was Sara Mosby by birth. Upon returning from her honeymoon, she was going to begin the process of legally changing her name to Sara Jovish.

But that wasn't a surname she wished to carry any more. She loved Blake. The man he'd been. She wondered if one day she could learn to forgive him.

She also did not feel like Sara Mosby anymore. Her brother had cornered the market on that name and she would always be in his shadow.

"It's Sara," she said. "Sara Holloway." Nothing wrong with adopting a professional name.

The Baroness nodded and the helicopter began to lift off.

"Well, Sara Holloway," the Baroness said. "I can make you a very rich woman. There are treasures all over this world, and I would like you to help me find them."

It sounded crazy. Sara measured the Baroness' face, which was stone serious. The offer was sincere.

"What do you say?" the Baroness asked. "Do you want to work for me?"

Sara and Carly swapped looks. The actress nodded yes.

Sara didn't bother taking one last glance of the island. The chopper carted them off toward the rising sun and she basked in the warmth of the rays coming through the window. As far as she was concerned, she never wanted to see this atoll again.

I beat you, Sara thought of Roche, realizing the exhilaration this carried. Her name would go in the history books as the person who'd finally done it. And not without help. The names of which the world would also know.

Sara cleared her throat and eyed the Baroness, giving a confident nod.

"I do."

ABOUT THE AUTHOR

Matt Serafini is the author of *Rites of Extinction, Island Red, Under the Blade,* and many more.

He has written extensively on the subjects of film and literature for numerous websites including Dread Central and Shock Till You Drop. His nonfiction has appeared in Fangoria and HorrorHound magazines. He spends a significant portion of his free time tracking down obscure slasher films, and hopes one day to parlay that knowledge into a definitive history book on the subject.

His novels are available in ebook and paperback from Amazon, Barnes & Noble, and all other fine retailers.

Matt lives in Massachusetts with his wife and children.

Please visit https://mattserafini.com/ to learn more.

Made in the USA
Monee, IL
12 November 2020

47372280R00166